. DOVER · THRIFT · EDITIONS

The Decameron
Selected Tales

GIOVANNI BOCCACCIO

EDITED BY
BOB BLAISDELL

DOVER PUBLICATIONS, INC.
Mineola, New York

DOVER THRIFT EDITIONS

GENERAL EDITOR: PAUL NEGRI

EDITOR OF THIS VOLUME: JOHN BERSETH

Bibliographical Note

This Dover edition, first published in 2000, is a reprint of twenty-five stories from Boccaccio's *Decameron*, selected by Bob Blaisdell from the translation by J. M. Rigg, published by the Navarre Society Ltd., London. The text has been paragraphed in accordance with contemporary usage, and a new Introduction has been written specially for this edition.

Library of Congress Cataloging-in-Publication Data

Boccaccio, Giovanni, 1313–1375.
   [Decamerone. English. Selections]
   The decameron : selected tales / Giovanni Boccaccio ; edited by Bob Blaisdell.
     p. cm.
   Translation by J. M. Rigg.
   ISBN 0-486-41113-3 (pbk.)
    1. Rigg, J. M. (James Macmullen), 1855–1926. I. Blaisdell, Robert. II. Title.

PQ4272.E5 A37 2000
853'.1—dc21

99-0566149

Manufactured in the United States of America
Dover Publications, Inc., 31 East 2nd Street, Mineola, N.Y. 11501

Introduction

THOUGH GIOVANNI BOCCACCIO had probably composed some of the stories of his *Decameron* (Greek for "Ten Days") before the terrible plague of 1348 afflicted the city of Florence, it was the chaos brought by the Black Death that inspired the book's neat, symmetrical framework: Ten days of stories by ten attractive young women and men who assemble in various idyllic locales outside the plague-ravaged city. Boccaccio borrowed the plots of most of the one hundred tales in his book from sources great and small, old and new, exalted and low — from sermon-inspired anecdotes to the raw humor of French fabliaux. The lowest, funniest, and raciest stories have become the most famous. In the book's prefatory remarks, Boccaccio addresses his intended audience — young women with time of leisure. In these stories "will be found some passages of love rudely crossed, with other courses of events of which the issues are felicitous, in times as well modern as ancient: from which stories the said ladies, who shall read them, may derive both pleasure from the entertaining matters set forth therein, and also good counsel, in that they may learn what to shun, and likewise what to pursue. Which cannot, I believe, come to pass, unless the dumps be banished by diversion of mind. And if it so happen (as God grant it may) let them give thanks to Love, who, liberating me from his fetters, has given me the power to devote myself to their gratification."

Boccaccio also described the effects of the plague on the morality and the actions of the Florentines, as well as explaining the simple coincidence that brings together for the first time his ten storytellers in a church on the outskirts of Florence. There are seven more or less indistinguishable young women in mourning and three young and undaunted lovers (not even the raging plague stifles the men's pursuit of their ladyloves); all of these young people are acquainted with each other in one way or another, whether by love, blood, friendship, or neighborhood. One of the women, Pampinea, suggests storytelling as a

way for them to pass the next two weeks in an agreeable, scandal-free
way. With Fridays and Saturdays being holy—as well as hairwashing—
days, they will meet Sunday through Thursday, for a total of ten days.
The rules are simple; the queen or king for one day states the theme
and chooses the ruler for the following day. Pampinea is to start the pro-
gram, and one man, Dioneo, is designated a kind of wild card because
he insists on not being bound by any rules. Something of a Boccaccio,
Dioneo is even less restrained and usually more comic than the others.
He enjoys his position as last storyteller of each day, often choosing to
upset the mood and tone created by the previous nine stories.·

A list of themes for the ten days will help clarify the starting point of
the selected tales: (Day 1) any pleasing subject; (Day 2) "the fortunes
of such as after divers misadventures have at last attained a goal of
unexpected felicity"; (Day 3) "the fortunes of such as have painfully
acquired some much-coveted thing, or, having lost, have recovered it";
(Day 4) "discourse is had of those whose loves had a disastrous close";
(Day 5)"good fortune befalling loves after divers direful or disastrous
adventures"; (Day 6) "such as by some sprightly sally have repulsed an
attack, or by some ready retort or device have avoided loss, peril or
scorn"; (Day 7) "tricks, which, either for love or for their deliverance
from peril, ladies have heretofore played their husbands, and whether
they were by the said husbands detected, or no"; (Day 8) "tricks that,
daily, woman plays on man, or man woman, or one man another";
(Day 9) "at the discretion of each, of such matters as most commend
themselves to each in turn"; (Day 10) "such as in matters of love, or
otherwise, have done something with liberality or magnificence." At
least some of the stories were circulating previous to the collection's
completion (in 1352 or 1353), and the critical responses to them
prompted the author's reply in the introduction to the Fourth Day:
"They say then, some of these my censors, that I am too fond of you,
young ladies, and am at too great pains to pleasure you. . . . I ask them
whether, considering only all that it means to have had, and to have
continually, before one's eyes your debonair demeanour, your bewitching
beauty and exquisite grace, and therewithal your modest womanliness,
not to speak of having known the amorous kisses, the caressing
embraces, the voluptuous comminglings, whereof our intercourse with
you, ladies most sweet, not seldom is productive, they do verily marvel
that I am fond of you. . . . Of a trust whoso taxes me thus must be one
that, feeling, knowing nought of the pleasure and power of natural
affection, loves you not, nor craves your love; and such an one I hold
in light esteem."

In his conclusion to the book Boccaccio, as in his introduction to
the fourth day, defends the book's subjects and their treatments:

"Peradventure, then, some of you will be found to say that I have used excessive license in the writing of these stories, in that I have caused ladies at times to tell, and oftentimes to list, matters that, whether to tell or to list, do not well become virtuous women. The which I deny, for that there is one of these stories so unseemly, but that it may without offence be told by any one, if but seemly words are used; which rule, methinks, has been very well observed." We may judge for ourselves whether Boccaccio's presentations of licentiousness are as innocent as he claims.

With its tight, simple frame and wondrous variety, nothing like *The Decameron* had ever before appeared in European literature. The book's significance reveals itself in many ways; its revelation of the culture and diversity of the Middle Ages; its historical influence on contemporary and later literature (including versions of tales by Chaucer, Shakespeare, and Keats); and, most of all, its comedy. The farces—for instance, Day 9, Story 2, about the abbess who, while condemning a young nun's fornication, is noticed to have a pair of priest's pants on her head; or Day 3, Story 10, where a too-clever-by-half monk teaches a naive but energetic young woman about "putting the devil in hell"—remind us that literature, and life, are not just about divine or serious topics. Some of the other stories, however, have gained esteem and favor for reasons that readers in today's world might find baffling, most notably the patient Griselda, who is the principal character in the book's closing story. Griselda, apparently suffering various outrages including her husband's apparent murder of her children, is not a character at all but a misogynistic conceit ("What I did was done of purpose aforethought," her husband Gaultieri smugly tells Griselda, "that thou mightst learn to be a wife"); in spite of the narrator's mild condemnation of the husband, Dioneo and Boccaccio took Griselda as an "example" to use in beating other women over the head for their "lack" of patience ("Who but Griselda had been able, with a countenance not only tearless, but cheerful, the hard and unheard-of trials to which Gaultieri subjected her?") Gaultieri is, unfortunately, all too typical an example of self-justifying male aggression then and now. So, if we take a lesson from the tale in the present day, it is from Gaultieri, not Griselda.

Before the twentieth century, many of Boccaccio's tales were expurgated in translation into English because of their portrayal of sexual license and their often ribald lampoonery. But as Boccaccio tells us in the book's conclusion, "However, whoso goes a reading among these stories, let him pass over those that vex him, and read those that please him. That none may be misled, each bears on its brow the epitome of that which it hides within its bosom."

This selection of twenty-five out of the hundred tales from the translation by J. M. Rigg provides a representative sampling of the more famous or notorious of them. The introductory comments that link the stories to their fictional narrators and refer to the common theme of the day have been excised as well as Boccaccio's various addresses to the reader.

Contents

The Decameron

FIRST DAY

STORY I.

Ser Ciappelletto cheats a holy friar by a false confession, and dies; and, having lived as a very bad man, is, on his death, reputed a saint, and called San Ciappelletto.

The story goes, then, that Musciatto Franzcsi, a great and wealthy merchant, being made a knight in France, and being to attend Charles Sansterre, brother of the King of France, when he came into Tuscany at the instance and with the support of Pope Boniface, found his affairs, as often happens to merchants, to be much involved in divers quarters, and neither easily nor suddenly to be adjusted; wherefore he determined to place them in the hands of commissioners, and found no difficulty except as to certain credits given to some Burgundians, for the recovery of which he doubted whether he could come by a competent agent; for well he knew that the Burgundians were violent men and ill-conditioned and faithless; nor could he call to mind any man so bad that he could with confidence oppose his guile to theirs. After long pondering the matter, he recollected one Ser Ciapperello da Prato, who much frequented his house in Paris. Who being short of stature and very affected, the French who knew not the meaning of Cepparello,[1] but supposed that it meant the same as Cappello, *i.e.* garland, in their vernacular, called him not Cappello, but Ciappelletto by reason of his diminutive size; and as Ciappelletto he was known everywhere, whereas few people knew him as Ciapperello.

Now Ciappelletto's manner of life was thus. He was by profession a notary, and his pride was to make false documents; he would have made them as often as he was asked, and more readily without fee than another at a great price; few indeed he made that were not false, and

---

[1] The diminutive of *ceppo*, stump or log: more commonly written *cepperello* (cf. p. 9) or *ceppatello*. The form *ciapperello* seems to be found only here.

1

great was his shame when they were discovered. False witness he bore, solicited or unsolicited, with boundless delight; and, as oaths were in those days had in very great respect in France, he, scrupling not to forswear himself, corruptly carried the day in every case in which he was summoned faithfully to attest the truth. He took inordinate delight, and bestirred himself with great zeal, in fomenting ill-feeling, enmities, dissensions between friends, kinsfolk and all other folk; and the more calamitous were the consequences the better he was pleased. Set him on murder, or any other foul crime, and he never hesitated, but went about it with alacrity; he had been known on more than one occasion to inflict wounds or death by preference with his own hands. He was a profuse blasphemer of God and His saints, and that on the most trifling occasions, being of all men the most irascible. He was never seen at church, held all the sacraments vile things, and derided them in language of horrible ribaldry. On the other hand he resorted readily to the tavern and other places of evil repute, and frequented them. He was as fond of women as a dog is of the stick: in the use against nature he had not his match among the most abandoned. He would have pilfered and stolen as a matter of conscience, as a holy man would make an oblation. Most gluttonous he was and inordinately fond of his cups, whereby he sometimes brought upon himself both shame and suffering. He was also a practised gamester and thrower of false dice. But why enlarge so much upon him? Enough that he was, perhaps, the worst man that ever was born.

The rank and power of Musciatto Franzesi had long been this reprobate's mainstay, serving in many instances to secure him considerate treatment on the part of the private persons whom he frequently, and the court which he unremittingly, outraged. So Musciatto, having bethought him of this Ser Cepparello, with whose way of life he was very well acquainted, judged him to be the very sort of person to cope with the guile of the Burgundians. He therefore sent for him, and thus addressed him:—"Ser Ciappelletto, I am, as thou knowest, about to leave this place for good; and among those with whom I have to settle accounts are certain Burgundians, very wily knaves; nor know I the man whom I could more fitly entrust with the recovery of my money than thyself. Wherefore, as thou hast nothing to do at present, if thou wilt undertake this business, I will procure thee the favour of the court, and give thee a reasonable part of what thou shalt recover."

Ser Ciappelletto, being out of employment, and by no means in easy circumstances, and about to lose Musciatto, so long his mainstay and support, without the least demur, for in truth he had hardly any choice, made his mind up and answered that he was ready to go. So the bargain was struck. Armed with the power of attorney and the royal letters

commendatory, Ser Ciappelletto took leave of Messer Musciatto and
hied him to Burgundy, where he was hardly known to a soul. He set
about the business which had brought him thither, the recovery of the
money, in a manner amicable and considerate, foreign to his nature, as
if he were minded to reserve his severity to the last. While thus occupied, he was frequently at the house of two Florentine usurers, who
treated him with great distinction out of regard for Messer Musciatto;
and there it so happened that he fell sick. The two brothers forthwith
placed physicians and servants in attendance upon him, and omitted
no means meet and apt for the restoration of his health. But all remedies proved unavailing; for being now old, and having led, as the physicians reported, a disorderly life, he went daily from bad to worse like
one stricken with a mortal disease.

This greatly disconcerted the two brothers; and one day, hard by the
room in which Ser Ciappelletto lay sick, they began to talk about him;
saying one to the other:—"What shall we do with this man? We are
hard bested indeed on his account. If we turn him out of the house,
sick as he is, we shall not only incur grave censure, but shall evince a
signal want of sense; for folk must know the welcome we gave him in
the first instance, the solicitude with which we have had him treated
and tended since his illness, during which time he could not possibly
do aught to displease us, and yet they would see him suddenly turned
out of our house sick unto death. On the other hand he has been so
bad a man that he is sure not to confess or receive any of the Church's
sacraments; and dying thus unconfessed, he will be denied burial in
church, but will be cast out into some ditch like a dog; nay, 'twill be all
one if he do confess, for such and so horrible have been his crimes that
no friar or priest either will or can absolve him; and so, dying without
absolution, he will still be cast out into the ditch. In which case the folk
of these parts, who reprobate our trade as iniquitous and revile it all day
long, and would fain rob us, will seize their opportunity, and raise a tu-
mult, and make a raid upon our houses, crying:—'Away with these
Lombard dogs, whom the Church excludes from her pale'; and will
certainly strip us of our goods, and perhaps take our lives also; so that
in any case we stand to lose if this man die."

Ser Ciappelletto, who, as we said, lay close at hand while they thus
spoke, and whose hearing was sharpened, as is often the case, by his
malady, overheard all that they said about him. So he called them to
him, and said to them:—"I would not have you disquiet yourselves in
regard of me, or apprehend loss to befall you by my death. I have heard
what you have said of me and have no doubt that 'twould be as you say,
if matters took the course you anticipate; but I am minded that it shall
be otherwise. I have committed so many offences against God in the

course of my life, that one more in the hour of my death will make no difference whatever to the account. So seek out and bring hither the worthiest and most holy friar you can find, and leave me to settle your affairs and mine upon a sound and solid basis, with which you may rest satisfied."

The two brothers had not much hope of the result, but yet they went to a friary and asked for a holy and discreet man to hear the confession of a Lombard that was sick in their house, and returned with an aged man of just and holy life, very learned in the Scriptures, and venerable and held in very great and especial reverence by all the citizens. As soon as he had entered the room where Ser Ciappelletto was lying, and had taken his place by his side, he began gently to comfort him: then he asked him how long it was since he was confessed.

Whereto Ser Ciappelletto, who had never been confessed, answered:—"Father, it is my constant practice to be confessed at least once a week, and many a week I am confessed more often; but true it is, that, since I have been sick, now eight days, I have made no confession, so sore has been my affliction."

"Son," said the friar, "thou hast well done, and well for thee, if so thou continue to do; as thou dost confess so often, I see that my labour of hearkening and questioning will be slight."

"Nay but, master friar," said Ser Ciappelletto, "say not so; I have not confessed so often but that I would fain make a general confession of all my sins that I have committed, so far as I can recall them, from the day of my birth to the present time; and therefore I pray you, my good father, to question me precisely in every particular just as if I had never been confessed. And spare me not by reason of my sickness, for I had far rather do despite to my flesh than, sparing it, risk the perdition of my soul, which my Saviour redeemed with His precious blood."

The holy man was mightily delighted with these words, which seemed to him to betoken a soul in a state of grace. He therefore signified to Ser Ciappelletto his high approval of this practice; and then began by asking him whether he had ever sinned carnally with a woman. Whereto Ser Ciappelletto answered with a sigh:—"My father, I scruple to tell you the truth in this matter, fearing lest I sin in vainglory."

"Nay, but," said the friar, "speak boldly; none ever sinned by telling the truth, either in confession or otherwise."

"Then," said Ser Ciappelletto, "as you bid me speak boldly, I will tell you the truth of this matter. I am virgin even as when I issued from my mother's womb."

"Now God's blessing on thee," said the friar, "well done; and the greater is thy merit in that, hadst thou so willed, thou mightest have done otherwise far more readily than we who are under constraint of rule."

He then proceeded to ask, whether he had offended God by gluttony. Whereto Ser Ciappelletto, heaving a heavy sigh, answered that he had frequently so offended; for, being wont to fast not only in Lent like other devout persons, but at least three days in every week, taking nothing but bread and water, he had quaffed the water with as good a gusto and as much enjoyment, more particularly when fatigued by devotion or pilgrimage, as great drinkers quaff their wine; and oftentimes he had felt a craving for such dainty dishes of herbs as ladies make when they go into the country, and now and again he had relished his food more than seemed to him meet in one who fasted, as he did, for devotion.

"Son," said the friar, "these sins are natural and very trifling; and therefore I would not have thee burden thy conscience too much with them. There is no man, however holy he may be, but must sometimes find it pleasant to eat after a long fast and to drink after exertion."

"O, my father," said Ser Ciappelletto, "say not this to comfort me. You know well that I know, that the things which are done in the service of God ought to be done in perfect purity of an unsullied spirit; and whoever does otherwise sins."

The friar, well content, replied: — "Glad I am that thou dost think so, and I am mightily pleased with thy pure and good conscience which therein appears; but tell me: hast thou sinned by avarice, coveting more than was reasonable, or withholding more than was right?"

"My father," replied Ser Ciappelletto, "I would not have you disquiet yourself, because I am in the house of these usurers: no part have I in their concerns; nay, I did but come here to admonish and reprehend them, and wean them from this abominable traffic; and so, I believe, I had done, had not God sent me this visitation. But you must know, that my father left me a fortune, of which I dedicated the greater part to God; and since then for my own support and the relief of Christ's poor I have done a little trading, whereof I have desired to make gain; and all that I have gotten I have shared with God's poor, reserving one half for my own needs and giving the other half to them; and so well has my Maker prospered me, that I have ever managed my affairs to better and better account."

"Well done," said the friar; "but how? hast thou often given way to anger?"

"Often indeed, I assure you," said Ser Ciappelletto. "And who could refrain therefrom, seeing men doing frowardly all day long, breaking the commandments of God and recking nought of His judgments? Many a time in the course of a single day I had rather be dead than alive, to see the young men going after vanity, swearing and forswearing themselves, haunting taverns, avoiding the churches, and in short walking in the way of the world rather than in God's way."

"My son," said the friar, "this is a righteous wrath; nor could I find occasion therein to lay a penance upon thee. But did anger ever by any chance betray thee into taking human life, or affronting or otherwise wronging any?"

"Alas," replied Ser Ciappelletto, "alas, sir, man of God though you seem to me, how come you to speak after this manner? If I had had so much as the least thought of doing any of the things of which you speak, should I believe, think you, that I had been thus supported of God? These are the deeds of robbers and such like evil men, to whom I have ever said, when any I saw:—'Go, God change your heart.'"

Said then the friar:—"Now, my son, as thou hopest to be blest of God, tell me, hast thou never borne false witness against any, or spoken evil of another, or taken the goods of another without his leave?"

"Yes, master friar," answered Ser Ciappelletto, "most true it is that I have spoken evil of another; for I had once a neighbour who without the least excuse in the world was ever beating his wife, and so great was my pity of the poor creature, whom, when he was in his cups, he would thrash as God alone knows how, that once I spoke evil of him to his wife's kinsfolk."

"Well, well," said the friar, "thou tellest me thou hast been a merchant; hast thou ever cheated any, as merchants use to do?"

"I'faith, yes, master friar," said Ser Ciappelletto; "but I know not who he was; only that he brought me some money which he owed me for some cloth that I had sold him, and I put it in a box without counting it, where a month afterwards I found four farthings more than there should have been, which I kept for a year to return to him, but not seeing him again, I bestowed them in alms for the love of God."

"This," said the friar, "was a small matter; and thou didst well to bestow them as thou didst." The holy friar went on to ask him many other questions, to which he made answer in each case in this sort. Then, as the friar was about to give him absolution, Ser Ciappelletto interposed:—"Sir, I have yet a sin to confess."

"What?" asked the friar.

"I remember," he said, "that I once caused my servant to sweep my house on a Saturday after none; and that my observance of Sunday was less devout than it should have been."

"O, my son," said the friar, "this is a light matter."

"No," said Ser Ciappelletto, "say not a light matter; for Sunday is the more to be had in honour because on that day our Lord rose from the dead."

Then said the holy friar:—"Now is there aught else that thou hast done?"

"Yes, master friar," replied Ser Ciappelletto, "once by inadvertence I spat in the church of God."

At this the friar began to smile, and said:— "My son, this is not a matter to trouble about; we, who are religious, spit there all day long."

"And great impiety it is when you so do," replied Ser Ciappelletto, "for there is nothing that is so worthy to be kept from all impurity as the holy temple in which sacrifice is offered to God." More he said in the same strain, which I pass over; and then at last he began to sigh, and by and by to weep bitterly, as he was well able to do when he chose. And the friar demanding:— "My son, why weepest thou?"

"Alas, master friar," answered Ser Ciappelletto, "a sin yet remains, which I have never confessed, such shame were it to me to tell it; and as often as I call it to mind, I weep as you now see me weep, being well assured that God will never forgive me this sin."

Then said the holy friar:— "Come, come, son, what is this that thou sayst? If all the sins of all the men, that ever were or ever shall be, as long as the world shall endure, were concentrated in one man, so great is the goodness of God that He would freely pardon them all, were he but penitent and contrite as I see thou art, and confessed them: wherefore tell me thy sin with a good courage."

Then said Ser Ciappelletto, still weeping bitterly:— "Alas, my father, mine is too great a sin, and scarce can I believe, if your prayers do not co-operate, that God will ever grant me His pardon thereof."

"Tell it with a good courage," said the friar; "I promise thee to pray God for thee."

Ser Ciappelletto, however, continued to weep, and would not speak, for all the friar's encouragement. When he had kept him for a good while in suspense, he heaved a mighty sigh, and said:— "My father, as you promise me to pray God for me, I will tell it you. Know, then, that once, when I was a little child, I cursed my mother"; and having so said he began again to weep bitterly.

"O, my son," said the friar, "does this seem to thee so great a sin? Men curse God all day long, and He pardons them freely, if they repent them of having so done; and thinkest thou He will not pardon thee this? Weep not, be comforted, for truly, hadst thou been one of them that set Him on the Cross, with the contrition that I see in thee, thou wouldst not fail of His pardon."

"Alas! my father," rejoined Ser Ciappelletto, "what is this you say? To curse my sweet mother that carried me in her womb for nine months day and night, and afterwards on her shoulder more than a hundred times! Heinous indeed was my offence; 'tis too great a sin; nor will it be pardoned, unless you pray God for me."

The friar now perceiving that Ser Ciappelletto had nothing more to

say, gave him absolution and his blessing, reputing him for a most holy
man, fully believing that all that he had said was true. And who would
not have so believed, hearing him so speak at the point of death? Then,
when all was done, he said: — "Ser Ciappelletto, if God so will, you will
soon be well; but should it so come to pass that God call your blessed
soul to Himself in this state of grace, is it well pleasing to you that your
body be buried in our convent?"

"Yea, verily, master friar," replied Ser Ciappelletto; "there would I
be, and nowhere else, since you have promised to pray God for me; besides which I have ever had a special devotion to your order. Wherefore
I pray you, that, on your return to your convent, you cause to be sent
me that very Body of Christ, which you consecrate in the morning on
the altar; because (unworthy though I be) I purpose with your leave to
take it, and afterwards the holy and extreme unction, that, though I
have lived as a sinner, I may die at any rate as a Christian." The holy
man said that he was greatly delighted, that it was well said of Ser
Ciappelletto, and that he would cause the Host to be forthwith brought
to him; and so it was.

The two brothers, who much misdoubted Ser Ciappelletto's power
to deceive the friar, had taken their stand on the other side of a wooden
partition which divided the room in which Ser Ciappelletto lay from
another, and hearkening there they readily heard and understood what
Ser Ciappelletto said to the friar; and at times could scarce refrain their
laughter as they followed his confession; and now and again they said
one to another: — "What manner of man is this, whom neither age nor
sickness, nor fear of death, on the threshold of which he now stands,
nor yet of God, before whose judgment-seat he must soon appear, has
been able to turn from his wicked ways, that he die not even as he has
lived?" But seeing that his confession had secured the interment of his
body in church, they troubled themselves no further.

Ser Ciappelletto soon afterwards communicated, and growing im-
mensely worse, received the extreme unction, and died shortly after
vespers on the same day on which he had made his good confession.
So the two brothers, having from his own moneys provided the wherewith to procure him honourable sepulture, and sent word to the friars
to come at even to observe the usual vigil, and in the morning to fetch
the corpse, set all things in order accordingly. The holy friar who had
confessed him, hearing that he was dead, had audience of the prior of
the friary; a chapter was convened and the assembled brothers heard
from the confessor's own mouth how Ser Ciappelletto had been a holy
man, as had appeared by his confession, and were exhorted to receive
the body with the utmost veneration and pious care, as one by which
there was good hope that God would work many miracles. To this the

prior and the rest of the credulous confraternity assenting, they went in
a body in the evening to the place where the corpse of Ser Ciappelletto
lay, and kept a great and solemn vigil over it; and in the morning they
made a procession habited in their surplices and copes, with books in
their hands and crosses in front; and chanting as they went, they
fetched the corpse and brought it back to their church with the utmost
pomp and solemnity, being followed by almost all the folk of the city,
men and women alike. So it was laid in the church, and then the holy
friar who had heard the confession got up in the pulpit and began to
preach marvellous things of Ser Ciappelletto's life, his fasts, his virginity, his simplicity and guilelessness and holiness; narrating among other
matters that of which Ser Ciappelletto had made tearful confession as
his greatest sin, and how he had hardly been able to make him conceive that God would pardon him; from which he took occasion to reprove his hearers; saying: — "And you, accursed of God, on the least
pretext, blaspheme God and His Mother, and all the celestial court."
    And much beside he told of his loyalty and purity; and, in short, so
wrought upon the people by his words, to which they gave entire credence, that they all conceived a great veneration for Ser Ciappelletto,
and at the close of the office came pressing forward with the utmost vehemence to kiss the feet and the hands of the corpse, from which they
tore off the cerements, each thinking himself blessed to have but a
scrap thereof in his possession; and so it was arranged that it should be
kept there all day long, so as to be visible and accessible to all. At nightfall it was honourably interred in a marble tomb in one of the chapels,
where on the morrow, one by one, folk came and lit tapers and prayed
and paid their vows, setting there the waxen images which they had
dedicated. And the fame of Ciappelletto's holiness and the devotion to
him grew in such measure that scarce any there was that in any adversity would vow aught to any saint but he, and they called him and still
call him San Ciappelletto, affirming that many miracles have been and
daily are wrought by God through him for such as devoutly crave his
intercession.
    So lived, so died Ser Cepperello da Prato, and came to be reputed
a saint, as you have heard. Nor would I deny that it is possible that he
is of the number of the blessed in the presence of God, seeing that,
though his life was evil and depraved, yet he might in his last moments
have made so complete an act of contrition that perchance God had
mercy on him and received him into His kingdom. But, as this is hidden from us, I speak according to that which appears, and I say that he
ought rather to be in the hands of the devil in hell than in Paradise.
Which, if so it be, is a manifest token of the superabundance of the
goodness of God to usward, inasmuch as He regards not our error but

the sincerity of our faith, and hearkens unto us when, mistaking one who is at enmity with Him for a friend, we have recourse to him, as to one holy indeed, as our intercessor for His grace. Wherefore, that we of this gay company may by His grace be preserved safe and sound throughout this time of adversity, commend we ourselves in our need to Him, whose name we began by invoking, with lauds and reverent devotion and good confidence that we shall be heard.

And so he was silent.

STORY IV.

A monk lapses into a sin meriting the most severe punishment, justly censures the same fault in his abbot, and thus evades the penalty.

In the not very remote district of Lunigiana there flourished formerly a community of monks more numerous and holy than is there to be found to-day, among whom was a young brother, whose vigour and lustihood neither the fasts nor the vigils availed to subdue. One afternoon, while the rest of the confraternity slept, our young monk took a stroll around the church, which lay in a very sequestered spot, and chanced to espy a young and very beautiful girl, a daughter, perhaps, of one of the husbandmen of those parts, going through the fields and gathering herbs as she went. No sooner had he seen her than he was sharply assailed by carnal concupiscence, insomuch that he made up to and accosted her; and (she hearkening) little by little they came to an understanding, and unobserved by any entered his cell together. Now it so chanced that, while they fooled it within somewhat reck lessly, he being overwrought with passion, the abbot awoke and passing slowly by the young monk's cell, heard the noise which they made within, and the better to distinguish the voices, came softly up to the door of the cell, and listening discovered that beyond all doubt there was a woman within. His first thought was to force the door open; but, changing his mind, he returned to his chamber and waited until the monk should come out.

Delightsome beyond measure though the monk found his intercourse with the girl, yet was he not altogether without anxiety. He had heard, as he thought, the sound of footsteps in the dormitory, and having applied his eye to a convenient aperture had had a good view of the abbot as he stood by the door listening. He was thus fully aware that the abbot might have detected the presence of a woman in the cell. Whereat he was exceedingly distressed, knowing that he had a severe punishment to expect; but he concealed his vexation from the girl while he busily cast about in his mind for some way of escape from his embarrassment. He thus hit on a novel stratagem which was exactly

11

suited to his purpose. With the air of one who had had enough of the
girl's company he said to her: — "I shall now leave you in order that I
may arrange for your departure hence unobserved. Stay here quietly
until I return." So out he went, locking the door of the cell, and withdrawing the key, which he carried straight to the abbot's chamber and
handed to him, as was the custom when a monk was going out, saying
with a composed air: — "Sir, I was not able this morning to bring in all
the faggots which I had made ready, so with your leave I will go to the
wood and bring them in."

The abbot, desiring to have better cognisance of the monk's offence,
and not dreaming that the monk knew that he had been detected, was
pleased with the turn matters had taken, and received the key gladly, at
the same time giving the monk the desired leave. So the monk withdrew, and the abbot began to consider what course it were best for him
to take, whether to assemble the brotherhood and open the door in
their presence, that, being witnesses of the delinquency, they might
have no cause to murmur against him when he proceeded to punish
the delinquent, or whether it were not better first to learn from the girl's
own lips how it had come about. And reflecting that she might be the
wife or daughter of some man who would take it ill that she should be
shamed by being exposed to the gaze of all the monks, he determined
first of all to find out who she was, and then to make up his mind. So
he went softly to the cell, opened the door, and, having entered, closed
it behind him. The girl, seeing that her visitor was none other than the
abbot, quite lost her presence of mind, and quaking with shame began
to weep. Master abbot surveyed her from head to foot, and seeing that
she was fresh and comely, fell a prey, old though he was, to fleshly cravings no less poignant and sudden than those which the young monk
had experienced, and began thus to commune with himself: — "Alas!
why take I not my pleasure when I may, seeing that I never need lack
for occasions of trouble and vexation of spirit? Here is a fair wench, and
no one in the world to know. If I can bring her to pleasure me, I know
not why I should not do so. Who will know? No one will ever know;
and sin that is hidden is half forgiven; this chance may never come
again; so, methinks, it were the part of wisdom to take the boon which
God bestows."

So musing, with an altogether different purpose from that with
which he had come, he drew near the girl, and softly bade her to be
comforted, and besought her not to weep; and so little by little he came
at last to show her what he would be at. The girl, being made neither
of iron nor of adamant, was readily induced to gratify the abbot, who
after bestowing upon her many an embrace and kiss, got upon the
monk's bed, where, being sensible, perhaps, of the disparity between

his reverend portliness and her tender youth, and fearing to injure her by his excessive weight, he refrained from lying upon her, but laid her upon him, and in that manner disported himself with her for a long time.

The monk, who had only pretended to go to the wood, and had concealed himself in the dormitory, no sooner saw the abbot enter his cell than he was overjoyed to think that his plan would succeed; and when he saw that he had locked the door, he was well assured thereof. So he stole out of his hiding-place, and set his eye to an aperture through which he saw and heard all that the abbot did and said. At length the abbot, having had enough of dalliance with the girl, locked her in the cell and returned to his chamber. Catching sight of the monk soon afterwards, and supposing him to have returned from the wood, he determined to give him a sharp reprimand and have him imprisoned, that he might thus secure the prey for himself alone. He therefore caused him to be summoned, chid him very severely and with a stern countenance, and ordered him to be put in prison.

The monk replied trippingly:— "Sir, I have not been so long in the order of St. Benedict as to have every particular of the rule by heart; nor did you teach me before to-day in what posture it behoves the monk to have intercourse with women, but limited your instruction to such matters as fasts and vigils. As, however, you have now given me my lesson, I promise you, if you also pardon my offence, that I will never repeat it, but will always follow the example which you have set me."

The abbot, who was a shrewd man, saw at once that the monk was not only more knowing than he, but had actually seen what he had done; nor, conscience-stricken himself, could he for shame mete out to the monk a measure which he himself merited. So pardon given, with an injunction to bury what had been seen in silence, they decently conveyed the young girl out of the monastery, whither, it is to be believed, they now and again caused her to return.

STORY X.

Master Alberto da Bologna honourably puts to shame a lady who sought occasion to put him to shame in that he was in love with her.

As stars in the serene expanse of heaven, as in spring-time flowers in the green pastures, so, honourable damsels, in the hour of rare and excellent converse is wit with its bright sallies. Which, being brief, are much more proper for ladies than for men, seeing that prolixity of speech, when brevity is possible, is much less allowable to them; albeit (shame be to us all and all our generation) few ladies or none are left to-day who understand aught that is wittily said, or understanding are able to answer it. For the place of those graces of the spirit which distinguished the ladies of the past has now been usurped by adornments of the person; and she whose dress is most richly and variously and curiously dight, accounts herself more worthy to be had in honour, forgetting, that, were one but so to array him, an ass would carry a far greater load of finery than any of them, and for all that be not a whit the more deserving of honour.

I blush to say this, for in censuring others I condemn myself. Tricked out, bedecked, bedizened thus, we are either silent and impassive as statues, or, if we answer aught that is said to us, much better were it we had held our peace. And we make believe, forsooth, that our failure to acquit ourselves in converse with our equals of either sex does but proceed from guilelessness; dignifying stupidity by the name of modesty, as if no lady could be modest and converse with other folk than her maid or laundress or bake-house woman; which if Nature had intended, as we feign she did, she would have set other limits to our garrulousness. True it is that in this, as in other matters, time and place and person are to be regarded; because it sometimes happens that a lady or gentleman thinking by some sally of wit to put another to shame, has rather been put to shame by that other, having failed duly to estimate their relative powers. Wherefore, that you may be on your guard against such error, and, further, that in you be not exemplified the common proverb, to wit, that women do ever and on all occasions choose the worst, I trust

14

that this last of to-day's stories, which falls to me to tell, may serve
you as a lesson; that, as you are distinguished from others by nobility
of nature, so you may also shew yourselves separate from them by
excellence of manners.

There lived not many years ago, perhaps yet lives, in Bologna, a very
great physician, so great that the fame of his skill was noised abroad
throughout almost the entire world.

Now Master Alberto (such was his name) was of so noble a temper
that, being now nigh upon seventy years of age, and all but devoid of
natural heat of body, he was yet receptive of the flames of love; and
having at an assembly seen a very beautiful widow lady, Madonna
Malgherida de' Ghisolieri, as some say, and being charmed with her
beyond measure, was, notwithstanding his age, no less ardently enamoured than a young man, insomuch that he was not well able to sleep
at night, unless during the day he had seen the fair lady's lovely and
delicate features. Wherefore he began to frequent the vicinity of her
house, passing to and fro in front of it, now on foot now on horseback,
as occasion best served. Which she and many other ladies perceiving,
made merry together more than once, to see a man of his years and discretion in love, as if they deemed that this most delightful passion of
love were only fit for empty-headed youths, and could not in men be
either harboured or engendered. Master Alberto thus continuing to
haunt the front of the house, it so happened that one feast-day the lady
with other ladies was seated before her door, and Master Alberto's
approach being thus observed by them for some time before he arrived,
they complotted to receive him and shew him honour, and then to rally
him on his love; and so they did, rising with one accord to receive him,
bidding him welcome, and ushering him into a cool courtyard, where
they regaled him with the finest wines and comfits; which done, in a
tone of refined and sprightly banter they asked him how it came about
that he was enamoured of this fair lady, seeing that she was beloved of
many a fine gentleman of youth and spirit.

Master Alberto, being thus courteously assailed, put a blithe face on
it, and answered:—"Madam, my love for you need surprise none that
is conversant with such matters, and least of all you that are worthy of
it. And though old men, of course, have lost the strength which love
demands for its full fruition, yet are they not therefore without the good
intent and just appreciation of what beseems the accepted lover, but
indeed understand it far better than young men, by reason that they
have more experience. My hope in thus old aspiring to love you, who
are loved by so many young men, is founded on what I have frequently
observed of ladies' ways at lunch, when they trifle with the lupin and
the leek. In the leek no part is good, but the head is at any rate not so

bad as the rest, and indeed not unpalatable; you, however, for the most part, following a depraved taste, hold it in your hand and munch the leaves, which are not only of no account but actually distasteful. How am I to know, madam, that in your selection of lovers, you are not equally eccentric? In which case I should be the man of your choice, and the rest would be cast aside."

Whereto the gentle lady, somewhat shame-stricken, as were also her fair friends, thus made answer:—"Master Alberto, our presumption has received from you a most just and no less courteous reproof; but your love is dear to me, as should ever be that of a wise and worthy man. And therefore, saving my honour, I am yours, entirely and devotedly at your pleasure and command."

This speech brought Master Alberto to his feet, and the others also rising, he thanked the lady for her courtesy, bade her a gay and smiling adieu, and so left the house. Thus the lady, not considering on whom she exercised her wit, thinking to conquer was conquered herself: against which mishap you, if you are discreet, will ever be most strictly on your guard.

As the young ladies and the three young men finished their story-telling the sun was westering and the heat of the day in great measure abated. Which their queen observing, debonairly thus she spoke:— "Now, dear gossips, my day of sovereignty draws to a close, and nought remains for me to do but to give you a new queen, by whom on the morrow our common life may be ordered as she may deem best in a course of seemly pleasure; and though there seems to be still some interval between day and night, yet, as whoso does not in some degree anticipate the course of time, cannot well provide for the future; and in order that what the new queen shall decide to be meet for the morrow may be made ready beforehand, I decree that from this time forth the days begin at this hour. And so in reverent submission to Him, in whom is the life of all beings, for our comfort and solace we commit the governance of our realm for the morrow into the hands of Queen Filomena, most discreet of damsels." So saying she arose, took the laurel wreath from her brow, and with a gesture of reverence set it on the brow of Filomena, whom she then, and after her all the other ladies and the young men, saluted as queen, doing her due and graceful homage.

Queen Filomena modestly blushed a little to find herself thus invested with the sovereignty; but, being put on her mettle by Pampinea's recent admonitions, she was minded not to seem awkward, and soon recovered her composure. She then began by confirming all the appointments made by Pampinea, and making all needful arrangements for the following morning and evening, which they were to pass where they then were. Whereupon she thus spoke:—"Dearest gossips, though, thanks rather to Pampinea's courtesy than to merit of mine, I am made queen of you all; yet I am not on that account minded to have respect merely to my own judgment in the governance of our life, but to unite your wisdom with mine; and that you may understand what I think of doing, and by consequence may be able to amplify or curtail it at your pleasure, I will in few words make known to you my purpose. The course observed by Pampinea to-day, if I have judged aright, seems to be alike commendable and delectable; wherefore, until by lapse of time, or for some other cause, it grows tedious, I purpose not to alter it. So when we have arranged for what we have already taken in hand, we will go hence and enjoy a short walk; at sundown we will sup in the cool; and we will then sing a few songs and otherwise divert ourselves, until it is time to go to sleep. To-morrow we will rise in the cool of the morning, and after enjoying another walk, each at his or her sweet will, we will return, as to-day, and in due time break our fast, dance, sleep, and having risen, will here resume our story-telling, wherein, methinks, pleasure and profit unite in superabundant measure. True it is that Pampinea, by reason of her late election to the sovereignty, neglected one matter, which I mean to introduce, to wit, the circumscription of the topic of our story-telling, and its preassignment, that each may be able to premeditate some apt story bearing upon the theme; and seeing that from the beginning of the world Fortune has made men the sport of divers accidents, and so it will continue until the end, the theme, so please you, shall in each case be the same; to wit, the fortune of such as after divers adventures have at last attained a goal of unexpected felicity.

The ladies and the young men alike commended the rules thus laid down, and agreed to follow it. Dioneo, however, when the rest had done speaking, said:—"Madam, as all the rest have said, so say I, briefly, that the rule prescribed by you is commendable and delectable; but of your especial grace I crave a favour, which, I trust, may be granted and continued to me, so long as our company shall endure; which favour is this: that I be not bound by the assigned theme if I am not so minded, but that I have leave to choose such topic as best shall please me. And lest any suppose that I crave this grace as one that has not stories ready to hand, I am henceforth content that mine be always the last."

The queen, knowing him to be a merry and facetious fellow, and feeling sure that he only craved his favour in order that, if the company were jaded, he might have an opportunity to recreate them by some amusing story, gladly, with the consent of the rest, granted his petition. She then rose, and attended by the rest sauntered towards a stream, which, issuing clear as crystal from a neighbouring hill, precipitated itself into a valley shaded by trees close set amid living rock and fresh

green herbage. Bare of foot and arm they entered the stream, and roving
hither and thither amused themselves in divers ways till in due time
they returned to the palace, and gaily supped. Supper ended, the
queen sent for instruments of music, and bade Lauretta lead a dance,
while Emilia was to sing a song accompanied by Dioneo on the lute.

Accordingly Lauretta led a dance, while Emilia with passion sang
the following song:—

> So fain I am of my own loveliness,
>   I hope, nor think not e'er
> The weight to feel of other amorousness.
>
> When in the mirror I my face behold,
>   That see I there which doth my mind content,
> Nor any present hap or memory old
> May me deprive of such sweet ravishment.
> Where else, then, should I find such blandishment
>   Of sight and sense that e'er
> My heart should know another amorousness?
>
> Nor need I fear lest the fair thing retreat,
>   When fain I am my solace to renew;
> Rather, I know, 'twill me advance to meet,
> To pleasure me, and shew so sweet a view
> That speech or thought of none in its semblance true
>   Paint or conceive may e'er,
> Unless he burn with ev'n such amorousness.
>
> Thereon as more intent I gaze, the fire
>   Waxeth within me hourly more and more,
> Myself I yield thereto, myself entire,
> And foretaste have of what it hath in store,
> And hope of greater joyance than before,
>   Nay, such as ne'er
> None knew; for ne'er was felt such amorousness.

This ballade, to which all heartily responded, albeit its words furnished much matter of thought to some, was followed by some other
dances, and part of the brief night being thus spent, the queen pro-
claimed the first day ended, and bade light the torches, that all might
go to rest until the following morning; and so, seeking their several
chambers, to rest they went.

SECOND DAY

STORY II.

Rinaldo d' Asti is robbed, arrives at Castel Guglielmo, and is entertained by a widow lady; his property is restored to him, and he returns home safe and sound.

Fair ladies, 'tis on my mind to tell you a story in which are mingled things sacred and passages of adverse fortune and love, which to hear will perchance be not unprofitable, more especially to travellers in love's treacherous lands, of whom if any fail to say St. Julian's paternoster, it often happens that, though he may have a good bed, he is ill lodged.

Know, then, that in the time of the Marquis Azzo da Ferrara, a merchant, Rinaldo d' Asti by name, having disposed of certain affairs which had brought him to Bologna, set his face homeward, and having left Ferrara behind him was on his way to Verona, when he fell in with some men that looked like merchants, but were in truth robbers and men of evil life and condition, whose company he imprudently joined, riding and conversing with them. They, perceiving that he was a merchant, and judging that he must have money about him, complotted to rob him on the first opportunity; and to obviate suspicion they played the part of worthy and reputable men, their discourse of nought but what was seemly and honourable and leal, their demeanour at once as respectful and as cordial as they could make it; so that he deemed himself very lucky to have met with them, being otherwise alone save for a single mounted servant. Journeying thus, they conversed, after the desultory manner of travellers, of divers matters, until at last they fell a talking of the prayers which men address to God, and one of the robbers—there were three of them—said to Rinaldo:—"And you, gentle sir, what is your wonted orison when you are on your travels?"

Rinaldo answered:—"Why, to tell the truth, I am a man unskilled, unlearned in such matters, and few prayers have I at my command, being one that lives in the good old way and lets two soldi count for

19

twenty-four deniers; nevertheless it has always been my custom in journeying to say of a morning, as I leave the inn, a paternoster and an avemaria for the souls of the father and mother of St. Julian, after which I pray God and St. Julian to provide me with a good inn for the night. And many a time in the course of my life have I met with great perils by the way, and evading them all have found comfortable quarters for the night: whereby my faith is assured, that St. Julian, in whose honour I say my paternoster, has gotten me this favour of God; nor should I look for a prosperous journey and a safe arrival at night, if I had not said it in the morning."

Then said his interrogator: — "And did you say it this morning?"

Whereto Rinaldo answered, "Troth, did I," which caused the other, who by this time knew what course matters would take, to say to himself: — "'Twill prove to have been said in the nick of time; for if we do not miscarry, I take it thou wilt have but a sorry lodging." Then turning to Rinaldo he said: — "I also have travelled much, and never a prayer have I said, through I have heard them much commended by many; nor has it ever been my lot to find other than good quarters for the night; it may be that this very evening you will be able to determine which of us has the better lodging, you that have said the paternoster, or I that have not said it. True, however, it is that in its stead I am accustomed to say the 'Dirupisti,' or the 'Intemerata,' or the 'De profundis,' which, if what my grandmother used to say is to be believed, are of the greatest efficacy."

So, talking of divers matters, and ever on the look-out for time and place suited to their evil purpose, they continued their journey, until towards evening, some distance from Castel Guglielmo, as they were about to ford a stream, these three ruffians, profiting by the lateness of the hour, and the loneliness and straitness of the place, set upon Rinaldo and robbed him, and leaving him afoot and in his shirt, said by way of adieu: — "Go now, and see if thy St. Julian will provide thee with good lodging to-night; our saint, we doubt not, will do as much by us"; and so crossing the stream, they went their way.

Rinaldo's servant, coward that he was, did nothing to help his master when he saw him attacked, but turned his horse's head, and was off at a smart pace; nor did he draw rein until he was come to Castel Guglielmo; where, it being now evening, he put up at an inn and gave himself no further trouble.

Rinaldo, left barefoot, and stripped to his shirt, while the night closed in very cold and snowy, was at his wits' end, and shivering so that his teeth chattered in his head, began to peer about, if haply he might find some shelter for the night, that so he might not perish with the cold; but, seeing none (for during a recent war the whole country had been wasted by fire), he set off for Castel Guglielmo, quickening his pace by reason of the cold. Whether his servant had taken refuge in Castel Guglielmo or elsewhere, he knew not, but he thought that, could he but enter the town, God would surely send him some succour. However, dark night overtook him while he was still about a mile from the castle; so that on his arrival he found the gates already locked and the bridges raised, and he could not pass in. Sick at heart, disconsolate and bewailing his evil fortune, he looked about for some place where he might ensconce himself, and at any rate find shelter from the snow. And by good luck he espied a house, built with a balcony a little above the castle-wall, under which balcony he purposed to shelter himself until daybreak. Arrived at the spot, he found beneath the balcony a postern, which, however, was locked; and having gathered some bits of straw that lay about, he placed them in front of the postern, and there in sad and sorrowful plight took up his quarters, with many a piteous appeal to St. Julian, whom he reproached for not better rewarding the faith which he reposed in him. St. Julian, however, had not abandoned him, and in due time provided him with a good lodging.

There was in the castle a widow lady of extraordinary beauty (none fairer) whom Marquis Azzo loved as his own life, and kept there for his pleasure. She lived in the very same house beneath the balcony of which Rinaldo had posted himself. Now it chanced that that very day the Marquis had come to Castel Guglielmo to pass the night with her, and had privily caused a bath to be made ready, and a supper suited to his rank, in the lady's own house. The arrangements were complete; and only the Marquis was stayed for, when a servant happened to present himself at the castle-gate, bringing tidings for the Marquis which obliged him suddenly to take horse. He therefore sent word to the lady that she must not wait for him, and forthwith took his departure. The lady, somewhat disconsolate, found nothing better to do than to get into the bath which had been intended for the Marquis, sup and go to bed: so into the bath she went. The bath was close to the postern on the other side of which hapless Rinaldo had ensconced himself, and thus the mournful and quavering music which Rinaldo made as he shuddered in the cold, and which seemed rather to proceed from a stork's beak than from the mouth of a human being, was audible to the lady in the bath. She therefore called her maid, and said to her:—"Go up and look out over the wall and down at the postern, and mark who is there, and what he is, and what he does there."

The maid obeyed, and, the night being fine, had no difficulty in making out Rinaldo as he sate there, barefoot, as I have said, and in his

shirt, and trembling in every limb. So she called out to him, to know
who he was. Rinaldo, who could scarcely articulate for shivering, told
as briefly as he could, who he was, and how and why he came to be
there; which done, he began piteously to beseech her not, if she could
avoid it, to leave him there all night to perish of cold. The maid went
back to her mistress full of pity for Rinaldo, and told her all she had
seen and heard.

The lady felt no less pity for Rinaldo; and bethinking her that she
had the key of the postern by which the Marquis sometimes entered
when he paid her a secret visit, she said to the maid:—"Go, and let him
in softly; here is this supper, and there will be none to eat it; and we can
very well put him up for the night."

Cordially commending her mistress's humanity, the maid went and
let Rinaldo in, and brought him to the lady, who, seeing that he was all
but dead with cold, said to him:—"Quick, good man, get into that
bath, which is still warm."

Gladly he did so, awaiting no second invitation, and was so much
comforted by its warmth that he seemed to have passed from death to
life. The lady provided him with a suit of clothes, which had been worn
by her husband shortly before his death, and which, when he had them
on, looked as if they had been made for him. So he recovered heart,
and, while he awaited the lady's commands, gave thanks to God and
St. Julian for delivering him from a woful night and conducting him,
as it seemed, to comfortable quarters.

The lady meanwhile took a little rest, after which she had a roaring
fire put in one of her large rooms, whither presently she came, and
asked her maid how the good man did. The maid replied:—"Madam,
he has put on the clothes, in which he shews to advantage, having a
handsome person, and seeming to be a worthy man, and well-bred."

"Go, call him then," said the lady, "tell him to come hither to the
fire, and we will sup; for I know that he has not supped."

Rinaldo, on entering the room and seeing the lady, took her to be of
no small consequence. He therefore made her a low bow, and did his
utmost to thank her worthily for the service she had rendered him. His
words pleased her no less than his person, which accorded with
what the maid had said: so she made him heartily welcome, installed
him at his ease by her side before the fire, and questioned him of
the adventure which had brought him thither. Rinaldo detailed all
the circumstances, of which the lady had heard somewhat when
Rinaldo's servant made his appearance at the castle. She therefore gave
entire credence to what he said, and told him what she knew about his

servant, and how he might easily find him on the morrow. She then bade set the table, which done, Rinaldo and she washed their hands and sate down together to sup.

Tall he was and comely of form and feature, debonair and gracious of mien and manner, and in his lusty prime. The lady had eyed him again and again to her no small satisfaction, and, her wantonness being already kindled for the Marquis, who was to have come to lie with her, she had let Rinaldo take the vacant place in her mind. So when supper was done, and they were risen from the table, she conferred with her maid, whether, after the cruel trick played upon her by the Marquis, it were not well to take the good gift which Fortune had sent her. The maid knowing the bent of her mistress's desire, left no word unsaid that might encourage her to follow it. Wherefore the lady, turning towards Rinaldo, who was standing where she had left him by the fire, began thus:—"So! Rinaldo, why still so pensive? Will nothing console you for the loss of a horse and a few clothes? Take heart, put a blithe face on it, you are at home; nay more, let me tell you that, seeing you in those clothes which my late husband used to wear, and taking you for him, I have felt, not once or twice, but perhaps a hundred times this evening, a longing to throw my arms round you and kiss you; and, in faith, I had so done, but that I feared it might displease you."

Rinaldo, hearing these words, and marking the flame which shot from the lady's eyes, and being no laggard, came forward with open arms, and confronted her and said:— "Madam, I am not unmindful that I must ever acknowledge that to you I owe my life, in regard of the peril whence you rescued me. If then there be any way in which I may pleasure you, churlish indeed were I not to devise it. So you may even embrace and kiss me to your heart's content, and I will embrace and kiss you with the best of good wills."

There needed no further parley. The lady, all aflame with amorous desire, forthwith threw herself into his arms, and straining him to her bosom with a thousand passionate embraces, gave and received a thousand kisses before they sought her chamber. There with all speed they went to bed, nor did day surprise them until again and again and in full measure they had satisfied their desire. With the first streaks of dawn they rose, for the lady was minded that none should surmise aught of the affair. So, having meanly habited Rinaldo, and replenished his purse, she enjoined him to keep the secret, shewed him the way to the castle, where he was to find his servant, and let him out by the same postern by which he had entered.

When it was broad day the gates were opened, and Rinaldo, passing himself off as a traveller from distant parts, entered the castle, and found his servant. Having put on the spare suit which was in his valise, he was about to mount the servant's horse, when, as if by miracle, there were brought into the castle the three gentlemen of the road who had robbed him the evening before, having been taken a little while after for another offence. Upon their confession Rinaldo's horse was restored to him, as were also his clothes and money; so that he lost nothing except a pair of garters, of which the robbers knew not where they had bestowed them.

Wherefore Rinaldo, giving thanks to God and St. Julian, mounted his horse, and returned home safe and sound, and on the morrow the three robbers kicked heels in the wind.

STORY V.

Andreuccio da Perugia comes to Naples to buy horses, meets with three serious adventures in one night, comes safe out of them all, and returns home with a ruby.

In Perugia, by what I once gathered, there lived a young man, Andreuccio di Pietro by name, a horse-dealer, who, having learnt that horses were to be had cheap at Naples, put five hundred florins of gold in his purse, and in company with some other merchants went thither, never having been away from home before. On his arrival at Naples, which was on a Sunday evening, about vespers, he learnt from his host that the fair would be held on the following morning. Thither accordingly he then repaired, and looked at many horses which pleased him much, and cheapening them more and more, and failing to strike a bargain with any one, he from time to time, being raw and unwary, drew out his purse of florins in view of all that came and went, to shew that he meant business.

While he was thus chaffering, and after he had shewn his purse, there chanced to come by a Sicilian girl, fair as fair could be, but ready to pleasure any man for a small consideration. He did not see her, but she saw him and his purse, and forthwith said to herself:— "Who would be in better luck than I if all those florins were mine?" and so she passed on. With the girl was an old woman, also a Sicilian, who, when she saw Andreuccio, dropped behind the girl, and ran towards him, making as if she would tenderly embrace him. The girl observing this said nothing, but stopped and waited a little way off for the old woman to rejoin her. Andreuccio turned as the old woman came up, recognised her, and greeted her very cordially; but time and place not permitting much converse, she left him, promising to visit him at his inn; and he resumed his chaffering, but bought nothing that morning.

Her old woman's intimate acquaintance with Andreuccio had no more escaped the girl's notice than the contents of Andreuccio's purse;

and with the view of devising, if possible, some way to make the money, either in whole or in part, her own, she began cautiously to ask the old woman, who and whence he was, what he did there, and how she came to know him. The old woman gave her almost as much and as circumstantial information touching Andreuccio and his affairs as he might have done himself, for she had lived a great while with his father, first in Sicily, and afterwards at Perugia. She likewise told the girl the name of his inn, and the purpose with which he had come to Naples. Thus fully armed with the names and all else that it was needful for her to know touching Andreuccio's kith and kin, the girl founded thereon her hopes of gratifying her cupidity, and forthwith devised a cunning stratagem to effect her purpose.

Home she went, and gave the old woman work enough to occupy her all day, that she might not be able to visit Andreuccio; then, summoning to her aid a little girl whom she had well trained for such services, she sent her about vespers to the inn where Andreuccio lodged. Arrived there, the little girl asked for Andreuccio of Andreuccio himself, who chanced to be just outside the gate.

On his answering that he was the man, she took him aside, and said:— "Sir, a lady of this country, so please you, would fain speak with you."

Whereto he listened with all his ears, and having a great conceit of his person, made up his mind that the lady was in love with him, as if there were ne'er another handsome fellow in Naples but himself; so forthwith he replied, that he would wait on the lady, and asked where and when it would be her pleasure to speak with him.

"Sir," replied the little girl, "she expects you in her own house, if you be pleased to come."

"Lead on then, I follow thee," said Andreuccio promptly, vouchsafing never a word to any in the inn. So the little girl guided him to her mistress's house, which was situated in a quarter the character of which may be inferred from its name, Evil Hole.

Of this, however, he neither knew nor suspected aught, but, supposing that the quarter was perfectly reputable and that he was going to see a sweet lady, strode carelessly behind the little girl into the house of her mistress, whom she summoned by calling out, "Andreuccio is here"; and Andreuccio then saw her advance to the head of the stairs to await his ascent. She was tall, still in the freshness of her youth, very fair of face, and very richly and nobly clad.

As Andreuccio approached, she descended three steps to meet him with open arms, and clasped him round the neck, but for a while stood silent as if from excess of tenderness; then, bursting into a flood of tears, she kissed his brow, and in slightly broken accents said:—"O Andreuccio, welcome, welcome, my Andreuccio."

Quite lost in wonder to be the recipient of such caresses, Andreuccio could only answer:—"Madam, well met." Whereupon she took him by the hand, led him up into her saloon, and thence without another word into her chamber, which exhaled throughout the blended fragrance of roses, orange-blossoms and other perfumes. He observed a handsome curtained bed, dresses in plenty hanging, as is customary in that country, on pegs, and other appointments very fair and sumptuous; which sights, being strange to him, confirmed his belief that he was in the house of no other than a great lady.

They sate down side by side on a chest at the foot of the bed, and thus she began to speak:—"Andreuccio, I cannot doubt that thou dost marvel both at the caresses which I bestow upon thee, and at my tears, seeing that thou knowest me not, and, maybe, hast never so much as heard my name; wait but a moment and thou shalt learn what perhaps will cause thee to marvel still more, to wit, that I am thy sister; and I tell thee, that, since of God's especial grace it is granted me to see one, albeit I would fain see all, of my brothers before I die, I shall not meet death, when the hour comes, without consolation; but thou, perchance, hast never heard aught of this; wherefore listen to what I shall say to thee. Pietro, my father and thine, as I suppose thou mayst have herd, dwelt a long while at Palermo, where his good heart and gracious bearing caused him to be (as he still is) much beloved by all that knew him; but by none was he loved so much as by a gentlewoman, afterwards my mother, then a widow, who, casting aside all respect for her father and brothers, ay, and her honour, grew so intimate with him that a child was born, which child am I, thy sister, whom thou seest before thee. Shortly after my birth it so befell that Pietro must needs leave Palermo and return to Perugia, and I, his little daughter, was left behind with my mother at Palermo; nor, so far as I have been able to learn, did he ever again bestow a thought upon either of us. Wherefore—to say nothing of the love which he should have borne me, his daughter by no servant or woman of low degree—I should, were he not my father, gravely censure the ingratitude which he shewed towards my mother, who, prompted by a most loyal love, committed her fortune and herself to his keeping, without so much as knowing who he was.

"But to what end? The wrongs of long-ago are much more easily censured than redressed; enough that so it was. He left me a little girl at Palermo, where, when I was grown to be almost as thou seest me, my

mother, who was a rich lady, gave me in marriage to an honest gentleman of the Girgenti family, who for love of my mother and myself
settled in Palermo, and there, being a staunch Guelf, entered into
correspondence with our King Charles;[1] which being discovered by
King Frederic[2] before the time was ripe for action, we had perforce to
flee from Sicily just when I was expecting to become the greatest lady
that ever was in the island. So, taking with us such few things as we
could, few, I say, in comparison of the abundance which we possessed,
we bade adieu to our estates and palaces, and found a refuge in this
country, and such favour with King Charles that, in partial compensation for the losses which we had sustained on his account, he has
granted us estates and houses and an ample pension, which he
regularly pays to my husband and thy brother-in-law, as thou mayst yet
see. In this manner I live here; but that I am blest with the sight of thee,
I ascribe entirely to the mercy of God; and no thanks to thee, my sweet
brother." So saying she embraced him again, and melting anew into
tears kissed his brow.

This story, so congruous, so consistent in every detail, came trippingly and without the least hesitancy from her tongue. Andreuccio
remembered that his father had indeed lived at Palermo; he knew by
his own experience the ways of young folk, how prone they are to love;
he saw her melt into tears, he felt her embraces and sisterly kisses; and
he took all she said for gospel. So, when she had done, he answered:—
"Madam, it should not surprise you that I marvel, seeing that, in sooth,
my father, for whatever cause, said never a word of you and your
mother, or, if he did so, it came not to my knowledge, so that I knew
no more of you than if you had not been; wherefore, the lonelier I
am here, and the less hope I had of such good luck, the better pleased
I am to have found here my sister. And indeed, I know not any man,
however exalted his station, who ought not to be well pleased to have
such a sister; much more, then, I, who am but a petty merchant; but, I
pray you, resolve me of one thing: how came you to know that I
was here?"

Then answered she:— "'Twas told me this morning by a poor woman
who is much about the house, because, as she tells me, she was long in
the service of our father both at Palermo and at Perugia; and, but that
it seemed more fitting that thou shouldst come to see me at home than
that I should visit thee at an inn, I had long ago sought thee out."

She then began to inquire particularly after all his kinsfolk by name,
and Andreuccio, becoming ever more firmly persuaded of that which

[1]Charles II. of Naples, son of Charles of Anjou.
[2]Frederic II. of Sicily, younger son of Peter III. of Arragon.

it was least for his good to believe, answered all her questions. Their conversation being thus prolonged and the heat great, she had Greek wine and sweetmeats brought in, and gave Andreuccio to drink; and when towards supper-time he made as if he would leave, she would in no wise suffer it; but, feigning to be very much vexed, she embraced him, saying:—"Alas! now 'tis plain how little thou carest for me: to think that thou art with thy sister, whom thou seest for the first time, and in her own house, where thou shouldst have alighted on thine arrival, and thou wouldst fain depart hence to go sup at an inn! Nay but, for certain, thou shalt sup with me; and albeit, to my great regret, my husband is not here, thou shalt see that I can do a lady's part in shewing thee honour."

Andreuccio, not knowing what else to say, replied:—"Sister, I care for you with all a brother's affection; but if I go not, supper will await me all the evening at the inn, and I shall justly be taxed with discourtesy."

Then said she:—"Blessed be God, there is even now in the house one by whom I can send word that they are not to expect thee at the inn, albeit thou wouldst far better discharge the debt of courtesy by sending word to thy friends, that they come here to sup; and then, if go thou must, you might all go in a body."

Andreuccio replied, that he would have none of his friends that evening, but since she would have him stay, he would even do her the pleasure. She then made a shew of sending word to the inn that they should not expect him at dinner.

Much more talk followed; and then they sate down to a supper of many courses splendidly served, which she cunningly protracted until nightfall; nor, when they were risen from table, and Andreuccio was about to take his departure, would she by any means suffer it, saying, that Naples was no place to walk about in after dark, least of all for a stranger, and that, as she had sent word to the inn that they were not to expect him at supper, so she had done the like in regard of his bed. Believing what she said, and being (in his false confidence) overjoyed to be with her, he stayed. After supper there was matter enough for talk both various and prolonged; and, when the night was in a measure spent, she gave up her own chamber to Andreuccio, leaving him with a small boy to shew him aught that he might have need of, while she retired with her women to another chamber.

It was a very hot night; so, no sooner was Andreuccio alone than he stripped himself to his doublet, and drew off his stockings and laid them on the bed's head; and nature demanding a discharge of the surplus weight which he carried within him, he asked the lad where this might be done, and was shewn a door in a corner of the room, and told to go in there. Andreuccio, nothing doubting, did so, but, by ill luck, set his foot on a plank which was detached from the joist at the further end, whereby down it went, and he with it. By God's grace he took no hurt by the fall, though it was from some height, beyond sousing himself from head to foot in the ordure which filled the whole place, which, that you may the better understand what has been said, and that which is to follow, I will describe to you.

A narrow and blind alley, such as we commonly see between two houses, was spanned by planks supported by joists on either side, and on the planks was the stool; of which planks that which fell with Andreuccio was one. Now Andreuccio, finding himself down there in the alley, fell to calling on the lad, who, as soon as he heard him fall, had run off, and promptly let the lady know what had happened. She hied forthwith to her chamber, and after a hasty search found Andreuccio's clothes and the money in them, for he foolishly thought to secure himself against risk by carrying it always on his person, and thus being possessed of the prize for which she had played her ruse, passing herself off as the sister of a man of Perugia, whereas she was really of Palermo, she concerned herself no further with Andreuccio except to close with all speed the door by which he had gone out when he fell.

As the lad did not answer, Andreuccio began to shout more loudly; but all to no purpose. Whereby his suspicions were aroused, and he began at last to perceive the trick that had been played upon him; so he climbed over a low wall that divided the alley from the street, and hied him to the door of the house, which he knew very well. There for a long while he stood shouting and battering the door till it shook on its hinges; but all again to no purpose. No doubt of his misadventure now lurking in his mind, he fell to bewailing himself, saying:—"Alas! in how brief a time have I lost five hundred florins and a sister!" with much more of the like sort.

Then he recommenced battering the door and shouting, to such a tune that not a few of the neighbours were roused, and finding the nuisance intolerable, got up; and one of the lady's servant-girls presented herself at the window with a very sleepy air, and said angrily:—"Who knocks below there?"

"Oh!" said Andreuccio, "dost not know me? I am Andreuccio, Madam Fiordaliso's brother."

"Good man," she rejoined, "if thou hast had too much to drink, go, sleep it off, and come back to-morrow. I know not Andreuccio, nor aught of the fantastic stuff thou pratest; prithee begone and be so good as to let us sleep in peace."

"How?" said Andreuccio, "dost not understand what I say? For sure thou dost understand; but if Sicilian kinships are of such a sort that folk forget them so soon, at least return me my clothes, which I left within, and right glad shall I be to be off."

Half laughing she rejoined: — "Good man, methinks thou dost dream": and so saying, she withdrew and closed the window. Andreuccio by this time needed no further evidence of his wrongs; his wrath knew no bounds, and mortification well-nigh converted it into frenzy; he was minded to exact by force what he had failed to obtain by entreaties; and so, arming himself with a large stone, he renewed his attack upon the door with fury, dealing much heavier blows than at first. Wherefore, not a few of the neighbours, whom he had already roused from their beds, set him down as an ill-conditioned rogue, and his story as a mere fiction intended to annoy the good woman,[1] and resenting the din which he now made, came to their windows, just as, when a stranger dog makes his appearance, all the dogs of the quarter will run to bark at him, and called out in chorus: — "'Tis a gross affront to come at this time of night to the house of the good woman with this silly story. Prithee, good man, let us sleep in peace; begone in God's name; and if thou hast a score to settle with her, come to-morrow, but a truce to thy pestering to-night."

Emboldened, perhaps, by these words, a man who lurked within the house, the good woman's bully, whom Andreuccio had as yet neither seen nor heard, shewed himself at the window, and said in a gruff voice and savage, menacing tone: — "Who is below there?"

Andreuccio looked up in the direction of the voice, and saw standing at the window, yawning and rubbing his eyes as if he had just been roused from his bed, or at any rate from deep sleep, a fellow with a black and matted beard, who, as far as Andreuccio's means of judging went, bade fair to prove a most redoubtable champion. It was not without fear, therefore, that he replied: — "I am a brother of the lady who is within."

The bully did not wait for him to finish his sentence, but, addressing him in a much sterner tone than before, called out: — "I know not why I come not down and give thee play with my cudgel, whilst thou givest me sign of life, ass, tedious driveller that thou must needs be, and drunken sot, thus to disturb our night's rest." Which said, he withdrew, and closed the window.

Some of the neighbours who best knew the bully's quality gave Andreuccio fair words. "For God's sake," said they, "good man, take thyself off, stay not here to be murdered. 'Twere best for thee to go."

---

[1] I.e. the bawd.

These counsels, which seemed to be dictated by charity, reinforced
the fear which the voice and aspect of the bully had inspired in
Andreuccio, who, thus despairing of recovering his money and in the
deepest of dumps, set his face towards the quarter whence in the day-
time he had blindly followed the little girl, and began to make his way
back to the inn. But so noisome was the stench which he emitted that
he resolved to turn aside and take a bath in the sea. So he bore leftward
up a street called Ruga Catalana, and was on his way towards the steep
of the city, when by chance he saw two men coming towards him, bearing a lantern, and fearing that they might be patrols or other men who
might do him a mischief, he stole away and hid himself in a disman-
tled house to avoid them. The house, however, was presently entered
by the two men, just as if they had been guided thither; and one of
them having disburdened himself of some iron tools which he carried
on his shoulder, they both began to examine them, passing meanwhile
divers comments upon them.

While they were thus occupied, "What," said one, "means this? Such
a stench as never before did I smell the like!"

So saying, he raised the lantern a little; whereby they had a view of
hapless Andreuccio, and asked in amazement:—"Who is there?"

Whereupon Andreuccio was at first silent, but when they flashed the
light close upon him, and asked him what he did there in such a filthy
state, he told them all that had befallen him.

Casting about to fix the place where it occurred, they said one to
another:—"Of a surety 'twas in the house of Scarabone Buttafuoco."

Then said one, turning to Andreuccio:—"Good man, albeit thou
hast lost thy money, thou hast cause enough to praise God that thou
hadst the luck to fall; for hadst thou not fallen, be sure that, no sooner
wert thou asleep, than thou hadst been knocked on the head, and lost
not only thy money but thy life. But what boots it now to bewail thee?
Thou mightest as soon pluck a star from the firmament as recover a
single denier; nay, 'tis as much as thy life is worth if he do but hear that
thou breathest a word of the affair."

The two men then held a short consultation, at the close of which
they said:—"Lo now; we are sorry for thee, and so we make thee a fair
offer. If thou wilt join with us in a little matter which we have in hand,
we doubt not but thy share of the gain will greatly exceed what thou
hast lost."

Andreuccio, being now desperate, answered that he was ready to join
them. Now Messer Filippo Minutolo, Archbishop of Naples, had that
day been buried with a ruby on his finger, worth over five hundred
florins of gold, besides other ornaments of extreme value. The two men
were minded to despoil the Archbishop of his fine trappings, and

imparted their design to Andreuccio, who, cupidity getting the better of caution, approved it; and so they all three set forth. But as they were on their way to the cathedral, Andreuccio gave out so rank an odour that one said to the other: — "Can we not contrive that he somehow wash himself a little, that he stink not so shrewdly?"

"Why yes," said the other, "we are now close to a well, which is never without the pulley and a large bucket; 'tis but a step thither, and we will wash him out of hand."

Arrived at the well, they found that the rope was still there, but the bucket had been removed; so they determined to attach him to the rope, and lower him into the well, there to wash himself, which done, he was to jerk the rope, and they would draw him up. Lowered accordingly he was; but just as, now washen, he jerked the rope, it so happened that a company of patrols, being thirsty because 'twas a hot night and some rogue had led them a pretty dance, came to the well to drink.

The two men fled, unobserved, as soon as they caught sight of the newcomers, who, parched with thirst, laid aside their bucklers, arms and surcoats, and fell to hauling on the rope, supposing that it bore the bucket, full of water. When, therefore, they saw Andreuccio, as he neared the brink of the well, loose the rope and clutch the brink with his hands, they were stricken with a sudden terror, and without uttering a word let go the rope, and took to flight with all the speed they could make. Whereat Andreuccio marvelled mightily, and had he not kept a tight grip on the brink of the well, he would certainly have gone back to the bottom and hardly have escaped grievous hurt, or death. Still greater was his astonishment, when, fairly landed on *terra firma*, he found the patrols' arms lying there, which he knew had not been carried by his comrades. He felt a vague dread, he knew not why; he bewailed once more his evil fortune; and without venturing to touch the arms, he left the well and wandered he knew not whither.

As he went, however, he fell in with his two comrades, now returning to draw him out of the well; who no sooner saw him than in utter amazement they demanded who had hauled him up. Andreuccio answered that he knew not, and then told them in detail how it had come about, and what he had found beside the well. They laughed as they apprehended the circumstances, and told him why they had fled, and who they were that had hauled him up. Then without further parley, for it was now midnight, they hied them to the cathedral. They had no difficulty in entering and finding the tomb, which was a magnificent structure of marble, and with their iron implements they raised the lid, albeit it was very heavy, to a height sufficient to allow a man to enter, and propped it up. This done, a dialogue ensued.

"Who shall go in?" said one.

"Not I," said the other.

"Nor I," rejoined his companion; "let Andreuccio go in."

"That will not I," said Andreuccio.

Whereupon both turned upon him and said:—"How? thou wilt not go in? By God, if thou goest not in, we will give thee that over the pate with one of these iron crowbars that thou shalt drop down dead."

Terror-stricken, into the tomb Andreuccio went, saying to himself as he did so:—"These men will have me go in, that they may play a trick upon me: when I have handed everything up to them, and am sweating myself to get out of the tomb, they will be off about their business, and I shall be left with nothing for my pains."

So he determined to make sure of his own part first; and bethinking him of the precious ring of which he had heard them speak, as soon as he had completed the descent, he drew the ring off the Archbishop's finger, and put it on his own: he then handed up one by one the crosier, mitre and gloves, and other of the Archbishop's trappings, stripping him to his shirt; which done, he told his comrades that there was nothing more. They insisted that the ring must be there, and bade him search everywhere. This he feigned to do, ejaculating from time to time that he found it not; and thus he kept them a little while in suspense. But they, who were in their way as cunning as he, kept on exhorting him to make a careful search, and, seizing their opportunity, withdrew the prop that supported the lid of the tomb, and took to their heels, leaving him there a close prisoner.

You will readily conceive how Andreuccio behaved when he understood his situation. More than once he applied his head and shoulders to the lid and sought with might and main to heave it up; but all his efforts were fruitless; so that at last, overwhelmed with anguish he fell in a swoon on the corpse of the Archbishop, and whether of the twain were the more lifeless, Andreuccio or the Archbishop, 'twould have puzzled an observer to determine.

When he came to himself he burst into a torrent of tears, seeing now nothing in store for him but either to perish there of hunger and fetid odours beside the corpse and among the worms, or, should the tomb be earlier opened, to be taken and hanged as a thief. These most lugubrious meditations were interrupted by a sound of persons walking and talking in the church. They were evidently a numerous company, and their purpose, as Andreuccio surmised, was the very same with which he and his comrades had come thither: whereby his terror was mightily increased.

Presently the folk opened the tomb, and propped up the lid, and then fell to disputing as to who should go in. None was willing, and the

contention was protracted; but at length one—'twas a priest—said:—
"Of what are ye afeared? Think ye to be eaten by him? Nay, the dead
eat not the living. I will go in myself."

So saying he propped his breast upon the edge of the lid, threw his
head back, and thrust his legs within, that he might go down feet foremost. On sight whereof Andreuccio started to his feet, and seizing hold
of one of the priest's legs, made as if he would drag him down; which
caused the priest to utter a prodigious yell, and bundle himself out of
the tomb with no small celerity. The rest took to flight in a panic, as if
a hundred thousand devils were at their heels. The tomb being thus left
open, Andreuccio, the ring still on his finger, sprang out. The way by
which he had entered the church served him for egress, and roaming
at random, he arrived towards daybreak at the coast. Diverging thence
he came by chance upon his inn, where he found that his host and his
comrades had been anxious about him all night. When he told them
all that had befallen him, they joined with the host in advising him to
leave Naples at once. He accordingly did so, and returned to Perugia,
having invested in a ring the money with which he had intended to
buy horses.

STORY VI.

Madam Beritola loses two sons, is found with two kids on an island, goes thence to Lunigiana, where one of her sons takes service with her master, and lies with his daughter, for which he is put in prison. Sicily rebels against King Charles, the son is recognized by the mother, marries the master's daughter, and, his brother being discovered, is reinstated in great honour.

Grave and grievous are the vicissitudes with which Fortune makes us acquainted, and as discourse of such matter serves to awaken our minds, which are so readily lulled to sleep by her flatteries, I deem it worthy of attentive hearing by all, whether they enjoy her favour or endure her frown, in that it ministers counsel to the one sort and consolation to the other. Wherefore, albeit great matters have preceded it, I mean to tell you a story, not less true than touching, of adventures whereof the issue was indeed felicitous, but the antecedent bitterness so long drawn out that scarce can I believe that it was ever sweetened by ensuing happiness.

Dearest ladies, you must know that after the death of the Emperor Frederic II. the crown of Sicily passed to Manfred; whose favour was enjoyed in the highest degree by a gentleman of Naples, Arrighetto Capece by name, who had to wife Madonna Beritola Caracciola, a fair and gracious lady, likewise a Neapolitan. Now when Manfred was conquered and slain by King Charles I. at Benevento, and the whole realm transferred its allegiance to the conqueror, Arrighetto, who was then governor of Sicily, no sooner received the tidings than he prepared for instant flight, knowing that little reliance was to be placed on the fleeting faith of the Sicilians, and not being minded to become a subject of his master's enemy. But the Sicilians having intelligence of his plans, he and many other friends and servants of King Manfred were surprised, taken prisoners and delivered over to King Charles, to whom the whole island was soon afterwards surrendered.

In this signal reversal of the wonted course of things Madam Beritola, knowing not what was become of Arrighetto, and from the past ever auguring future evil, lest she should suffer foul dishonour, abandoned all that she possessed, and with a son of, perhaps, eight years, Giusfredi by name, being also pregnant, fled in a boat to Lipari, where she gave birth to another male child, whom she named Outcast. Then with her sons and a hired nurse she took ship for Naples, intending there to rejoin her family. Events, however, fell out otherwise than she expected; for by stress of weather the ship was carried out of her course to the desert island of Ponza,[1] where they put in to a little bay until such time as they might safely continue their voyage. Madam Beritola landed with the rest on the island, and, leaving them all, sought out a lonely and secluded spot, and there abandoned herself to melancholy brooding on the loss of her dear Arrighetto. While thus she spent her days in solitary preoccupation with her grief it chanced that a galley of corsairs swooped down upon the island, and, before either the mariners or any other folk were aware of their peril, made an easy capture of them all and sailed away; so that, when Madam Beritola, her wailing for that day ended, returned, as was her wont, to the shore to solace herself with the sight of her sons, she found none there.

At first she was lost in wonder, then with a sudden suspicion of the truth she bent her eyes seaward, and there saw the galley still at no great distance, towing the ship in her wake. Thus apprehending beyond all manner of doubt that she had lost her sons as well as her husband, and that, alone, desolate and destitute, she might not hope that any of her lost ones would ever be restored to her, she fell down on the shore in a swoon with the names of her husband and sons upon her lips. None was there to administer cold water or aught else that might recall her truant powers; her animal spirits might even wander whithersoever they would at their sweet will: strength, however, did at last return to her poor exhausted frame, and therewith tears and lamentations, as, plaintively repeating her sons' names, she roamed in quest of them from cavern to cavern. Long time she sought them thus; but when she saw that her labour was in vain, and that night was closing in, hope, she knew not why, began to return, and with it some degree of anxiety on her own account. Wherefore she left the shore and returned to the cavern where she had been wont to indulge her plaintive mood.

She passed the night in no small fear and indescribable anguish; the new day came, and, as she had not supped, she was fain after tierce to appease her hunger, as best she could, by a breakfast of herbs: this done, she wept and began to ruminate on her future way of life. While thus engaged, she observed a she-goat come by and go into an adjacent cavern, and after a while come forth again and go into the wood: thus

---

[1]The largest, now inhabited, of a group of islets in the Gulf of Gaeta.

roused from her reverie she got up, went into the cavern from which the she-goat had issued, and there saw two kids, which might have been born that very day, and seemed to her the sweetest and the most delicious things in the world: and, having, by reason of her recent delivery, milk still within her, she took them up tenderly, and set them to her breast. They, nothing loath, sucked at her teats as if she had been their own dam; and thenceforth made no distinction between her and the dam. Which caused the lady to feel that she had found company in the desert; and so, living on herbs and water, weeping as often as she bethought her of her husband and sons and her past life, she disposed herself to live and die there, and became no less familiar with the she-goat than with her young.

The gentle lady thus leading the life of a wild creature, it chanced that after some months stress of weather brought a Pisan ship to the very same bay in which she had landed. The ship lay there for several days, having on board a gentleman, Currado de' Malespini by name (of the same family as the Marquis), who with his noble and most devout lady was returning home from a pilgrimage, having visited all the holy places in the realm of Apulia. To beguile the tedium of the sojourn Currado with his lady, some servants and his dogs, set forth one day upon a tour through the island. As they neared the place where Madam Beritola dwelt, Currado's dogs on view of the two kids, which, now of a fair size, were grazing, gave chase. The kids, pursued by the dogs, made straight for Madam Beritola's cavern. She, seeing what was toward, started to her feet, caught up a stick, and drove the dogs back. Currado and his lady coming up after the dogs, gazed on Madam Beritola, now tanned and lean and hairy, with wonder, which she more than reciprocated. At her request Currado called off the dogs; and then he and his lady besought her again and again to say who she was and what she did there. So she told them all about herself, her rank, her misfortunes, and the savage life which she was minded to lead.

Currado, who had known Arrighetto Capece very well, was moved to tears by compassion, and exhausted all his eloquence to induce her to change her mind, offering to escort her home, or to take her to live with him in honourable estate as his sister until God should vouchsafe her kindlier fortune. The lady declining all his offers, Currado left her with his wife, whom he bade see that food was brought thither, and let Madam Beritola, who was all in rags, have one of her own dresses to wear, and do all that she could to persuade her to go with them. So the gentle lady stayed with Madam Beritola, and after condoling with her at large on her misfortunes had food and clothing brought to her, and with the greatest difficulty in the world prevailed upon her to eat and dress herself. At last, after much beseeching, she induced her to depart from her oft-declared intention never to go where she might meet any that knew her, and accompany them to Lunigiana, taking with her the two kids and the dam, which latter had in the meantime returned, and to the gentle lady's great surprise had greeted Madam Beritola with the utmost affection.

So with the return of fair weather Madam Beritola, taking with her the dam and the two kids, embarked with Currado and his lady on their ship, being called by them—for her true name was not to be known of all—Cavriuola;[1] and the wind holding fair, they speedily reached the mouth of the Magra,[2] and landing hied them to·Currado's castle; where Madam Beritola abode with Currado's lady in the quality of her maid, serving her well and faithfully, wearing widow's weeds, and feeding and tending her kids with assiduous and loving care.

The corsairs, who, not espying Madam Beritola, had left her at Ponza when they took the ship on which she had come thither, had made a course to Genoa, taking with them all the other folk. On their arrival the owners of the galley shared the booty, and so it happened that as part thereof Madam Beritola's nurse and her two boys fell to the lot of one Messer Guasparrino d'Oria, who sent all three to his house, being minded to keep them there as domestic slaves. The nurse, beside herself with grief at the loss of her mistress and the woful plight in which she found herself and her two charges, shed many a bitter tear. But, seeing that they were unavailing, and that she and the boys were slaves together, she, having, for all her low estate, her share of wit and good sense, made it her first care to comfort them; then, regardful of the condition to which they were reduced, she bethought her, that, if the lads were recognised, 'twould very likely be injurious to them. So, still hoping that some time or another Fortune would change her mood, and they be able, if living, to regain their lost estate, she resolved to let none know who they were, until she saw a fitting occasion; and accordingly, whenever she was questioned thereof by any, she gave them out as her own children. The name of the elder she changed from Giusfredi to Giannotto di Procida; the name of the younger she did not think it worth while to change. She spared no pains to make Giusfredi understand the reason why she had changed his name, and the risk which he might run if he were recognised. This she impressed upon him not once only but many times; and the boy, who was apt to learn, followed the instructions of the wise nurse with perfect exactitude.

So the two boys, ill clad and worse shod, continued with the nurse in Messer Guasparrino's house for two years, patiently performing all kinds of menial offices. But Giannotto, being now sixteen years old, and of a spirit that consorted ill with servitude, brooked not the baseness of

---

[1]*I.e.* she-goat.
[2]Between Liguria and Tuscany.

his lot, and dismissed himself from Messer Guasparrino's service by getting aboard a galley bound for Alexandria, and travelled far and wide, and fared never the better. In the course of his wanderings he learned that his father, whom he had supposed to be dead, was still living, but kept in prison under watch and ward by King Charles. He was grown a tall handsome young man, when, perhaps three or four years after he had given Messer Guasparrino the slip, weary of roaming and all but despairing of his fortune, he came to Lunigiana, and by chance took service with Currado Malespini, who found him handy, and was well-pleased with him. His mother, who was in attendance on Currado's lady, he seldom saw, and never recognised her, nor she him; so much had time changed both from their former aspect since they last met.

While Giannotto was thus in the service of Currado, it fell out by the death of Niccolò da Grignano that his widow, Spina, Currado's daughter, returned to her father's house. Very fair she was and loveable, her age not more than sixteen years, and so it was that she saw Giannotto with favour, and he her, and both fell ardently in love with one another. Their passion was early gratified; but several months elapsed before any detected its existence. Wherefore, growing overbold, they began to dispense with the precautions which such an affair demanded. So one day, as they walked with others through a wood, where the trees grew fair and close, the girl and Giannotto left the rest of the company some distance behind, and, thinking that they were well in advance, found a fair pleasaunce girt in with trees and carpeted with abundance of grass and flowers, and fell to solacing themselves after the manner of lovers. Long time they thus dallied, though such was their delight that all too brief it seemed to them, and so it befell that they were surprised first by the girl's mother and then by Currado.

Pained beyond measure by what he had seen, Currado, without assigning any cause, had them both arrested by three of his servants and taken in chains to one of his castles; where in a frenzy of passionate wrath he left them, resolved to put them to an ignominious death. The girl's mother was also very angry, and deemed her daughter's fall deserving of the most rigorous chastisement, but, when by one of Currado's chance words she divined the doom which he destined for the guilty pair, she could not reconcile herself to it, and hasted to intercede with her angry husband, beseeching him to refrain the impetuous wrath which would hurry him in his old age to murder his daughter and imbrue his hands in the blood of his servant, and vent it in some other way, as by close confinement and duress, whereby the culprits should be brought to repent them of their fault in tears. Thus, and with much more to the like effect, the devout lady urged her suit, and at length prevailed upon her husband to abandon his murderous design. Wherefore, he commanded that the pair should be confined in separate prisons, and closely guarded, and kept short of food and in sore discomfort, until further order; which was accordingly done; and the life which the captives led, their endless tears, their fasts of inordinate duration, may be readily imagined.

Giannotto and Spina had languished in this sorry plight for full a year, entirely ignored by Currado, when in concert with Messer Gian di Procida, King Peter of Arragon raised a rebellion[1] in the island of Sicily, and wrested it from King Charles, whereat Currado, being a Ghibelline, was overjoyed. Hearing the tidings from one of his warders, Giannotto heaved a great sigh, and said: — "Alas, fourteen years have I been a wanderer upon the face of the earth, looking for no other than this very event; and now, that my hopes of happiness may be for ever frustrate, it has come to pass only to find me in prison, whence I may never think to issue alive."

"How?" said the warder; "what signify to thee these doings of these mighty monarchs? What part hadst thou in Sicily?"

Giannotto answered: — "'Tis as if my heart were breaking when I bethink me of my father and what part he had in Sicily. I was but a little lad when I fled the island, but yet I remember him as its governor in the time of King Manfred."

"And who then was thy father?" demanded the warder.

"His name," rejoined Giannotto, "I need no longer scruple to disclose, seeing that I find myself in the very strait which I hoped to avoid by concealing it. He was and still is, if he live, Arrighetto Capece; and my name is not Giannotto but Giusfredi; and I doubt not but, were I once free, and back in Sicily, I might yet hold a very honourable position in the island."

The worthy man asked no more questions, but, as soon as he found opportunity, told what he had learned to Currado; who, albeit he made light of it in the warder's presence, repaired to Madam Beritola, and asked her in a pleasant manner, whether she had had by Arrighetto a son named Giusfredi. The lady answered, in tears, that, if the elder of her two sons were living, such would be his name, and his age twenty-two years. This inclined Currado to think that Giannotto and Giusfredi were indeed one and the same; and it occurred to him, that, if so it were, he might at once shew himself most merciful and blot out his daughter's shame and his own by giving her to him in marriage; wherefore he sent for Giannotto privily, and questioned him in detail touching

[1]The Sicilian Vespers, Easter, 1282.

his past life. And finding by indubitable evidence that he was indeed Giusfredi, son of Arrighetto Capece, he said to him:—

"Giannotto, thou knowest the wrong which thou hast done me in the person of my daughter, what and how great it is, seeing that I used thee well and kindly, and thou shouldst therefore, like a good servant, have shewn thyself jealous of my honour, and zealous in my interest; and many there are who, hadst thou treated them as thou hast treated me, would have caused thee to die an ignominious death; which my clemency would not brook. But now, as it is even so as thou sayst, and thou art of gentle blood by both thy parents, I am minded to put an end to thy sufferings as soon as thou wilt, releasing thee from the captivity in which thou languishest, and setting thee in a happy place, and rein-stating at once thy honour and my own. Thy intimacy with Spina— albeit shameful to both—was yet prompted by love. Spina, as thou knowest, is a widow, and her dower is ample and secure. What her breeding is, and her father's and her mother's, thou knowest: of thy present condition I say nought. Wherefore, when thou wilt, I am con-senting, that, having been with dishonour thy friend, she become with honour thy wife, and that, so long as it seem good to thee, thou tarry here with her and me as my son."

Captivity had wasted Giannotto's flesh, but had in no degree impaired the generosity of spirit which he derived from his ancestry, or the whole-hearted love which he bore his lady. So, albeit he ardently desired that which Currado offered, and knew that he was in Currado's power, yet, even as his magnanimity prompted, so, unswervingly, he made answer:—"Currado, neither ambition nor cupidity nor aught else did ever beguile me to any treacherous machination against either thy person or thy property. Thy daughter I loved, and love and shall ever love, because I deem her worthy of my love; and, if I dealt with her after a fashion which to the mechanic mind seems hardly honourable, I did but commit that fault which is ever congenial to youth, which can never be eradicated so long as youth continues, and which, if the aged would but remember that they were once young and would measure the delinquencies of others by their own and their own by those of others, would not be deemed so grave as thou and many others depict it; and what I did, I did as a friend, not as an enemy. That which thou offerest I have ever desired, and should long ago have sought, had I sup-posed that thou wouldst grant it, and 'twill be the more grateful to me in proportion to the depth of my despair. But if thy intent be not such as thy words import, feed me not with vain hopes, but send me back to prison there to suffer whatever thou mayst be pleased to inflict; nor doubt that even as I love Spina, so for love of her shall I ever love thee, though thou do thy worst, and still hold thee in reverent regard."

Currado marvelled to hear him thus speak, and being assured of his magnanimity and the fervour of his love, held him the more dear; wherefore he rose, embraced and kissed him, and without further delay bade privily bring thither Spina, who left her prison wasted and wan and weak, and so changed that she seemed almost another woman than of yore, even as Giannotto was scarce his former self. Then and there in Currado's presence they plighted their troth according to our custom of espousals; and some days afterwards Currado, having in the meantime provided all things meet for their convenience and solace, yet so as that none should surmise what had happened, deemed it now time to gladden their mothers with the news. So he sent for his lady and Cavriuola, and thus, addressing first Cavriuola, he spoke:—"What would you say, madam, were I to restore you your elder son as the husband of one of my daughters?"

Cavriuola answered:—"I should say, that, were it possible for you to strengthen the bond which attaches me to you, then assuredly you had so done, in that you restored to me that which I cherish more tenderly than myself, and in such a guise as in some measure to renew within me the hope which I had lost: more I could not say."

And so, weeping, she was silent. Then, turning to his lady, Currado said:—"And thou, madam, what wouldst thou think if I were to present thee with such a son-in-law?"

"A son-in-law," she answered, "that was not of gentle blood, but a mere churl, so he pleased you, would well content me."

"So!" returned Currado; "I hope within a few days to gladden the hearts of both of you."

He waited only until the two young folk had recovered their wonted mien, and were clad in a manner befitting their rank. Then, addressing Giusfredi, he said:—"Would it not add to thy joy to see thy mother here?"

"I dare not hope," returned Giusfredi, "that she has survived calamities and sufferings such as hers; but were it so, great indeed would be my joy, and none the less that by her counsel I might be aided to the recovery (in great measure) of my lost heritage in Sicily."

Whereupon Currado caused both the ladies to come thither, and presented to them the bride. The gladness with which they both greeted her was a wonder to behold, and no less great was their wonder at the benign inspiration that had prompted Currado to unite her in wedlock with Giannotto, whom Currado's words caused Madam Beritola to survey with some attention.

A hidden spring of memory was thus touched; she recognised in the man the lineaments of her boy, and awaiting no further evidence she ran with open arms and threw herself upon his neck. No word did she utter, for very excess of maternal tenderness and joy; but, every avenue of sense closed, she fell as if bereft of life within her son's embrace. Giannotto, who had often seen her in the castle and never recognised her, marvelled not a little, but nevertheless it at once flashed upon him that 'twas his mother, and blaming himself for his past inadvertence he took her in his arms and wept and tenderly kissed her. With gentle solicitude Currado's lady and Spina came to her aid, and restored her suspended animation with cold water and other remedies. She then with many tender and endearing words kissed him a thousand times or more, which tokens of her love he received with a look of reverential acknowledgment. Thrice, nay a fourth time were these glad and gracious greetings exchanged, and joyful indeed were they that witnessed them, and hearkened while mother and son compared their past adventures.

Then Currado, who had already announced his new alliance to his friends, and received their felicitations, proceeded to give order for the celebration of the event with all becoming gaiety and splendour. As he did so, Giusfredi said to him:—"Currado, you have long given my mother honourable entertainment, and on me you have conferred many boons; wherefore, that you may fill up the measure of your kindness, 'tis now my prayer that you be pleased to gladden my mother and my marriage feast and me with the presence of my brother, now in servitude in the house of Messer Guasparrino d'Oria, who, as I have already told you, made prize of both him and me; and that then you send some one to Sicily, who shall make himself thoroughly acquainted with the circumstances and condition of the country, and find out how it has fared with my father Arrighetto, whether he be alive or dead, and if alive, in what circumstances, and being thus fully informed, return to us with the tidings."

Currado assented, and forthwith sent most trusty agents both to Genoa and to Sicily. So in due time an envoy arrived at Genoa, and made instant suit to Guasparrino on Currado's part for the surrender of Outcast and the nurse, setting forth in detail all that had passed between Currado and Giusfredi and his mother. Whereat Messer Guasparrino was mightily astonished, and said:—"Of a surety there is nought that, being able, I would not do to pleasure Currado; and true it is that I have had in my house for these fourteen years the boy whom thou dost now demand of me, and his mother, and gladly will I surrender them; but tell Currado from me to beware of excessive credulity, and to put no faith in the idle tales of Giannotto, or Giusfredi, as thou sayest he calls himself, who is by no means so guileless as he supposes."

Then, having provided for the honourable entertainment of the worthy envoy, he sent privily for the nurse, and cautiously sounded her as to the affair. The nurse had heard of the revolt of Sicily, and had learned that Arrighetto was still alive. She therefore banished fear, and told Messer Guasparrino the whole story, and explained to him the reasons why she had acted as she had done. Finding that what she said accorded very well with what he had learned from Currado's envoy, he inclined to credit the story, and most astutely probing the matter in divers ways, and always finding fresh grounds for confidence, he reproached himself for the sorry manner in which he had treated the boy, and by way of amends gave him one of his own daughters, a beautiful girl of eleven years, to wife with a dowry suited to Arrighetto's rank, and celebrated their nuptials with great festivity. He then brought the boy and girl, Currado's envoy, and the nurse in a well-armed galliot to Lerici, being there met by Currado, who had a castle not far off, where great preparations had been made for their entertainment: and thither accordingly he went with his whole company.

What cheer the mother had of her son, the brothers of one another, and all the three of the faithful nurse; what cheer Messer Guasparrino and his daughter had of all, and all of them, and what cheer all had of Currado and his lady and their sons and their friends, words may not describe; wherefore, my ladies, I leave it to your imagination. And that their joy might be full, God, who, when He gives, gives most abundantly, added the glad tidings that Arrighetto Capece was alive and prosperous. For, when in the best of spirits the ladies and gentlemen had sat them down to feast, and they were yet at the first course, the envoy from Sicily arrived, and among other matters reported, that, no sooner had the insurrection broken out in the island than the people hied them in hot haste to the prison where Arrighetto was kept in confinement by King Charles, and despatching the guards, brought him forth, and knowing him to be a capital enemy to King Charles made him their captain, and under his command fell upon and massacred the French. Whereby he had won the highest place in the favour of King Peter, who had granted him restitution of all his estates and honours, so that he was now both prosperous and mighty. The envoy added that Arrighetto had received him with every token of honour, and manifested the utmost delight on hearing of his lady and son, of whom no tidings had reached him since his arrest, and had sent, to bring them home, a brigantine with some gentlemen aboard, whose arrival might hourly be expected.

The envoy, and the good news which he brought, were heartily welcome; and presently Currado, with some of his friends, encountered the gentlemen who came for Madam Beritola and Giusfredi, and saluting them cordially invited them to his feast, which was not yet half done. Joy unheard-of was depicted on the faces of the lady, of Giusfredi, and of all the rest as they greeted them; nor did they on their part take their places at the table before, as best they might, they had conveyed to

Currado and his lady Arrighetto's greetings and grateful acknowledgments of the honour which they had conferred upon his lady and his son, and had placed Arrighetto, to the uttermost of his power, entirely at their service. Then, turning to Messer Guasparrino, of whose kindness Arrighetto surmised nothing, they said that they were very sure that, when he learned the boon which Outcast had received at his hands, he would pay him the like and an even greater tribute of gratitude.

This speech ended, they feasted most joyously with the brides and bridegrooms. So passed the day, the first of many which Currado devoted to honouring his son-in-law and his other intimates, both kinsfolk and friends. The time of festivity ended, Madam Beritola and Giusfredi and the rest felt that they must leave: so, taking Spina with them, they parted, not without many tears, from Currado and his lady and Guasparrino, and went aboard the brigantine, which, wafted by a prosperous wind, soon brought them to Sicily. At Palermo they were met by Arrighetto, who received them all, ladies and sons alike, with such cheer as it were vain to attempt to describe. There it is believed that they all lived long and happily and in amity with God, being not unmindful of the blessings which He had conferred upon them.

STORY VIII.

The Count of Antwerp, labouring under a false accusation, goes into exile. He leaves his two children in different places in England, and takes service in Ireland. Returning to England an unknown man, he finds his sons prosperous. He serves as a groom in the army of the King of France; his innocence is established, and he is restored to his former honours.

Vast indeed is the field that lies before us, wherein to roam at large; 'twould readily afford each of us not one course but ten, so richly has Fortune diversified it with episodes both strange and sombre; wherefore selecting one such from this infinite store, I say:—That, after the transference of the Roman Empire from the Franks to the Germans, the greatest enmity prevailed between the two nations, with warfare perpetual and relentless: wherefore, deeming that the offensive would be their best defence, the King of France and his son mustered all the forces they could raise from their own dominions and those of their kinsmen and allies, and arrayed a grand army for the subjugation of their enemies. Before they took the field, as they could not leave the realm without a governor, they chose for that office Gautier, Count of Antwerp, a true knight and sage counsellor, and their very loyal ally and vassal, choosing him the rather, because, albeit he was a thorough master of the art of war, yet they deemed him less apt to support its hardships than for the conduct of affairs of a delicate nature. Him, therefore, they set in their place as their vicar-general and regent of the whole realm of France, and having so done, they took the field.

Count Gautier ordered his administration wisely and in a regular course, discussing all matters with the queen and her daughter-in-law; whom, albeit they were left under his charge and jurisdiction, he nevertheless treated as his ladies paramount. The Count was about forty years of age, and the very mould of manly beauty; in bearing as courteous and chivalrous as ever a gentleman might be, and withal so debonair and dainty, so feat and trim of person that he had not his peer among the gallants of that day. His wife was dead, leaving him two children and no more, to wit, a boy and a girl, still quite young.

47

Now the King and his son being thus away at the war, and the Count frequenting the court of the two said ladies, and consulting with them upon affairs of state, it so befell that the Prince's lady regarded him with no small favour, being very sensible alike of the advantages of his person and the nobility of his bearing; whereby she conceived for him a passion which was all the more ardent because it was secret. And, as he was without a wife, and she was still in the freshness of her youth, she saw not why she should not readily be gratified; but supposing that nothing stood in the way but her own shamefastness, she resolved to be rid of that, and disclose her mind to him without any reserve. So one day, when she was alone, she seized her opportunity, and sent for him, as if she were desirous to converse with him on indifferent topics.

The Count, his mind entirely aloof from the lady's purpose, presented himself forthwith, and at her invitation sate down by her side on a settee. They were quite alone in the room; but the Count had twice asked her the reason why she had so honoured him, before, overcome by passion, she broke silence, and crimson from brow to neck with shame, half sobbing, trembling in every limb, and faltering at every word, she thus spoke:—

"Dearest friend and sweet my lord, sagacity such as yours cannot but be apt to perceive how great is the frailty of men and women, and how, for divers reasons, it varies in different persons in such a degree that no just judge would mete out the same measure to each indifferently, though the fault were apparently the same. Who would not acknowledge that a poor man or woman, fain to earn daily bread by the sweat of the brow, is far more reprehensible in yielding to the solicitations of love, than a rich lady, whose life is lapped in ease and unrestricted luxury? Not a soul, I am persuaded, but would so acknowledge!

"Wherefore I deem that the possession of these boons of fortune should go far indeed to acquit the possessor, if she, perchance, indulge an errant love; and, for the rest, that, if she have chosen a wise and worthy lover, she should be entirely exonerated. And as I think I may fairly claim the benefit of both these pleas, and of others beside, to wit, my youth and my husband's absence, which naturally incline me to love, 'tis meet that I now urge them in your presence in defence of my passion; and if they have the weight with you which they should have with the wise, I pray you to afford me your help and counsel in the matter wherein I shall demand it.

"I avow that in the absence of my husband I have been unable to withstand the promptings of the flesh and the power of love, forces of such potency that even the strongest men—not to speak of delicate women—have not seldom been, nay daily are, overcome by them; and so, living thus, as you see me, in ease and luxury, I have allowed the allurements of love to draw me on until at last I find myself a prey to passion. Wherein were I discovered, I were, I confess, dishonoured; but discovery being avoided, I count the dishonour all but nought. Moreover, love has been so gracious to me that not only has he spared to blind me in the choice of my lover, but he has even lent me his most effective aid, pointing me to one well worthy of the love of a lady such as I, even to yourself; whom, if I misread not my mind, I deem the most handsome and courteous and debonair, and therewithal the sagest cavalier that the realm of France may shew. And as you are without a wife, so may I say that I find myself without a husband. Wherefore in return for this great love I bear you, deny me not, I pray you, yours; but have pity on my youth, which wastes away for you like ice before the fire."

These words were followed by such a flood of tears, that, albeit she had intended yet further to press her suit, speech failed her; her eyes drooped, and, almost swooning with emotion, she let her head fall upon the Count's breast.

The Count, who was the most loyal of knights, began with all severity to chide her mad passion and to thrust her from him—for she was now making as if she would throw her arms around his neck—and to asseverate with oaths that he would rather be hewn in pieces than either commit, or abet another in committing such an offence against the honour of his lord; when the lady, catching his drift, and forgetting all her love in a sudden frenzy of rage, cried out:—"So! unknightly knight, is it thus you flout my love? Now Heaven forbid, but, as you would be the death of me, I either do you to death or drive you from the world!"

So saying, she dishevelled and tore her hair and rent her garments to shreds about her bosom. Which done, she began shrieking at the top of her voice:—"Help! help! The Count of Antwerp threatens to violate me!"

Whereupon the Count, who knew that a clear conscience was no protection against the envy of courtiers, and doubted that his innocence would prove scarce a match for the cunning of the lady, started to his feet, and hied him with all speed out of the room, out of the palace, and back to his own house. Counsel of none he sought; but forthwith set his children on horseback, and taking horse himself, departed post haste for Calais. The lady's cries brought not a few to her aid, who, observing her plight, not only gave entire credence to her story, but improved upon it, alleging that the debonair and accomplished Count had long employed all the arts of seduction to compass his end. So they rushed in hot haste to the Count's house, with intent to arrest him, and not finding him, sacked it and razed it to the ground. The news, as glosed and garbled, being carried to the King and Prince in the field, they were mightily incensed, and offered a great reward for the Count, dead or alive, and condemned him and his posterity to perpetual banishment.

Meanwhile the Count, sorely troubled that by his flight his innocence shewed as guilt, pursued his journey, and concealing his identity,
and being recognised by none, arrived with his two children at Calais.
Thence he forthwith crossed to England, and, meanly clad, fared on for
London, taking care as he went to school his children in all that
belonged to their new way of life, and especially in two main articles:
to wit, that they should bear with resignation the poverty to which, by
no fault of theirs, but solely by one of Fortune's caprices, they and he
were reduced, and that they should be most sedulously on their guard
to betray to none, as they valued their lives, whence they were, or who
their father was. The son, Louis by name, was perhaps nine, and the
daughter, Violante, perhaps seven years of age. For years so tender they
proved apt pupils, and afterwards shewed by their conduct that they had
well learned their father's lesson. He deemed it expedient to change
their names, and accordingly called the boy Perrot and the girl Jeannette.
So, meanly clad, the Count and his two children arrived at London,
and there made shift to get a living by going about soliciting alms in the
guise of French mendicants.

Now, as for this purpose they waited one morning outside a church,
it so befell that a great lady, the wife of one of the marshals of the King
of England, observed them, as she left the church, asking alms, and
demanded of the Count whence he was, and whether the children
were his. He answered that he was from Picardy, that the children were
his, and that he had been fain to leave Picardy by reason of the mis-
conduct of their reprobate elder brother. The lady looked at the girl,
who being fair, and of gentle and winning mien and manners, found
much favour in her eyes. So the kind-hearted lady said to the Count:—
"My good man, if thou art willing to leave thy little daughter with me,
I like her looks so well that I will gladly take her; and if she grow up a
good woman, I will see that she is suitably married when the right time
comes." The Count was much gratified by the proposal, which he
forthwith accepted, and parted with the girl, charging the lady with
tears to take every care of her.

Having thus placed the girl with one in whom he felt sure that he
might trust, he determined to tarry no longer in London; wherefore,
taking Perrot with him and begging as he went, he made his way to
Wales, not without great suffering, being unused to go afoot. Now in
Wales another of the King's marshals had his court, maintaining great
state and a large number of retainers; to which court the Count and his
son frequently repaired, there to get food; and there Perrot, finding the
marshal's son and other gentlemen's sons vying with one another in
boyish exercises, as running and leaping, little by little joined their
company, and shewed himself a match or more for them all in all their

contests. The marshal's attention being thus drawn to him, he was well pleased with the boy's mien and bearing, and asked who he was. He was told that he was the son of a poor man who sometimes came there to solicit alms. Whereupon he asked the Count to let him have the boy, and the Count, to whom God could have granted no greater boon, readily consented, albeit he was very loath to part with Perrot.

Having thus provided for his son and daughter, the Count resolved to quit the island; and did so, making his way as best he could to Stamford, in Ireland, where he obtained a menial's place in the service of a knight, retainer to one of the earls of that country, and so abode there a long while, doing all the irksome and wearisome drudgery of a lackey or groom.

Meanwhile under the care of the gentle lady at London Violante or Jeannette increased, as in years and stature so also in beauty, and in such favour with the lady and her husband and every other member of the household and all who knew her that 'twas a wonder to see; nor was there any that, observing her bearing and manners, would not have said that estate or dignity there was none so high or honourable but she was worthy of it. So the lady, who, since she had received her from her father, had been unable to learn aught else about him than what he had himself told, was minded to marry her honourably according to what she deemed to be her rank. But God, who justly apportions reward according to merit, having regard to her noble birth, her innocence, and the load of suffering which the sin of another had laid upon her, ordered otherwise; and in His good providence, lest the young gentlewoman should be mated with a churl, permitted, we must believe, events to take the course they did.

The gentle lady with whom Jeannette lived had an only son, whom she and her husband loved most dearly, as well because he was a son as for his rare and noble qualities, for in truth there were few that could compare with him in courtesy and courage and personal beauty. Now the young man marked the extraordinary beauty and grace of Jeannette, who was about six years his junior, and fell so desperately in love with her that he had no eyes for any other maiden; but, deeming her to be of low degree, he not only hesitated to ask her of his parents in marriage, but, fearing to incur reproof for indulging a passion for an inferior, he did his utmost to conceal his love. Whereby it gave him far more disquietude than if he had avowed it; insomuch that—so extreme waxed his suffering—he fell ill, and that seriously. Divers physicians were called in, but, for all their scrutiny of his symptoms, they could not determine the nature of his malady, and one and all gave him up for lost. Nothing could exceed the sorrow and dejection of his father and mother, who again and again piteously implored him to discover to them the cause of his malady, and received no other answer than sighs or complaints that he seemed to be wasting away.

Now it so happened that one day, Jeannette, who from regard for his mother was sedulous in waiting upon him, for some reason or another came into the room where he lay, while a very young but skilful physician sate by him and held his pulse. The young man gave her not a word or other sign of recognition; but his passion waxed, his heart smote him, and the acceleration of his pulse at once betrayed his inward commotion to the physician, who, albeit surprised, remained quietly attentive to see how long it would last, and observing that it ceased when Jeannette left the room, conjectured that he was on the way to explain the young man's malady. So, after a while, still holding the young man's pulse, he sent for Jeannette, as if he had something to ask of her. She returned forthwith; the young man's pulse mounted as soon as she entered the room, and fell again as soon as she left it.

Wherefore the physician no longer hesitated, but rose, and taking the young man's father and mother aside, said to them:—"The restoration of your son's health rests not with medical skill, but solely with Jeannette, whom, as by unmistakable signs I have discovered, he ardently loves, though, so far I can see, she is not aware of it. So you know what you have to do, if you value his life."

The prospect thus afforded of their son's deliverance from death reassured the gentleman and his lady, albeit they were troubled, misdoubting it must be by his marriage with Jeannette.

So, when the physician was gone, they went to the sick lad, and the lady thus spoke:—"My son, never would I have believed that thou wouldst have concealed from me any desire of thine, least of all if such it were that privation should cause thee to languish; for well assured thou shouldst have been and shouldst be, that I hold thee dear as my very self, and that whatever may be for thy contentment, even though it were scarce seemly, I would do it for thee; but, for all thou hast so done, God has shewn Himself more merciful to theeward than thyself, and, lest thou die of this malady, has given me to know its cause, which is nothing else than the excessive love which thou bearest to a young woman, be she who she may. Which love in good sooth thou needest not have been ashamed to declare; for it is but natural at thy age; and hadst thou not loved, I should have deemed thee of very little worth. So, my son, be not shy of me, but frankly discover to me thy whole heart; and away with this gloom and melancholy whereof thy sickness is engendered, and be comforted, and assure thyself that there is nought that thou mayst require of me which I will not do to give thee ease, so far as my powers may reach, seeing that thou art dearer to me than my own life. Away with thy shamefastness and fears, and tell me if there is aught wherein I may be helpful to thee in the matter of thy love; and if I bestir not myself and bring it to pass, account me the most harsh mother that ever bore son."

The young man was at first somewhat shamefast to hear his mother thus speak, but, reflecting that none could do more for his happiness than she, he took courage, and thus spoke:—"Madam, my sole reason for concealing my love from you was that I have observed that old people for the most part forget that they once were young; but, as I see that no such unreasonableness is to be apprehended in you, I not only acknowledge the truth of what you say that you have discerned, but I will also disclose to you the object of my passion, on the understanding that your promise shall to the best of your power be performed, as it must be, if I am to be restored to you in sound health."

Whereupon the lady, making too sure of that which was destined to fall out otherwise than she expected, gave him every encouragement to discover all his heart, and promised to lose no time and spare no pains in endeavouring to compass his gratification. "Madam," said then the young man, "the rare beauty and exquisite manners of our Jeannette, my powerlessness to make her understand—I do not say commiserate—my love, and my reluctance to disclose it to any, have brought me to the condition in which you see me; and if your promise be not in one way or another performed, be sure that my life will be brief."

The lady, deeming that the occasion called rather for comfort than for admonition, replied with a smile:—"Ah! my son, was this then of all things the secret of thy suffering? Be of good cheer, and leave me to arrange the affair, when you are recovered."

So, animated by a cheerful hope, the young man speedily gave sign of a most marked improvement, which the lady observed with great satisfaction, and then began to cast about how she might keep her promise.

So one day she sent for Jeannette, and in a tone of gentle raillery asked her if she had a lover. Jeannette turned very red as she answered:—"Madam, 'twould scarce, nay, 'twould ill become a damsel such as I, poor, outcast from home, and in the service of another, to occupy herself with thoughts of love."

Whereto the lady answered:—"So you have none, we will give you one, who will brighten all your life and give you more joy of your beauty; for it is not right that so fair a damsel as you remain without a lover."

"Madam," rejoined Jeannette, "you found me living in poverty with my father, you adopted me, you have brought me up as your daughter; wherefore I should, if possible, comply with your every wish; but in this matter I will render you no compliance, nor do I doubt that I do well. So you will give me a husband, I will love him, but no other will I love;

for, as patrimony I now have none save my honour, that I am minded to guard and preserve while my life shall last."

Serious though the obstacle was which these words opposed to the plan by which the lady had intended to keep her promise to her son, her sound judgment could not but secretly acknowledge that the spirit which they evinced was much to be commended in the damsel. Wherefore she said:—"Nay but, Jeannette; suppose that our Lord the King, who is a young knight as thou art a most fair damsel, craved some indulgence of thy love, wouldst thou deny him?"

"The King," returned Jeannette without the least hesitation, "might constrain me, but with my consent he should never have aught of me that was not honourable."

Whereto the lady made no answer, for she now understood the girl's temper; but, being minded to put her to the proof, she told her son that, as soon as he was recovered, she would arrange that he should be closeted with her in the same room, and be thus able to use all his arts to bring her to his will, saying that it ill became her to play the part of procuress and urge her son's suit upon her own maid. But as the young man, by no means approving this idea, suddenly grew worse, the lady at length opened her mind to Jeannette, whom she found in the same frame as before, and indeed even more resolute. Wherefore she told her husband all that she had done; and as both preferred that their son should marry beneath him, and live, than that he should remain single and die, they resolved, albeit much disconcerted, to give Jeannette to him to wife; and so after long debate they did. Whereat Jeannette was overjoyed, and with devout heart gave thanks to God that He had not forgotten her; nevertheless she still gave no other account of herself than that she was the daughter of a Picard. So the young man recovered, and blithe at heart as ne'er another, was married, and began to speed the time gaily with his bride.

Meanwhile Perrot, left in Wales with the marshal of the King of England, had likewise with increase of years increase of favour with his master, and grew up most shapely and well-favoured, and of such prowess that in all the island at tourney or joust or any other passage of arms he had not his peer; being everywhere known and renowned as Perrot the Picard. And as God had not forgotten Jeannette, so likewise He made manifest by what follows that He had not forgotten Perrot. Wellnigh half the population of those parts being swept off by a sudden visitation of deadly pestilence, most of the survivors fled therefrom in a panic, so that the country was, to all appearance, entirely deserted. Among those that died of the pest were the marshal, his lady, and his son, besides brothers and nephews and kinsfolk in great number; whereby of his entire household there were left only one of his daughters, now marriageable, and a few servants, among them Perrot. Now Perrot being a man of such notable prowess, the damsel, soon after the pestilence had spent itself, took him, with the approval and by the advice of the few folk that survived, to be her husband, and made him lord of all that fell to her by inheritance. Nor was it long before the King of England, learning that the marshal was dead, made Perrot the Picard, to whose merit he was no stranger, marshal in the dead man's room. Such, in brief, was the history of the two innocent children, with whom the Count of Antwerp had parted, never expecting to see them again.

'Twas now the eighteenth year since the Count of Antwerp had taken flight from Paris, when, being still in Ireland, where he had led a very sorry and suffering sort of life, and feeling that age was now come upon him, he felt a longing to learn, if possible, what was become of his children. The fashion of his outward man was now completely changed; for long hardship had (as he well knew) given to his age a vigour which his youth, lapped in ease, had lacked. So he hesitated not to take his leave of the knight with whom he had so long resided, and poor and in sorry trim he crossed to England, and made his way to the place where he had left Perrot—to find him a great lord and marshal of the King, and in good health, and withal a hardy man and very handsome. All which was very grateful to the old man; but yet he would not make himself known to his son, until he had learned the fate of Jeannette.

So forth he fared again, nor did he halt until he was come to London, where, cautiously questing about for news of the lady with whom he had left his daughter, and how it fared with her, he learned that Jeannette was married to the lady's son. Whereat, in the great gladness of his heart, he counted all his past adversity but a light matter, since he had found his children alive and prosperous. But sore he yearned to see Jeannette. Wherefore he took to loitering, as poor folk are wont, in the neighbourhood of the house. And so one day Jacques Lamiens— such was the name of Jeannette's husband—saw him and had pity on him, observing that he was poor and aged, and bade one of his servants take him indoors, and for God's sake give him something to eat; and nothing loath the servant did so.

Now Jeannette had borne Jacques several children, the finest and the most winsome children in the world, the eldest no more than eight years old; who gathered about the Count as he ate, and, as if by instinct divining that he was their grandfather, began to make friends with him. He, knowing them for his grandchildren, could not conceal his love, and repaid them with caresses; insomuch that they would not hearken to their governor when he called them, but remained with the Count. Which being reported to Jeannette, she came out of her room, crossed to where the Count was sitting with the children, and bade them do as their master told them, or she would certainly have them whipped. The children began to cry, and to say that they would rather stay with the worthy man, whom they liked much better than their master; whereat both the lady and the Count laughed in sympathy.

The Count had risen, with no other intention—for he was not minded to disclose his paternity—than to pay his daughter the respect due from his poverty to her rank, and the sight of her had thrilled his soul with a wondrous delight. By her he was and remained unrecognised; utterly changed as he was from his former self; aged, grey-haired, bearded, lean and tanned—in short to all appearance another man than the Count.

However, seeing that the children were unwilling to leave him, but wept when she made as if she would constrain them, she bade the master let them be for a time. So the children remained with the worthy man, until by chance Jacques' father came home, and learned from the master what had happened. Whereupon, having a grudge against Jeannette, he said:—"Let them be; and God give them the ill luck which He owes them: whence they sprang, thither they must needs return; they descend from a vagabond on the mother's side, and so 'tis no wonder that they consort readily with vagabonds."

The Count caught these words and was sorely pained, but, shrugging his shoulders, bore the affront silently as he had borne many another. Jacques, who had noted his children's fondness for the worthy man, to wit, the Count, was displeased; but nevertheless, such was the love he bore them, that, rather than see them weep, he gave order that, if the worthy man cared to stay there in his service, he should be received. The Count answered that he would gladly do so, but that he was fit for nothing except to look after horses, to which he had been used all his life. So a horse was assigned him, and when he had groomed him, he occupied himself in playing with the children.

While Fortune thus shaped the destinies of the Count of Antwerp and his children, it so befell that after a long series of truces made with the Germans the King of France died, and his crown passed to his son, whose wife had been the occasion of the Count's banishment. The new king, as soon as the last truce with the Germans was run out, renewed hostilities with extraordinary vigour, being aided by his brother of England with a large army under the command of his marshal, Perrot, and his other marshal's son, Jacques Lamiens. With them went the worthy man, that is to say, the Count, who, unrecognised by any, served for a long while in the army in the capacity of groom, and acquitted himself both in counsel and in arms with a wisdom and valour unwonted in one of his supposed rank. The war was still raging when the Queen of France fell seriously ill, and, as she felt her end approach, made a humble and contrite confession of all her sins to the Archbishop of Rouen, who was universally reputed a good and most holy man. Among her other sins she confessed the great wrong that she had done to the Count of Antwerp; nor was she satisfied to confide it to the Archbishop, but recounted the whole affair, as it had passed, to not a few other worthy men, whom she besought to use their influence with the King to procure the restitution of the Count, if he were still alive, and if not, of his children, to honour and estate. And so, dying shortly afterwards, she was honourably buried. The Queen's confession wrung from the King a sigh or two of compunction for a brave man cruelly wronged; after which he caused proclamation to be made throughout the army and in many other parts, that whoso should bring him tidings of the Count of Antwerp, or his children, should receive from him such a guerdon for each of them as should justly be matter of marvel; seeing that he held him acquitted, by confession of the Queen, of the crime for which he had been banished, and was therefore now minded to grant him not only restitution but increase of honour and estate.

Now the Count, being still with the army in his character of groom, heard the proclamation, which he did not doubt was made in good faith. Wherefore he hied him forthwith to Jacques, and begged a private interview with him and Perrot, that he might discover to them that whereof the King was in quest. So the meeting was had; and Perrot was on the point of declaring himself, when the Count anticipated him: "Perrot," he said, "Jacques here has thy sister to wife, but never a dowry had he with her. Wherefore that thy sister be not doweiless, 'tis my will that he, and no other, have this great reward which the King offers for thee, son, as he shall certify, of the Count of Antwerp, and for his wife and thy sister, Violante, and for me, Count of Antwerp, thy father."

So hearing, Perrot scanned the Count closely, and forthwith recognising him, burst into tears, and throwing himself at his feet embraced him, saying:—"My father, welcome, welcome indeed art thou."

Whereupon, between what he had heard from the Count and what he had witnessed on the part of Perrot, Jacques was so overcome with wonder and delight, that at first he was at a loss to know how to act. However, giving entire credence to what he had heard, and recalling insulting language which he had used towards the quondam groom, the Count, he was sore stricken with shame, and wept, and fell at the Count's feet, and humbly craved his pardon for all past offences; which the Count, raising him to his feet, most graciously granted him. So with many a tear and many a hearty laugh the three men compared their several fortunes; which done, Perrot and Jacques would have arrayed the Count in manner befitting his rank, but he would by no means

suffer it, being minded that Jacques, so soon as he was well assured that
the guerdon was forthcoming, should present him to the King in his
garb of groom, that thereby the King might be the more shamed. So
Jacques, with the Count and Perrot, went presently to the King and
offered to present to him the Count and his children, provided the
guerdon were forthcoming according to the proclamation. Jacques
wondered not a little as forthwith at a word from the King a guerdon
was produced ample for all three, and he was bidden take it away with
him, so only that he should in very truth produce, as he had promised,
the Count and his children in the royal presence.

Then, withdrawing a little and causing his quondam groom, now
Count, to come forward with Perrot, he said:— "Sire, father and son are
before you; the daughter, my wife, is not here, but, God willing, you
shall soon see her."

So hearing, the King surveyed the Count, whom, notwithstanding
his greatly changed appearance, he at length recognised, and well-nigh
moved to tears, he raised him from his knees to his feet, and kissed and
embraced him. He also gave a kindly welcome to Perrot, and bade
forthwith furnish the Count with apparel, servants and horses, suited to
his rank; all which was no sooner said than done. Moreover the King
shewed Jacques no little honour, and particularly questioned him of all
his past adventures.

As Jacques was about to take the noble guerdons assigned him for the
discovery of the Count and his children, the Count said to him:—
"Take these tokens of the magnificence of our Lord the King, and
forget not to tell thy father that that 'tis from no vagabond that thy
children, his and my grandchildren, descend on the mother's side."

So Jacques took the guerdons, and sent for his wife and mother to
join him at Paris. Thither also came Perrot's wife: and there with all
magnificence they were entertained by the Count, to whom the King
had not only restored all his former estates and honours, but added
thereto others, whereby he was now become a greater man than he had
ever been before. Then with the Count's leave they all returned to their
several houses. The Count himself spent the rest of his days at Paris in
greater glory than ever.

THIRD DAY

STORY I.

Masetto da Lamporecchio feigns to be dumb, and obtains a gardener's place at a convent of women, who with one accord make haste to lie with him.

In this very country-side of ours there was and yet is a convent of women of great repute for sanctity—name it I will not, lest I should in some measure diminish its repute—the nuns being at the time of which I speak but nine in number, including the abbess, and all young women. Their very beautiful garden was in charge of a foolish fellow, who, not being content with his wage, squared accounts with their steward, and hied him back to Lamporecchio, whence he came.

Among others who welcomed him home was a young husbandman, Masetto by name, a stout and hardy fellow, and handsome for a contadino, who asked him where he had been so long. Nuto, as our good friend was called, told him. Masetto then asked how he had been employed at the convent, and Nuto answered:—"I kept their large and beautiful garden in good trim, and, besides, I sometimes went to the wood to fetch the faggots, I drew water, and did some other trifling services; but the ladies gave so little wage that it scarce kept me in shoes. And moreover they are all young, and, I think, they are one and all possessed of the devil, for 'tis impossible to do anything to their mind; indeed, when I would be at work in the kitchen-garden, 'put this here,' would say one, 'put that here,' would say another, and a third would snatch the hoe from my hand, and say, 'that is not as it should be'; and so they would worry me until I would give up working and go out of the garden; so that, what with this thing and that, I was minded to stay there no more, and so I am come hither. The steward asked me before I left to send him any one whom on my return I might find fit for the work, and I promised; but God bless his loins, I shall be at no pains to find out and send him any one."

59

As Nuto thus ran on, Masetto was seized by such a desire to be with these nuns that he quite pined, as he gathered from what Nuto said that his desire might be gratified. And as that could not be, if he said nothing to Nuto, he remarked:—"Ah! 'twas well done of thee to come hither. A man to live with women! he might as well live with so many devils: six times out of seven they know not themselves what they want."

There the conversation ended; but Masetto began to cast about how he should proceed to get permission to live with them. He knew that he was quite competent for the services of which Nuto spoke, and had therefore no fear of failing on that score; but he doubted he should not be received, because he was too young and well-favoured. So, after much pondering, he fell into the following train of thought:—The place is a long way off, and no one there knows me; if I make believe that I am dumb, doubtless I shall be admitted. Whereupon he made his mind up, laid a hatchet across his shoulder, and saying not a word to any of his destination, set forth, intending to present himself at the convent in the character of a destitute man. Arrived there, he had no sooner entered than he chanced to encounter the steward in the courtyard, and making signs to him as dumb folk do, he let him know that of his charity he craved something to eat, and that, if need were, he would split firewood. The steward promptly gave him to eat, and then set before him some logs which Nuto had not been able to split, all which Masetto, who was very strong, split in a very short time. The steward, having occasion to go to the wood, took him with him, and there set him at work on the lopping; which done he placed the ass in front of him, and by signs made him understand that he was to take the loppings back to the convent. This he did so well that the steward kept him for some days to do one or two odd jobs. Whereby it so befell that one day the abbess saw him, and asked the steward who he was.

"Madam," replied the steward, "'tis a poor deaf mute that came here a day or two ago craving alms, so I have treated him kindly, and have let him make himself useful in many ways. If he knew how to do the work of the kitchen-garden and would stay with us, I doubt not we should be well served; for we have need of him, and he is strong, and would be able for whatever he might turn his hand to; besides which you would have no cause to be apprehensive lest he should be cracking his jokes with your young women."

"As I trust in God," said the abbess, "thou sayst sooth; find out if he can do the garden work, and if he can, do all thou canst to keep him with us; give him a pair of shoes, an old hood, and speak him well, make much of him, and let him be well fed." All which the steward promised to do.

Masetto, meanwhile, was close at hand, making as if he were sweeping

the courtyard, and heard all that passed between the abbess and the
steward, whereat he gleefully communed with himself on this wise:—
Put me once within there, and you will see that I will do the work of
the kitchen-garden as it never was done before. So the steward set him
to work in the kitchen-garden, and finding that he knew his business
excellently well, made signs to him to know whether he would stay, and
he made answer by signs that he was ready to do whatever the steward
wished. The steward then signified that he was engaged, told him to
take charge of the kitchen-garden, and shewed him what he had to do
there. Then, having other matters to attend to, he went away, and left
him there. Now, as Masetto worked there day by day, the nuns began
to tease him, and make him their butt (as it commonly happens that
folk serve the dumb) and used bad language to him, the worst they
could think of, supposing that he could not understand them: all
which passed scarce heeded by the abbess, who perhaps deemed him
as destitute of virility as of speech.

Now it so befell that after a hard day's work he was taking a little rest,
when two young nuns, who were walking in the garden, approached
the spot where he lay, and stopped to look at him, while he pretended
to be asleep. And so the bolder of the two said to the other:—
"If I thought thou wouldst keep the secret, I would tell thee what I
have sometimes meditated, and which thou perhaps mightest also
find agreeable."

The other replied:—"Speak thy mind freely and be sure that I will
never tell a soul."

Whereupon the bold one began:—"I know not if thou hast ever con-
sidered how close we are kept here, and that within these precincts dare
never enter any man, unless it be the old steward or this mute: and I
have often heard from ladies that have come hither, that all the other
sweets that the world has to offer signify not a jot in comparison of the
pleasure that a woman has in connexion with a man. Whereof I have
more than once been minded to make experiment with this mute, no
other man being available. Nor, indeed, could one find any man in the
whole world so meet therefor; seeing that he could not blab if he
would; thou seest that he is but a dull clownish lad, whose size has
increased out of all proportion to his sense; wherefore I would fain hear
what thou hast to say to it."

"Alas!" said the other, "what is 't thou sayst? Knowest thou not that
we have vowed our virginity to God?"

"Oh," rejoined the first, "think but how many vows are made to
Him all day long, and never a one performed: and so, for our vow, let Him
find another or others to perform it."

"But," said her companion, "suppose that we conceived, how then?"

"Nay but," protested the first, "thou goest about to imagine evil before it befalls thee: time enough to think of that when it comes to pass; there will be a thousand ways to prevent its ever being known, so only we do not publish it ourselves."

Thus reassured, the other was now the more eager of the two to test the quality of the male human animal. "Well then," she said, "how shall we go about it?" and was answered: — "Thou seest 'tis past none; I make no doubt but all the sisters are asleep, except ourselves; search we through the kitchen-garden, to see if there be any there, and if there be none, we have but to take him by the hand and lead him hither to the hut where he takes shelter from the rain; and then one shall mount guard while the other has him with her inside. He is such a simpleton that he will do just whatever we bid him."

No word of this conversation escaped Masetto, who, being disposed to obey, hoped for nothing so much as that one of them should take him by the hand. They, meanwhile, looked carefully all about them, and satisfied themselves that they were secure from observation: then she that had broached the subject came close up to Masetto, and shook him; whereupon he started to his feet. So she took him by the hand with a blandishing air, to which he replied with some clownish grins. And then she led him into the hut, where he needed no pressing to do what she desired of him. Which done, she changed places with the other, as loyal comradeship required; and Masetto, still keeping up the pretence of simplicity, did their pleasure. Wherefore before they left, each must needs make another assay of the mute's powers of riding; and afterwards, talking the matter over many times, they agreed that it was in truth not less but even more delightful than they had been given to understand; and so, as they found convenient opportunity, they continued to go and disport themselves with the mute.

Now it so chanced that one of their gossips, looking out of the window of her cell, saw what they did, and imparted it to two others. The three held counsel together whether they should not denounce the offenders to the abbess, but soon changed their mind, and came to an understanding with them, whereby they became partners in Masetto. And in course of time by divers chances the remaining three nuns also entered the partnership. Last of all the abbess, still witting nought of these doings, happened one very hot day, as she walked by herself through the garden, to find Masetto, who now rode so much by night that he could stand very little fatigue by day, stretched at full length asleep under the shade of an almond-tree, his person quite exposed in front by reason that the wind had disarranged his clothes. Which the lady observing, and knowing that she was alone, fell a prey to the same appetite to which her nuns had yielded: she aroused Masetto, and took him with her to her chamber, where, for some days, though the nuns loudly complained that the gardener no longer came to work in the kitchen-garden, she kept him, tasting and re-tasting the sweetness of that indulgence which she was wont to be the first to censure in others. And when at last she had sent him back from her chamber to his room, she must needs send for him again and again, and made such exorbitant demands upon him, that Masetto, not being able to satisfy so many women, bethought him that his part of mute, should he persist in it, might entail disastrous consequences.

So one night, when he was with the abbess, he cut the tongue-string, and thus broke silence: — "Madam, I have understood that a cock may very well serve ten hens, but that ten men are sorely tasked to satisfy a single woman; and here am I expected to serve nine, a burden quite beyond my power to bear; nay, by what I have already undergone I am now so reduced that my strength is quite spent; wherefore either bid me Godspeed, or find some means to make matters tolerable."

Wonder-struck to hear the supposed mute thus speak, the lady exclaimed: — "What means this? I took thee to be dumb."

"And in sooth, Madam, so was I," said Masetto, "not indeed from my birth, but through an illness which took from me the power of speech, which only this very night have I recovered; and so I praise God with all my heart."

The lady believed him, and asked him what he meant by saying that he had nine to serve. Masetto told her how things stood; whereby she perceived that of all her nuns there was not any but was much wiser than she; and lest, if Masetto were sent away, he should give the convent a bad name, she discreetly determined to arrange matters with the nuns in such sort that he might remain there. So, the steward having died within the last few days, she assembled all the nuns; and their and her own past errors being fully avowed, they by common consent, and with Masetto's concurrence, resolved that the neighbours should be given to understand that by their prayers and the merits of their patron saint, Masetto, long mute, had recovered the power of speech; after which they made him steward, and so ordered matters among themselves that he was able to endure the burden of their service. In the course of which, though he procreated not a few little monastics, yet 'twas all managed so discreetly that no breath of scandal stirred, until after the abbess's death, by which time Masetto was advanced in years and minded to return home with the wealth that he had gotten; which he was suffered to do as soon as he made his desire known.

And so Masetto, who had left Lamporecchio with a hatchet on his shoulder, returned thither in his old age rich and a father, having by the wisdom with which he employed his youth, spared himself the pains and expense of rearing children, and averring that such was the measure that Christ meted out to the man that set horns on his cap.

STORY IX.

Gillette of Narbonne cures the King of France of a fistula, craves for spouse Bertrand de Roussillon, who marries her against his will, and hies him in despite to Florence, where, as he courts a young woman, Gillette lies with him in her stead, and has two sons by him; for which cause he afterwards takes her into favour and entreats her as his wife.

Know, then, that in the realm of France there was a gentleman, Isnard, Comte de Roussillon, by name, who, being in ill-health, kept ever in attendance on him a physician, one Master Gerard of Narbonne. The said Count had an only son named Bertrand, a very fine and winsome little lad; with whom were brought up other children of his own age, among them the said physician's little daughter Gillette; who with a love boundless and ardent out of all keeping with her tender years became enamoured of this Bertrand. And so, when the Count died, and his son, being left a ward of the King, must needs go to Paris, the girl remained beside herself with grief, and, her father dying soon after, would gladly have gone to Paris to see Bertrand, might she but have found a fair excuse; but no decent pretext could she come by, being left a great and sole heiress and very closely guarded. So being come of marriageable age, still cherishing Bertrand's memory, she rejected not a few suitors, to whom her kinsfolk would fain have married her, without assigning any reason.

Now her passion waxing ever more ardent for Bertrand, as she learned that he was grown a most goodly gallant, tidings reached her that the King of France, in consequence of a tumour which he had had in the breast, and which had been ill tended, was now troubled with a fistula, which occasioned him extreme distress and suffering; nor had he as yet come by a physician that was able, though many had essayed, to cure him, but had rather grown worse under their hands; wherefore in despair he was minded no more to have recourse to any for counsel or aid. Whereat the damsel was overjoyed, deeming not only that she might find therein lawful occasion to go to Paris, but, that, if the disease was what she took it to be, it might well betide that she should be wedded

64

to Bertrand. So—for not a little knowledge had she gotten from her father—she prepared a powder from certain herbs serviceable in the treatment of the supposed disease, and straightway took horse, and hied her to Paris.

Arrived there she made it her first concern to have sight of Bertrand; and then, having obtained access to the King, she besought him of his grace to shew her his disease. The King knew not how to refuse so young, fair and winsome a damsel, and let her see the place.

Whereupon, no longer doubting that she should cure him, she said:— "Sire, so please you, I hope in God to cure you of this malady within eight days without causing you the least distress or discomfort."

The King inly scoffed at her words, saying to himself:—"How should a damsel have come by a knowledge and skill that the greatest physicians in the world do not possess?" He therefore graciously acknowledged her good intention, and answered that he had resolved no more to follow advice of physician.

"Sire," said the damsel, "you disdain my art, because I am young and a woman; but I bid you bear in mind that I rely not on my own skill, but on the help of God, and the skill of Master Gerard of Narbonne, my father, and a famous physician in his day."

Whereupon the King said to himself:—"Perchance she is sent me by God; why put I not her skill to the proof, seeing that she says that she can cure me in a short time, and cause me no distress?" And being minded to make the experiment, he said:—"Damsel, and if, having caused me to cancel my resolve, you should fail to cure me, what are you content should ensue?"

"Sire," answered the damsel, "set a guard upon me; and if within eight days I cure you not, have me burned; but if I cure you, what shall be my guerdon?"

"You seem," said the King, "to be yet unmarried; if you shall effect the cure, we will marry you well and in high place."

"Sire," returned the damsel, "well content indeed am I that you should marry me, so it be to such a husband as I shall ask of you, save that I may not ask any of your sons or any other member of the royal house."

Whereto the King forthwith consented, and the damsel, thereupon applying her treatment, restored him to health before the period assigned. Wherefore, as soon as the King knew that he was cured:— "Damsel," said he, "well have you won your husband."

She answered:—"In that case, Sire, I have won Bertrand de Roussillon, of whom, while yet a child, I was enamoured, and whom I have ever since most ardently loved."

To give her Bertrand seemed to the King no small matter; but, having pledged his word, he would not break it: so he sent for Bertrand, and said to him: — "Bertrand, you are now come to man's estate, and fully equipped to enter on it; 'tis therefore our will that you go back and assume the governance of your country, and that you take with you a damsel, whom we have given you to wife."

"And who is the damsel, Sire?" said Bertrand.

"She it is," answered the King, "that has restored us to health by her physic."

Now Bertrand, knowing Gillette, and that her lineage was not such as matched his nobility, albeit, seeing her, he had found her very fair, was overcome with disdain, and answered: — "So, Sire, you would fain give me a she-doctor to wife. Now God forbid that I should ever marry any such woman."

"Then," said the King, "you would have us fail of the faith which we pledged to the damsel, who asked you in marriage by way of guerdon for our restoration to health."

"Sire," said Bertrand, "you may take from me all that I possess, and give me as your man to whomsoever you may be minded; but rest assured that I shall never be satisfied with such a match."

"Nay, but you will," replied the King; "for the damsel is fair and discreet, and loves you well; wherefore we anticipate that you will live far more happily with her than with a dame of much higher lineage."

Bertrand was silent; and the King made great preparations for the celebration of the nuptials. The appointed day came, and Bertrand, albeit reluctantly, nevertheless complied, and in the presence of the King was wedded to the damsel, who loved him more dearly than herself. Which done, Bertrand, who had already taken his resolution, said that he was minded to go down to his county, there to consummate the marriage; and so, having craved and had leave of absence of the King, he took horse, but instead of returning to his county he hied him to Tuscany; where, finding the Florentines at war with the Sienese, he determined to take service with the Florentines, and being made heartily and honourably welcome, was appointed to the command of part of their forces, at a liberal stipend, and so remained in their service for a long while.

Distressed by this turn of fortune, and hoping by her wise management to bring Bertrand back to his county, the bride hied her to Roussillon, where she was received by all the tenants as their liege lady. She found that, during the long absence of the lord, everything had fallen into decay and disorder; which, being a capable woman, she rectified with great and sedulous care, to the great joy of the tenants, who held her in great esteem and love, and severely censured the Count, that he was not satisfied with her. When the lady had duly ordered all things in the county, she despatched two knights to the Count with the intelligence, praying him, that, if 'twas on her account that he came not home, he would so inform her; in which case she would gratify him by departing.

To whom with all harshness he replied: — "She may even please herself in the matter. For my part I will go home and live with her, when she has this ring on her finger and a son gotten of me upon her arm."

The ring was one which he greatly prized, and never removed from his finger, by reason of a virtue which he had been given to understand that it possessed. The knights appreciated the harshness of a condition which contained two articles, both of which were all but impossible; and, seeing that by no words of theirs could they alter his resolve, they returned to the lady, and delivered his message.

Sorely distressed, the lady after long pondering determined to try how and where the two conditions might be satisfied, that so her husband might be hers again. Having formed her plan, she assembled certain of the more considerable and notable men of the county, to whom she gave a consecutive and most touching narrative of all that she had done for love of the Count, with the result; concluding by saying that she was not minded to tarry there to the Count's perpetual exile, but to pass the rest of her days in pilgrimages and pious works for the good of her soul: wherefore she prayed them to undertake the defence and governance of the county, and to inform the Count that she had made entire and absolute cession of it to him, and was gone away with the intention of never more returning to Roussillon.

As she spoke, tears not a few coursed down the cheeks of the honest men, and again and again they besought her to change her mind, and stay. All in vain, however; she commended them to God, and, accompanied only by one of her male cousins and a chambermaid (all three habited as pilgrims and amply provided with money and precious jewels), she took the road, nor tarried until she was arrived at Florence. There she lodged in a little inn kept by a good woman that was a widow, bearing herself lowly as a poor pilgrim, and eagerly expectant of news of her lord.

Now it so befell that the very next day she saw Bertrand pass in front of the inn on horseback at the head of his company; and though she knew him very well, nevertheless she asked the good woman of the inn who he was.

The hostess replied: — "'Tis a foreign gentleman — Count Bertrand they call him — a very pleasant gentleman, and courteous, and much beloved in this city; and he is in the last degree enamoured of one of our neighbours here, who is a gentlewoman, but in poor circumstances. A very virtuous damsel she is too, and, being as yet unmarried by reason of her poverty, she lives with her mother, who is an excellent and most discreet lady, but for whom, perchance, she would before now have yielded and gratified the Count's desire."

No word of this was lost on the lady; she pondered and meditated every detail with the closest attention, and having laid it all to heart, took her resolution: she ascertained the names and abode of the lady and her daughter that the Count loved, and hied her one day privily, wearing her pilgrim's weeds, to their house, where she found the lady and her daughter in very evident poverty, and after greeting them, told the lady that, if it were agreeable to her, she would speak with her.

The gentlewoman rose and signified her willingness to listen to what she had to say; so they went into a room by themselves and sate down, and then the Countess began thus:—"Madam, methinks you are, as I am, under Fortune's frown; but perchance you have it in your power, if you are so minded, to afford solace to both of us."

The lady answered that, so she might honourably find it, solace indeed was what she craved most of all things in the world. Whereupon the Countess continued:—"I must first be assured of your faith, wherein if I confide and am deceived, the interests of both of us will suffer."

"Have no fear," said the gentlewoman, "speak your whole mind without reserve, for you will find that there is no deceit in me."

So the Countess told who she was, and the whole course of her love affair, from its commencement to that hour, on such wise that the gentlewoman, believing her story the more readily that she had already heard it in part from others, was touched with compassion for her. The narrative of her woes complete, the Countess added:—"Now that you have heard my misfortunes, you know the two conditions that I must fulfil, if I would come by my husband; nor know I any other person than you, that may enable me to fulfil them; but so you may, if this which I hear is true, to wit, that my husband is in the last degree enamoured of your daughter."

"Madam," replied the gentlewoman, "I know not if the Count loves my daughter, but true it is that he makes great shew of loving her; but how may this enable me to do aught for you in the matter that you have at heart?"

"The how, madam," returned the Countess, "I will shortly explain to you; but you shall first hear what I intend shall ensue, if you serve me. Your daughter, I see, is fair and of marriageable age, and, by what I have learned and may well understand, 'tis because you have not the wherewith to marry her that you keep her at home. Now, in recompense of the service that you shall do me, I mean to provide her forthwith from my own moneys with such a dowry as you yourself shall deem adequate for her marriage."

The lady was too needy not to be gratified by the proposal; but,

nevertheless, with the true spirit of the gentlewoman, she answered:—
"Nay but, madam, tell me that which I may do for you, and if it shall
be such as I may honourably do, gladly will I do it, and then you
shall do as you may be minded."

Said then the Countess:—"I require of you, that through some one
in whom you trust you send word to the Count, my husband, that your
daughter is ready to yield herself entirely to his will, so she may be sure
that he loves her even as he professes; whereof she will never be con-
vinced, until he send her the ring which he wears on his finger, and
which, she understands, he prizes so much: which, being sent, you
shall give to me, and shall then send him word that your daughter is
ready to do his pleasure, and, having brought him hither secretly, you
shall contrive that I lie by his side instead of your daughter. Perchance,
by God's grace I shall conceive, and so, having his ring on my finger,
and a son gotten of him on my arm, shall have him for my own again,
and live with him even as a wife should live with her husband, and owe
it all to you."

The lady felt that 'twas not a little that the Countess craved of her,
for she feared lest it should bring reproach upon her daughter: but she
reflected that to aid the good lady to recover her husband was an honourable enterprise, and that in undertaking it she would be subserving
a like end; and so, trusting in the good and virtuous disposition of the
Countess, she not only promised to do as she was required, but in no
long time, proceeding with caution and secrecy, as she had been bidden, she both had the ring from the Count, loath though he was to part
with it, and cunningly contrived that the Countess should lie with him
in place of her daughter. In which first commingling, so ardently
sought by the Count, it so pleased God that the lady was gotten, as in
due time her delivery made manifest, with two sons. Nor once only, but
many times did the lady gratify the Countess with the embraces of her
husband, using such secrecy that no word thereof ever got wind, the
Count all the while supposing that he lay, not with his wife, but with
her that he loved, and being wont to give her, as he left her in the
morning, some fair and rare jewel, which she jealously guarded.

When she perceived that she was with child, the Countess, being
minded no more to burden the lady with such service, said to her:—
"Madam, thanks be to God and to you, I now have that which I
desired, and therefore 'tis time that I make you grateful requital, and
take my leave of you."

The lady answered that she was glad if the Countess had gotten
aught that gave her joy; but that 'twas not as hoping to have guerdon
thereof that she had done her part, but simply because she deemed it
meet and her duty so to do.

"Well said, madam," returned the Countess, "and in like manner that which you shall ask of me I shall not give you by way of guerdon, but because I deem it meet and my duty to give it."

Whereupon the lady, yielding to necessity, and abashed beyond measure, asked of her a hundred pounds wherewith to marry her daughter. The Countess, marking her embarrassment, and the modesty of her request, gave her five hundred pounds besides jewels fair and rare, worth, perhaps, no less; and having thus much more than contented her, and received her superabundant thanks, she took leave of her and returned to the inn.

The lady, to render purposeless further visits or messages on Bertrand's part, withdrew with her daughter to the house of her kinsfolk in the country; nor was it long before Bertrand, on the urgent entreaty of his vassals and intelligence of the departure of his wife, quitted Florence and returned home. Greatly elated by this intelligence, the Countess tarried awhile in Florence, and was there delivered of two sons as like as possible to their father, whom she nurtured with sedulous care. But by and by she saw fit to take the road, and being come, unrecognized by any, to Montpellier, rested there a few days; and being on the alert for news of the Count and where he was, she learned that on All Saints' day he was to hold a great reception of ladies and gentlemen at Roussillon. Whither, retaining her now wonted pilgrim's weeds, she hied her, and finding that the ladies and gentlemen were all gathered in the Count's palace and on the point of going to table, she tarried not to change her dress, but went up into the hall, bearing her little ones in her arms, and threading her way through the throng to the place where she saw the Count stand, and threw herself at his feet, and sobbing, said to him:—

"My lord, thy hapless bride am I, who to ensure thy homecoming and abidance in peace have long time been a wanderer, and now demand of thee observance of the condition whereof word was brought me by the two knights whom I sent to thee. Lo in my arms not one son only but twain, gotten of thee, and on my finger thy ring. 'Tis time, then, that I be received of thee as thy wife according to thy word."

Whereat the Count was all dumbfounded, recognizing the ring and his own lineaments in the children, so like were they to him; but saying to himself nevertheless:—"How can it have come about?"

So the Countess, while the Count and all that were present marvelled exceedingly, told what had happened, and the manner of it, in precise detail. Wherefore the Count, perceiving that she spoke truth, and having regard to her perseverance and address and her two fine boys, and the wishes of all his vassals and the ladies, who with one

accord besought him to own and honour her thenceforth as his lawful
bride, laid aside his harsh obduracy, and raised the Countess to her
feet, and embraced and kissed her, and acknowledged her for his lawful wife, and the children for his own. Then, having caused her to be
rearrayed in garments befitting her rank, he, to the boundless delight of
as many as were there, and of all other his vassals, gave up that day and
some that followed to feasting and merrymaking; and did ever thenceforth honour, love and most tenderly cherish her as his bride and wife.

STORY X.

Alibech turns hermit, and is taught by Rustico, a monk, how the Devil is put in hell. She is afterwards conveyed thence, and becomes the wife of Neerbale.

Gracious ladies, perchance you have not yet heard how the Devil is put in hell; wherefore, without deviating far from the topic of which you have discoursed throughout the day, I will tell you how 'tis done; it may be the lesson will prove inspiring; besides which, you may learn therefrom that, albeit Love prefers the gay palace and the dainty chamber to the rude cabin, yet, for all that, he may at times manifest his might in wilds matted with forests, rugged with alps, and desolate with caverns: whereby it may be understood that all things are subject to his sway. But—to come to my story—I say that in the city of Capsa[1] in Barbary there was once a very rich man, who with other children had a fair and dainty little daughter, Alibech by name. Now Alibech, not being a Christian, and hearing many Christians, that were in the city, speak much in praise of the Christian Faith and the service of God, did one day inquire of one of them after what fashion it were possible to serve God with as few impediments as might be, and was informed that they served God best who most completely renounced the world and its affairs, like those who had fixed their abode in the wilds of the Thebaid desert. Whereupon, actuated by no sober predilection, but by childish impulse, the girl, who was very simple and about fourteen years of age, said never a word more of the matter, but stole away on the morrow, and quite alone set out to walk to the Thebaid desert; and, by force of resolution, albeit with no small suffering, she after some days reached those wilds; where, espying a cabin a great way off, she hied her thither, and found a holy man by the door, who, marvelling to see her there, asked her what she came there to seek. She answered that, guided by the spirit of God, she was come thither, seeking, if haply she might serve Him, and also find some one that might teach her how He

[1]Now Gafsa, in Tunis.

ought to be served. Marking her youth and great beauty, the worthy man, fearing lest, if he suffered her to remain with him, he should be ensnared by the Devil, commended her good intention, set before her a frugal repast of roots of herbs, crab-apples and dates, with a little water to wash them down, and said to her:—

"My daughter, there is a holy man not far from here, who is much better able to teach thee that of which thou art in quest than I am; go to him, therefore"; and she shewed her the way.

But when she was come whither she was directed, she met with the same answer as before, and so, setting forth again, she came at length to the cell of a young hermit, a worthy man and very devout—his name Rustico—whom she interrogated as she had the others. Rustico, being minded to make severe trial of his constancy, did not send her away, as the others had done, but kept her with him in his cell, and when night came, made her a little bed of palm-leaves; whereon he bade her compose herself to sleep. Hardly had she done so before the solicitations of the flesh joined battle with the powers of Rustico's spirit, and he, finding himself left in the lurch by the latter, endured not many assaults before he beat a retreat, and surrendered at discretion: wherefore he bade adieu to holy meditation and prayer and discipline, and fell a musing on the youth and beauty of his companion, and also how he might so order his conversation with her, that without seeming to her to be a libertine he might yet compass that which he craved of her. So, probing her by certain questions, he discovered that she was as yet entirely without cognizance of man, and as simple as she seemed: wherefore he excogitated a plan for bringing her to pleasure him under colour of serving God.

He began by giving her a long lecture on the great enmity that subsists between God and the Devil; after which he gave her to understand that, God, having condemned the Devil to hell, to put him there was of all services the most acceptable to God. The girl asking him how it might be done, Rustico answered:—"Thou shalt know it in a trice; thou hast but to do that which thou seest me do." Then, having divested himself of his scanty clothing, he threw himself stark naked on his knees, as if he would pray; whereby he caused the girl, who followed his example, to confront him in the same posture.[1] [Seeing her thus, with her beauty revealed in all its glory, he burned with desire more than ever, and his flesh was resurrected. Alibech gazed at this in amazement and said:

---

[1] The material in brackets was left in Italian by the translator, J. M. Rigg, with the explanatory footnote "No apology is needed for leaving, in accordance with precedent, the subsequent detail untranslated." In accordance with contemporary sensibilities, the Dover editors have freely translated the passage for this edition.

"Rustico, what is that thing I see sticking out in front of you, and which I do not possess?"

"Oh, my daughter," replied Rustico, "now you see for yourself that Devil I told you about. He is hurting me so much that I can hardly bear it."

"Praise God!" said the girl. "I see that I am better off than you are, for I do not possess such a Devil."

"You speak the truth," Rustico replied. "But you have something else which I do not have, and you have it in place of this."

"Oh?" answered Alibech. "What is that?"

"You possess hell," said Rustico, "and I truly believe that God has sent you here for the salvation of my soul. Because if this Devil persists in giving me so much pain, and if you take pity on me by letting me return him to hell, you would be giving me great comfort, and you would be rendering a great service, pleasing God, which is what you say you came here to do."

"Oh, father," replied the girl in all innocence, "since I possess hell, let us do as you suggest as soon as possible."

"God bless you, my daughter," Rustico said. "Let us go then and put him back in, and then he may leave me in peace at last."

He then led the girl over to one of the beds and showed her the way to incarcerate that cursed Devil. The young girl, who had never before put a single Devil into hell, felt some pain this first time, and so she said to Rustico:

"This Devil must surely be an evil thing, father, and a true enemy of God, for not only does he bring pain to mankind, but he also hurts hell when put back into it."

"My daughter," Rustico said, "it will not always be like that." And in order to show that this would not be the case, they returned him to hell several times before leaving the bed, having made it impossible for him to lift his arrogant head, and he was content to rest in peace. But the Devil's pride was to rise up again many times, and the young girl, who was always obedient and available to draw him in, began to take a liking to this sport. She expressed herself to Rustico: "Now I certainly see what those good men of Capsa meant when they said that serving God was so agreeable. Truly, I cannot recall anything that gave more pleasure and satisfaction than putting the Devil back in hell. The way I see it, anyone who does anything except give service to God is a fool."

For this reason she often came to Rustico, saying: "Father, I have not come to fritter away my time but to serve God. Now, let's get to work and return the Devil to hell." Sometimes, in the midst of their activities, she said to him: "Rustico, I cannot understand why the Devil would ever want to escape from hell. If he liked being in hell as much as hell likes holding him in there, he would never leave."

By enticing Rustico to engage in their sport with such frequency, constantly urging him on in service of God, the young girl depleted his physical resources to the point where he began to feel only cold where another man would be drenched in sweat from the heat. Because of this state of affairs, he explained to the girl that the Devil should only be put back in hell when he lifted his head in pride. "For we, by the grace of God, have so used him up that he prays God to leave him in peace." And thus he was able to quiet the girl for a while. But when she realized that Rustico was no longer asking her to put the Devil back into hell, she accosted him one day and said: "Rustico, it's all very well that your Devil has been punished and bothers you no more, but my hell refuses to leave me alone. Therefore, you should have your Devil help me to calm the rage of my hell—after all, it was with the aid of my hell that we tamed the arrogance of your Devil."

Rustico, who was living on nothing but herb roots and spring water, was unable to respond very well to her needs. He explained that it would take a number of Devils to adequately tame her hell, but he would do what he could. Thus it was that sometimes he was able to satisfy her, but most of the time it was like tossing a bean into the mouth of a hungry lion. The result was that the girl felt she was not serving God as well as she would have liked, and complained about it more often than not.] However, the case standing thus (deficiency of power against superfluity of desire) between Rustico's Devil and Alibech's hell, it chanced that a fire broke out in Capsa, whereby the house of Alibech's father was burned, and he and all his sons and the rest of his household perished; so that Alibech was left sole heiress of all his estate.

And a young gallant, Neerbale by name, who by reckless munificence had wasted all his substance, having discovered that she was alive, addressed himself to the pursuit of her, and, having found her in time to prevent the confiscation of her father's estate as an escheat for failure of heirs, took her, much to Rustico's relief and against her own will, back to Capsa, and made her his wife, and shared with her her vast patrimony. But before he had lain with her, she was questioned by the ladies of the manner in which she had served God in the desert; whereto she answered, that she had been wont to serve Him by putting the Devil in hell, and that Neerbale had committed a great sin, when he took her out of such service. The ladies being curious to know how the Devil was put in hell, the girl satisfied them, partly by words, partly by signs.

Whereat they laughed exorbitantly (and still laugh) and said to her:— "Be not down-hearted, daughter; 'tis done here too; Neerbale will know well how to serve God with you in that way."

And so the story passing from mouth to mouth throughout the city, it came at last to be a common proverb, that the most acceptable service that can be rendered to God is to put the Devil in hell; which proverb, having travelled hither across the sea, is still current. Wherefore, young ladies, you that have need of the grace of God, see to it that you learn how to put the Devil in hell, because 'tis mightily pleasing to God, and of great solace to both the parties, and much good may thereby be engendered and ensue.

A thousand times or more had Dioneo's story brought the laugh to the lips of the honourable ladies, so quaint and curiously entertaining found they the fashion of it. And now at its close the queen, seeing the term of her sovereignty come, took the laurel wreath from her head, and with mien most debonair, set it on the brow of Filostrato, saying:— "We shall soon see whether the wolf will know better how to guide the sheep than the sheep have yet succeeded in guiding the wolves."

Whereat Filostrato said with a laugh:—"Had I been hearkened to, the wolves would have taught the sheep to put the Devil in hell even as Rustico taught Alibech. Wherefore call us not wolves, seeing that you have not shewn yourselves sheep: however, as best I may be able, I will govern the kingdom committed to my charge."

Whereupon Neifile took him up: "Hark ye, Filostrato," she said, "while you thought to teach us, you might have learnt a lesson from us, as did Masetto da Lamporecchio from the nuns, and have recovered your speech when the bones had learned to whistle without a master."[1]

Filostrato, perceiving that there was a scythe for each of his arrows, gave up jesting, and addressed himself to the governance of his kingdom. He called the seneschal, and held him strictly to account in every particular; he then judiciously ordered all matters as he deemed would be best and most to the satisfaction of the company, while his sovereignty should last; and having so done, he turned to the ladies, and said:— "Loving ladies, as my ill luck would have it, since I have had wit to tell good from evil, the charms of one or other of you have kept me ever a slave to Love: and for all I shewed myself humble and obedient and conformable, so far as I knew how, to all his ways, my fate has been still the same, to be discarded for another, and go ever from bad to worse; and so, I suppose, 'twill be with me to the hour of my death. Wherefore I am minded that to-morrow our discourse be of no other topic than that which is most germane to my condition, to wit, of those whose loves had a disastrous close: because mine, I expect, will in the long run be most disastrous; nor for other cause was the name, by which you address me, given me by one that well knew its signification." Which said, he arose, and dismissed them all until supper-time.

---

[1] *I.e.* when you were so emaciated that your bones made music like a skeleton in the wind.

So fair and delightsome was the garden that none saw fit to quit it, and seek diversion elsewhere. Rather—for the sun now shone with a tempered radiance that caused no discomfort—some of the ladies gave chase to the kids and conies and other creatures that haunted it, and, scampering to and fro among them as they sate, had caused them a hundred times, or so, some slight embarrassment. Dioneo and Fiammetta fell a singing of Messer Guglielmo and the lady of Vergiù.[2] Filomena and Pamfilo sat them down to a game of chess; and, as thus they pursued each their several diversions, time sped so swiftly that the supper-hour stole upon them almost unawares: whereupon they ranged the tables round the beautiful fountain, and supped with all glad and festal cheer.

When the tables were removed, Filostrato, being minded to follow in the footsteps of his fair predecessors in sway, bade Lauretta lead a dance and sing a song. She answered:—"My lord, songs of others know I none, nor does my memory furnish me with any of mine own that seems meet for so gay a company; but, if you will be content with what I have, gladly will I give you thereof."

"Nought of thine," returned the king, "could be other than goodly and delectable. Wherefore give us even what thou hast." So encouraged, Lauretta, with dulcet voice, but manner somewhat languishing, raised the ensuing strain, to which the other ladies responded:—

> What dame disconsolate
> May so lament as I,
> That vainly sigh, to Love still dedicate?
>
> He that the heaven and every orb doth move
> Formed me for His delight
> Fair, debonair and gracious, apt for love;
> That here on earth each soaring spirit might
> Have foretaste how, above,
> That beauty shews that standeth in His sight.
> Ah! but dull wit and slight,
> For that it judgeth ill,
> Liketh me not, nay, doth me vilely rate.
>
> There was who loved me, and my maiden grace
> Did fondly clip and strain,
> As in his arms, so in his soul's embrace,
> And from mine eyes Love's fire did drink amain,

---

[2]Evidently some version of the tragical *conte* "de la Chastelaine de Vergi, qui mori por laialment amer son ami." See "Fabliaux et Contes," ed. Barbazan, iv. 296: and cf. Bandello, Pt. iv. Nov. v, and Heptameron, Journée vii. Nouvelle lxx.

And time that glides apace
In nought but courting me to spend was fain;
Whom courteous I did deign
Ev'n as my peer to entreat;
But am of him bereft! Ah! dolorous fate!

Came to me next a gallant swol'n with pride
    Brave, in his own conceit,
    And no less noble eke. Whom woe betide
That he me took, and holds in all unmeet
    Suspicion, jealous-eyed!
And I, who wot that me the world should greet
    As the predestined sweet
    Of many men, well-nigh
Despair, to be to one thus subjugate.

Ah! woe is me! cursed be the luckless day,
    When, a new gown to wear,
    I said the fatal ay; for blithe and gay
In that plain gown I lived, no whit less fair;
    While in this rich array
A sad and far less honoured life I bear!
    Would I had died, or e'er
    Sounded those notes of joy
(Ah! dolorous cheer!) my woe to celebrate!

So list my supplication, lover dear,
    Of whom such joyance I,
    As ne'er another, had. Thou that in clear
Light of the Maker's presence art, deny
    Not pity to thy fere,
Who thee may ne'er forget; but let one sigh
    Breathe tidings that on high
    Thou burnest still for me;
And sue of God that He me there translate.

So ended Lauretta her song, to which all hearkened attentively,
though not all interpreted it alike. Some were inclined to give it a moral
after the Milanese fashion, to wit, that a good porker was better than a
pretty quean. Others construed it in a higher, better and truer sense,
which 'tis not to the present purpose to unfold. Some more songs
followed by command of the king, who caused torches not a few to be
lighted and ranged about the flowery mead; and so the night was prolonged until the last star that had risen had begun to set. Then, bethinking him that 'twas time for slumber, the king bade all good-night, and
dismissed them to their several chambers.

FOURTH DAY

STORY I.

Tancred, Prince of Salerno, slays his daughter's lover, and sends her his heart in a golden cup: she pours upon it a poisonous distillation, which she drinks and dies.

Tancred, Prince of Salerno, a lord most humane and kind of heart, but that in his old age he imbrued his hands in the blood of a lover, had in the whole course of his life but one daughter; and had he not had her, he had been more fortunate.

Never was daughter more tenderly beloved of father than she of the Prince, who, for that cause not knowing how to part with her, kept her unmarried for many a year after she had come of marriageable age: then at last he gave her to a son of the Duke of Capua, with whom she had lived but a short while, when he died and she returned to her father. Most lovely was she of form and feature (never woman more so), and young and light of heart, and more knowing, perchance, than beseemed a woman. Dwelling thus with her loving father, as a great lady, in no small luxury, nor failing to see that the Prince, for the great love he bore her, was at no pains to provide her with another husband, and deeming it unseemly on her part to ask one of him, she cast about how she might come by a gallant to be her secret lover. And seeing at her father's court not a few men, both gentle and simple, that resorted thither, as we know men use to frequent courts, and closely scanning their mien and manners, she preferred before all others the Prince's page, Guiscardo by name, a man of very humble origin, but preeminent for native worth and noble bearing; of whom, seeing him frequently, she became hotly enamoured, hourly extolling his qualities more and more highly.

The young man, who for all his youth by no means lacked shrewdness, read her heart, and gave her his own on such wise that his love for her engrossed his mind to the exclusion of almost everything else.

79

While thus they burned in secret for one another, the lady, desiring of all things a meeting with Guiscardo, but being shy of making any her confidant, hit upon a novel expedient to concert the affair with him. She wrote him a letter containing her commands for the ensuing day, and thrust it into a cane in the space between two of the knots, which cane she gave to Guiscardo, saying:—"Thou canst let thy servant have it for a bellows to blow thy fire up to night."

Guiscardo took it, and feeling sure that 'twas not unadvisedly that she made him such a present, accompanied with such words, hied him straight home, where, carefully examining the cane, he observed that it was cleft, and, opening it, found the letter; which he had no sooner read, and learned what he was to do, than, pleased as ne'er another, he fell to devising how to set all in order that he might not fail to meet the lady on the following day, after the manner she had prescribed.

Now hard by the Prince's palace was a grotto, hewn in days of old in the solid rock, and now long disused, so that an artificial orifice, by which it received a little light, was all but choked with brambles and plants that grew about and overspread it. From one of the ground-floor rooms of the palace, which room was part of the lady's suite, a secret stair led to the grotto, though the entrance was barred by a very strong door. This stair, having been from time immemorial disused, had passed out of mind so completely that there was scarce any that remembered that it was there: but Love, whose eyes nothing, however secret, may escape, had brought it to the mind of the enamoured lady.

For many a day, using all secrecy, that none should discover her, she had wrought with her tools, until she had succeeded in opening the door; which done, she had gone down into the grotto alone, and having observed the orifice, had by her letter apprised Guiscardo of its apparent height above the floor of the grotto, and bidden him contrive some means of descending thereby. Eager to carry the affair through, Guiscardo lost no time in rigging up a ladder of ropes, whereby he might ascend and descend; and having put on a suit of leather to protect him from the brambles, he hied him the following night (keeping the affair close from all) to the orifice, made the ladder fast by one of its ends to a massive trunk that was rooted in the mouth of the orifice, climbed down the ladder, and awaited the lady.

On the morrow, making as if she would fain sleep, the lady dismissed her damsels, and locked herself into her room: she then opened the door of the grotto, hied her down, and met Guiscardo, to their marvellous mutual satisfaction. The lovers then repaired to her room, where in exceeding great joyance they spent no small part of the day. Nor were they neglectful of the precautions needful to prevent discovery of their amour; but in due time Guiscardo returned to the grotto; whereupon the lady locked the door and rejoined her damsels. At nightfall Guiscardo reascended his ladder, and, issuing forth of the orifice, hied him home; nor, knowing now the way, did he fail to revisit the grotto many a time thereafter.

But Fortune, noting with envious eye a happiness of such degree and duration, gave to events a dolorous turn, whereby the joy of the two lovers was converted into bitter lamentation. 'Twas Tancred's custom to come from time to time quite alone to his daughter's room, and tarry talking with her a while. Whereby it so befell that he came down there one day after breakfast, while Ghismonda—such was the lady's name—was in her garden with her damsels; so that none saw or heard him enter; nor would he call his daughter, for he was minded that she should not forgo her pleasure. But, finding the windows closed and the bed-curtains drawn down, he seated himself on a divan that stood at one of the corners of the bed, rested his head on the bed, drew the curtain over him, and thus, hidden as if of set purpose, fell asleep.

As he slept Ghismonda, who, as it happened, had caused Guiscardo to come that day, left her damsels in the garden, softly entered the room, and having locked herself in, unwitting that there was another in the room, opened the door to Guiscardo, who was in waiting. Straightway they got them to bed, as was their wont; and, while they were solaced and disported them together, it so befell that Tancred awoke, and heard and saw what they did: whereat he was troubled beyond measure, and at first was minded to upbraid them; but on second thoughts he deemed it best to hold his peace, and avoid discovery, if so he might with greater stealth and less dishonour carry out the design which was already in his mind.

The two lovers continued long together, as they were wont, all unwitting of Tancred; but at length they saw fit to get out of bed, when Guiscardo went back to the grotto, and the lady hied her forth of the room. Whereupon Tancred, old though he was, got out at one of the windows, clambered down into the garden, and, seen by none, returned sorely troubled to his room. By his command two men took Guiscardo early that same night, as he issued forth of the orifice accoutred in his suit of leather, and brought him privily to Tancred; who, as he saw him, all but wept, and said:—"Guiscardo, my kindness to thee is ill requited by the outrage and dishonour which thou hast done me in the person of my daughter, as to-day I have seen with my own eyes."

To whom Guiscardo could answer nought but:—"Love is more potent than either you or I."

Tancred then gave order to keep him privily under watch and ward in a room within the palace; and so 'twas done. Next day, while Ghismonda wotted nought of these matters, Tancred, after pondering divers novel expedients, hied him after breakfast, according to his wont, to his daughter's room, where, having called her to him and locked himself in with her, he began, not without tears, to speak on this wise:—

"Ghismonda, conceiving that I knew thy virtue and honour, never, though it had been reported to me, would I have credited, had I not seen with my own eyes, that thou wouldst so much as in idea, not to say fact, have ever yielded thyself to any man but thy husband: wherefore, for the brief residue of life that my age has in store for me, the memory of thy fall will ever be grievous to me. And would to God, as thou must needs demean thyself to such dishonour, thou hadst taken a man that matched thy nobility; but of all the men that frequent my court, thou must needs choose Guiscardo, a young man of the lowest condition, a fellow whom we brought up in charity from his tender years; for whose sake thou hast plunged me into the abyss of mental tribulation, insomuch that I know not what course to take in regard of thee. As to Guiscardo, whom I caused to be arrested last night as he issued from the orifice, and keep in durance, my course is already taken, but how I am to deal with thee, God knows, I know not. I am distraught between the love which I have ever borne thee, love such as no father ever bare to daughter, and the most just indignation evoked in me by thy signal folly; my love prompts me to pardon thee, my indignation bids me harden my heart against thee, though I do violence to my nature. But before I decide upon my course, I would fain hear what thou hast to say to this." So saying, he bent his head, and wept as bitterly as any child that had been soundly thrashed.

Her father's words, and the tidings they conveyed that not only was her secret passion discovered, but Guiscardo taken, caused Ghismonda immeasurable grief, which she was again and again on the point of evincing, as most women do, by cries and tears; but her high spirit triumphed over this weakness; by a prodigious effort she composed her countenance, and taking it for granted that her Guiscardo was no more, she inly devoted herself to death rather than a single prayer for herself should escape her lips. Wherefore, not as a woman stricken with grief or chidden for a fault, but unconcerned and unabashed, with tearless eyes, and frank and utterly dauntless mien, thus answered she her father:—

"Tancred, your accusation I shall not deny, neither will I cry you mercy, for nought should I gain by denial, nor aught would I gain by supplication: nay more; there is nought I will do to conciliate thy humanity and love; my only care is to confess the truth, to defend my honour by words of sound reason, and then by deeds most resolute to give effect to the promptings of my high soul. True it is that I have loved and love Guiscardo, and during the brief while I have yet to live shall love him, nor after death, so there be then love, shall I cease to love him; but that I love him, is not imputable to my womanly frailty so much as to the little zeal thou shewedst for my bestowal in marriage, and to Guiscardo's own worth. It should not have escaped thee, Tancred, creature of flesh and blood as thou art, that thy daughter was also a creature of flesh and blood, and not of stone or iron; it was, and is, thy duty to bear in mind (old though thou art) the nature and the might of the laws to which youth is subject; and, though thou hast spent part of thy best years in martial exercises, thou shouldst nevertheless have not been ignorant how potent is the influence even upon the aged—to say nothing of the young—of ease and luxury. And not only am I, as being thy daughter, a creature of flesh and blood, but my life is not so far spent but that I am still young, and thus doubly fraught with fleshly appetite, the vehemence whereof is marvellously enhanced by reason that, having been married, I have known the pleasure that ensues upon the satisfaction of such desire. Which forces being powerless to withstand, I did but act as was natural in a young woman, when I gave way to them, and yielded myself to love.

"Nor in sooth did I fail to the utmost of my power so to order the indulgence of my natural propensity that my sin should bring shame neither upon thee nor upon me. To which end Love in his pity, and Fortune in a friendly mood, found and discovered to me a secret way, whereby, none witting, I attained my desire: this, from whomsoever thou hast learned it, howsoever thou comest to know it, I deny not. 'Twas not at random, as many women do, that I loved Guiscardo; but by deliberate choice I preferred him before all other men, and of determinate forethought I lured him to my love, whereof, through his and my discretion and constancy, I have long had joyance. Wherein 'twould seem that thou, following rather the opinion of the vulgar than the dictates of truth, find cause to chide me more severely than in my sinful love, for, as if thou wouldst not have been vexed, had my choice fallen on a nobleman, thou complainest that I have forgathered with a man of low condition; and dost not see that therein thou censurest not my fault but that of Fortune, which not seldom raises the unworthy to high place and leaves the worthiest in low estate.

"But leave we this: consider a little the principles of things: thou seest that in regard of our flesh we are all moulded of the same substance, and that all souls are endowed by one and the same Creator with equal faculties, equal powers, equal virtues. 'Twas merit that made the first distinction between us, born as we were, nay, as we are, all equal, and those whose merits were and were approved in act the greatest were called noble, and the rest were not so denoted. Which law, albeit overlaid by the contrary usage of after times, is not yet abrogated, nor so impaired but that it is still traceable in nature and good manners; for which cause whoso with merit acts, does plainly shew himself a gentleman; and if any denote him otherwise, the default is his own and not his whom he so denotes. Pass in review all thy nobles, weigh their merits, their manners and bearing, and then compare Guiscardo's qualities with theirs: if thou wilt judge without prejudice, thou wilt pronounce him noble in the highest degree, and thy nobles one and all churls.

"As to Guiscardo's merits and worth I did but trust the verdict which thou thyself didst utter in words, and which mine own eyes confirmed. Of whom had he such commendation as of thee for all those excellences whereby a good man and true merits commendation? And in sooth thou didst him but justice; for, unless mine eyes have played me false, there was nought for which thou didst commend him but I had seen him practise it, and that more admirably than words of thine might express; and had I been at all deceived in this matter, 'twould have been by thee. Wilt thou say then that I have forgathered with a man of low condition? If so, thou wilt not say true. Didst thou say with a poor man, the impeachment might be allowed, to thy shame, that thou so ill hast known how to requite a good man and true that is thy servant; but poverty, though it take away all else, deprives no man of gentilesse. Many kings, many great princes, were once poor, and many a ditcher or herdsman has been and is very wealthy. As for thy last perpended doubt, to wit, how thou shouldst deal with me, banish it utterly from thy thoughts.

"If in thy extreme old age thou art minded to manifest a harshness unwonted in thy youth, wreak thy harshness on me, resolved as I am to cry thee no mercy, prime cause as I am that this sin, if sin it be, has been committed; for of this I warrant thee, that as thou mayst have done or shalt do to Guiscardo, if to me thou do not the like, I with my own hands will do it. Now get thee gone to shed thy tears with the women, and when thy melting mood is over, ruthlessly destroy Guiscardo and me, if such thou deem our merited doom, by one and the same blow."

The loftiness of his daughter's spirit was not unknown to the Prince; but still he did not credit her with a resolve quite as firmly fixed as her words implied, to carry their purport into effect. So, parting from her without the least intention of using harshness towards her in her own person, he determined to quench the heat of her love by wreaking his vengeance on her lover, and bade the two men that had charge of Guiscardo to strangle him noiselessly that same night, take the heart out of the body, and send it to him. The men did his bidding: and on the morrow the Prince had a large and beautiful cup of gold brought to him, and having put Guiscardo's heart therein, sent it by the hand of one of his most trusted servants to his daughter, charging the servant to say, as he gave it to her: — "Thy father sends thee this to give thee joy of that which thou lovest best, even as thou hast given him joy of that which he loved best."

Now when her father had left her, Ghismonda, wavering not a jot in her stern resolve, had sent for poisonous herbs and roots, and therefrom had distilled a water, to have it ready for use, if that which she apprehended should come to pass. And when the servant appeared with the Prince's present and message, she took the cup unblenchingly, and having lifted the lid, and seen the heart, and apprehended the meaning of the words, and that the heart was beyond a doubt Guiscardo's, she raised her head, and looking straight at the servant, said: — "Sepulture less honourable than of gold had ill befitted heart such as this: herein has my father done wisely."

Which said, she raised it to her lips, and kissed it saying: — "In all things and at all times, even to this last hour of my life, have I found my father most tender in his love, but now more so than ever before; wherefore I now render him the last thanks which will ever be due from me to him for this goodly present."

So she spoke, and straining the cup to her, bowed her head over it, and gazing at the heart, said: — "Ah! sojourn most sweet of all my joys, accursed be he by whose ruthless act I see thee with the bodily eye: 'twas enough that to the mind's eye thou wert hourly present. Thou has run thy course; thou hast closed the span that Fortune allotted thee; thou hast reached the goal of all; thou hast left behind thee the woes and weariness of the world; and thy enemy has himself granted thee sepulture accordant with thy deserts. No circumstance was wanting to duly celebrate thy obsequies, save the tears of her whom, while thou livedst, thou didst so dearly love; which that thou shouldst not lack, my remorseless father was prompted of God to send thee to me, and, albeit my resolve was fixed to die with eyes unmoistened and front all unperturbed by fear, yet will I accord thee my tears; which done, my care shall be forthwith by thy means to join my soul to that most precious soul which thou didst once enshrine. And is there other company than hers, in which with more of joy and peace I might fare to the abodes unknown? She is yet here within, I doubt not, contemplating the abodes of her and my delights, and — for sure I am that she loves me — awaiting my soul that loves her before all else."

Having thus spoken, she bowed herself low over the cup; and, while no womanish cry escaped her, 'twas as if a fountain of water were unloosed within her head, so wondrous a flood of tears gushed from her eyes, while times without number she kissed the dead heart. Her damsels that stood around her knew not whose the heart might be or what her words might mean, but melting in sympathy, they all wept, and compassionately, as vainly, enquired the cause of her lamentation, and in many other ways sought to comfort her to the best of their understanding and power.

When she had wept her fill, she raised her head, and dried her eyes. Then:—"O heart," said she, "much cherished heart, discharged is my every duty towards thee; nought now remains for me to do but to come and unite my soul with thine."

So saying, she sent for the vase that held the water which the day before she had distilled, and emptied it into the cup where lay the heart bathed in her tears; then, nowise afraid, she set her mouth to the cup, and drained it dry, and so with the cup in her hand she got her upon her bed, and having there disposed her person in guise as seemly as she might, laid her dead lover's heart upon her own, and silently awaited death. Meanwhile the damsels, seeing and hearing what passed, but knowing not what the water was that she had drunk, had sent word of each particular to Tancred; who, apprehensive of that which came to pass, came down with all haste to his daughter's room, where he arrived just as she got her upon her bed, and, now too late, addressed himself to comfort her with soft words, and seeing in what plight she was, burst into a flood of bitter tears. To whom the lady said:—

"Reserve thy tears, Tancred, till Fortune send thee hap less longed for than this: waste them not on me who care not for them. Whoever yet saw any but thee bewail the consummation of his desire? But, if of the love thou once didst bear me any spark still lives in thee, be it thy parting grace to me, that, as thou brookedst not that I should live with Guiscardo in privity and seclusion, so wherever thou mayst have caused Guiscardo's body to be cast, mine may be united with it in the common view of all."

The Prince replied not for excess of grief; and the lady, feeling that her end was come, strained the dead heart to her bosom, saying:— "Fare ye well; I take my leave of you"; and with eyelids drooped and every sense evanished departed this life of woe. Such was the lamentable end of the loves of Guiscardo and Ghismonda; whom Tancred, tardily repentant of his harshness, mourned not a little, as did also all the folk of Salerno, and had honourably interred side by side in the same tomb.

STORY V.

Lisabetta's brothers slay her lover: he appears to her in a dream, and shews her where he is buried: she privily disinters the head, and sets it in a pot of basil, whereon she daily weeps a great while. The pot being taken from her by her brothers, she dies not long after.

Know then that there were at Messina three young men, that were brothers and merchants, who were left very rich on the death of their father, who was of San Gimignano; and they had a sister, Lisabetta by name, a girl fair enough, and no less debonair, but whom, for some reason or another, they had not as yet bestowed in marriage. The three brothers had also in their shop a young Pisan, Lorenzo by name, who managed all their affairs, and who was so goodly of person and gallant, that Lisabetta bestowed many a glance upon him, and began to regard him with extraordinary favour; which Lorenzo marking from time to time, gave up all his other amours, and in like manner began to affect her, and so, their loves being equal, 'twas not long before they took heart of grace, and did that which each most desired. Wherein continuing to their no small mutual solace and delight, they neglected to order it with due secrecy, whereby one night as Lisabetta was going to Lorenzo's room, she, all unwitting, was observed by the eldest of the brothers, who, albeit much distressed by what he had learnt, yet, being a young man of discretion, was swayed by considerations more seemly, and, allowing no word to escape him, spent the night in turning the affair over in his mind in divers ways.

On the morrow he told his brothers that which, touching Lisabetta and Lorenzo, he had observed in the night, which, that no shame might thence ensue either to them or to their sister, they after long consultation determined to pass over in silence, making as if they had seen or heard nought thereof, until such time as they in a safe and convenient manner might banish this disgrace from their sight before it could go further. Adhering to which purpose, they jested and laughed with Lorenzo as they had been wont; and after a while pretending that they were all three going forth of the city on pleasure, they took Lorenzo with them; and being come to a remote and very lonely spot, seeing that 'twas apt for their design, they took Lorenzo, who was completely off his guard, and slew him, and buried him on such wise that none was ware of it.

On their return to Messina they gave out that they had sent him away on business; which was readily believed, because 'twas what they had been frequently used to do. But as Lorenzo did not return, and Lisabetta questioned the brothers about him with great frequency and urgency, being sorely grieved by his long absence, it so befell that one day, when she was very pressing in her enquiries, one of the brothers said: — "What means this? What hast thou to do with Lorenzo, that thou shouldst ask about him so often? Ask us no more, or we will give thee such answer as thou deservest." So the girl, sick at heart and sorrowful, fearing she knew not what, asked no questions; but many a time at night she called piteously to him, and besought him to come to her, and bewailed his long tarrying with many a tear, and ever yearning for his return, languished in total dejection.

But so it was that one night, when, after long weeping that her Lorenzo came not back, she had at last fallen asleep, Lorenzo appeared to her in a dream, wan and in utter disarray, his clothes torn to shreds and sodden; and thus, as she thought, he spoke: — "Lisabetta, thou dost nought but call me, and vex thyself for my long tarrying, and bitterly upbraid me with thy tears; wherefore be it known to thee that return to thee I may not, because the last day that thou didst see me thy brothers slew me."

After which, he described the place where they had buried him, told her to call and expect him no more, and vanished. The girl then awoke, and doubting not that the vision was true, wept bitterly. And when morning came, and she was risen, not daring to say aught to her brothers, she resolved to go to the place indicated in the vision, and see if what she had dreamed were even as it had appeared to her. So, having leave to go a little way out of the city for recreation in company with a maid that had at one time lived with them and knew all that she did, she hied her thither with all speed; and having removed the dry leaves that were strewn about the place, she began to dig where the earth seemed least hard. Nor had she dug long, before she found the body of her hapless lover, whereon as yet there was no trace of corruption or decay; and thus she saw without any manner of doubt that her vision was true.

And so, saddest of women, knowing that she might not bewail him there, she would gladly if she could, have carried away the body and given it more honourable sepulture elsewhere; but as she might not so do, she took a knife, and, as best she could, severed the head from the trunk, and wrapped it in a napkin and laid it in the lap of her maid; and having covered the rest of the corpse with earth, she left the spot, having been seen by none, and went home. There she shut herself up in her room with the head, and kissed it a thousand times in every part, and wept long and bitterly over it, till she had bathed it in her tears. She then wrapped it in a piece of fine cloth, and set it in a large and beautiful pot of the sort in which marjoram or basil is planted, and covered it with earth, and therein planted some roots of the goodliest basil of Salerno, and drenched them only with her tears, or water perfumed with roses or orange-blossoms. And 'twas her wont ever to sit beside this pot, and, all her soul one yearning, to pore upon it, as that which enshrined her Lorenzo, and when long time she had so done, she would bend over it, and weep a great while, until the basil was quite bathed in her tears.

Fostered with such constant, unremitting care, and nourished by the richness given to the soil by the decaying head that lay therein, the basil burgeoned out in exceeding great beauty and fragrance. And, the girl persevering ever in this way of life, the neighbours from time to time took note of it, and when her brothers marvelled to see her beauty ruined, and her eyes as it were evanished from her head, they told them of it, saying: — "We have observed that such is her daily wont."

Whereupon the brothers, marking her behaviour, chid her therefore once or twice, and as she heeded them not, caused the pot to be taken privily from her. Which, so soon as she missed it, she demanded with the utmost instance and insistence, and, as they gave it not back to her, ceased not to wail and weep, insomuch that she fell sick; nor in her sickness craved she aught but the pot of basil. Whereat the young men, marvelling mightily, resolved to see what the pot might contain; and having removed the earth they espied the cloth, and therein the head, which was not yet so decayed, but that by the curled locks they knew it for Lorenzo's head. Passing strange they found it, and fearing lest it should be bruited abroad, they buried the head, and, with as little said as might be, took order for their privy departure from Messina, and hied them thence to Naples.

The girl ceased not to weep and crave her pot, and, so weeping, died. Such was the end of her disastrous love; but not a few in course of time coming to know the truth of the affair, there was one that made the song that is still sung: to wit: —

> A thief he was, I swear,
> A sorry Christian he,
> That took my basil of Salerno fair, etc.[1]

---

[1] This Sicilian folk-song, of which Boccaccio quotes only the first two lines, is given in extenso from MS. Laurent. 38, plut. 42, by Fanfani in his edition of the *Decameron* (Florence, 1857). The following is a free rendering—

A thief he was, I swear,
  A sorry Christian he,
  That took my basil of Salerno fair,
  That flourished mightily.
  Planted by mine own hands with loving care
  What time they revelled free:
  To spoil another's goods is churlish spite.

To spoil another's goods is churlish spite,
  Ay, and most heinous sin.
  A basil had I (alas! luckless wight!),
  The fairest plant: within
  Its shade I slept: 'twas grown to such a height.
  But some folk for chagrin
  'Reft me thereof, ay, and before my door.

'Reft me thereof, ay, and before my door.
  Ah! dolorous day and drear!
  Ah! woe is me! Would God I were no more!
  My purchase was so dear!
  Ah! why that day did I to watch give o'er?
  For him my cherished fere
  With marjoram I bordered it about.

With marjoram I bordered it about
  In May-time fresh and fair,
  And watered it thrice ere each week was out,
  And marked it grow full yare:
  But now 'tis stolen. Ah! too well 'tis known![1]

But now 'tis stolen. Ah! too well 'tis known!
  That no more may I hide:
  But had to me a while before been shewn
  What then should me betide,
  At night before my door, I had laid me down
  To watch my plant beside.
  Yet God Almighty sure me succour might.

Ay, God Almighty sure me succour might,
  So were it but His will,
  'Gainst him that me hath done so foul despite,
  That in dire torment still
  I languish, since the thief reft from my sight
  My plant that did me thrill,
  And to my inmost soul such comfort lent!

---

[1]This stanza is defective in the original.

And to my inmost soul such comfort lent!
   So fresh its fragrance blew,
   That when, what time the sun uprose, I went
   My watering to do,
   I'd hear the people all in wonderment
   Say, whence this perfume new?
And I for love of it of grief shall die.

And I for love of it of grief shall die,
   Of my fair plant for dole.
   Would one but shew me how I might it buy!
   Ah! how 'twould me console!
   Ounces[1] an hundred of fine gold have I:
   Him would I give the whole,
Ay, and a kiss to boot, so he were fain.

---

[1]The "oncia" was a Sicilian gold coin worth rather more than a zecchino.

STORY X.

The wife of a leech, deeming her lover, who has taken an opiate, to be dead, puts him in a chest, which, with him therein, two usurers carry off to their house. He comes to himself, and is taken for a thief; but, the lady's maid giving the Signory to understand that she had put him in the chest which the usurers stole, he escapes the gallows, and the usurers are mulcted in moneys for the theft of the chest.

You are to know, then, fairest my damsels, that 'tis not long since there dwelt at Salerno a leech most eminent in surgery, his name, Master Mazzeo della Montagna, who in his extreme old age took to wife a fair damsel of the same city, whom he kept in nobler and richer array of dresses and jewels, and all other finery that the sex affects, than any other lady in Salerno. Howbeit, she was none too warm most of her time, being ill covered abed by the doctor; who gave her to understand— even as Messer Ricciardo di Chinzica, of whom we spoke a while since, taught his lady the feasts—that for once that a man lay with a woman he needed I know not how many days to recover, and the like nonsense: whereby she lived as ill content as might be; and, lacking neither sense nor spirit, she determined to economize at home, and taking to the street, to live at others' expense. So, having passed in review divers young men, she at last found one that was to her mind, on whom she set all her heart and hopes of happiness. Which the gallant perceiving was mightily flattered, and in like manner gave her all his love.

Ruggieri da Jeroli—such was the gallant's name—was of noble birth, but of life and conversation so evil and reprehensible that kinsman or friend he had none left that wished him well, or cared to see him; and all Salerno knew him for a common thief and rogue of the vilest character. Whereof the lady took little heed, having a mind to him for another reason; and so with the help of her maid she arranged a meeting with him. But after they had solaced themselves a while, the lady began to censure his past life, and to implore him for love of her to depart from such evil ways; and to afford him the means thereto, she from time to time furnished him with money. While thus with all discretion they continued their intercourse, it chanced that a man halt of one of his legs was placed under the leech's care. The leech saw what was amiss with him, and told his kinsfolk, that, unless a gangrened bone that he had in his leg were taken out, he must die, or have the whole leg amputated; that if the bone were removed he might recover; but that otherwise he would not answer for his life: whereupon the relatives assented that the bone should be removed, and left the patient in the hands of the leech; who, deeming that by reason of the pain 'twas not possible for him to endure the treatment without an opiate, caused to be distilled in the morning a certain water of his own concoction, whereby the patient, drinking it, might be ensured sleep during such time as he deemed the operation, which he meant to perform about vespers, would occupy.

In the meantime he had the water brought into his house, and set it in the window of his room, telling no one what it was. But when the vesper hour was come, and the leech was about to visit his patient, a messenger arrived from some very great friends of his at Amalfi, bearing tidings of a great riot there had been there, in which not a few had been wounded, and bidding him on no account omit to hie him thither forthwith. Wherefore the leech put off the treatment of the leg to the morrow, and took boat to Amalfi; and the lady, knowing that he would not return home that night, did as she was wont in such a case, to wit, brought Ruggieri in privily, and locked him in her chamber until certain other folk that were in the house were gone to sleep. Ruggieri, then, being thus in the chamber, awaiting the lady, and having—whether it were that he had had a fatiguing day, or eaten something salt, or, perchance, that 'twas his habit of body—a mighty thirst, glancing at the window, caught sight of the bottle containing the water which the leech had prepared for the patient, and taking it to be drinking water, set it to his lips and drank it all, and in no long time fell into a deep sleep.

So soon as she was able the lady hied her to the room, and there finding Ruggieri asleep, touched him and softly told him to get up: to no purpose, however; he neither answered nor stirred a limb. Wherefore the lady, rather losing patience, applied somewhat more force, and gave him a push, saying:—"Get up, sleepy-head; if thou hadst a mind to sleep, thou shouldst have gone home, and not have come hither."

Thus pushed Ruggieri fell down from a box on which he lay, and, falling, shewed no more sign of animation than if he had been a corpse. The lady, now somewhat alarmed, essayed to lift him, and shook him roughly, and took him by the nose, and pulled him by the beard; again to no purpose: he had tethered his ass to a stout pin. So the lady began to fear he must be dead: however, she went on to pinch him shrewdly, and singe him with the flame of a candle; but when these methods also failed she, being, for all she was a leech's wife, no leech herself, believed for sure that he was dead; and as there was nought in the world that she loved so much, it boots not to ask if she was sore distressed; wherefore silently, for she dared not lament aloud, she began to weep over him and bewail such a misadventure. But, after a while, fearing lest her loss should not be without a sequel of shame, she bethought her that she must contrive without delay to get the body out of the house; and standing in need of another's advice, she quietly summoned her maid, shewed her the mishap that had befallen her, and craved her counsel. Whereat the maid marvelled not a little; and she too fell to pulling Ruggieri this way and that, and pinching him, and, as she found no sign of life in him, concurred with her mistress that he was verily dead, and advised her to remove him from the house.

"And where," said the lady, "shall we put him, that to-morrow, when he is discovered, it be not suspected that 'twas hence he was carried?"

"Madam," answered the maid, "late last evening I marked in front of our neighbour the carpenter's shop a chest, not too large, which, if he have not put it back in the house, will come in very handy for our purpose, for we will put him inside, and give him two or three cuts with a knife, and so leave him. When he is found, I know not why it should be thought that 'twas from this house rather than from any other that he was put there; nay, as he was an evil-liver, 'twill more likely be supposed, that, as he hied him on some evil errand, some enemy slew him, and then put him in the chest."

The lady said there was nought in the world she might so ill brook as that Ruggieri should receive any wound; but with that exception she approved her maid's proposal, and sent her to see if the chest were still where she had seen it. The maid, returning, reported that there it was, and, being young and strong, got Ruggieri, with the lady's help, upon her shoulders; and so the lady, going before to espy if any folk came that way, and the maid following, they came to the chest, and having laid Ruggieri therein, closed it and left him there.

Now a few days before, two young men, that were usurers, had taken up their quarters in a house a little further on: they had seen the chest during the day, and being short of furniture, and having a mind to make great gain with little expenditure, they had resolved that, if it were still there at night, they would take it home with them. So at midnight forth they hied them, and finding the chest, were at no pains to examine it closely, but forthwith, though it seemed somewhat heavy, bore it off to their house, and set it down beside a room in which their women slept; and without being at pains to adjust it too securely they left it there for the time, and went to bed.

Towards matins Ruggieri, having had a long sleep and digested the draught and exhausted its efficacy, awoke, but albeit his slumber was broken, and his senses had recovered their powers, yet his brain remained in a sort of torpor which kept him bemused for some days; and when he opened his eyes and saw nothing, and stretched his hands hither and thither and found himself in the chest, it was with difficulty that he collected his thoughts.

"How is this?" he said to himself. "Where am I? Do I sleep or wake? I remember coming this evening to my lady's chamber; and now it seems I am in a chest. What means it? Can the leech have returned, or somewhat else have happened that caused the lady, while I slept, to hide me here? That was it, I suppose. Without a doubt it must have been so."

And having come to this conclusion, he composed himself to listen, if haply he might hear something, and being somewhat ill at ease in the chest, which was none too large, and the side on which he lay paining him, he must needs turn over to the other, and did so with such adroitness that, bringing his loins smartly against one of the sides of the chest, which was set on an uneven floor, he caused it to tilt and then fall; and such was the noise that it made as it fell that the women that slept there awoke, albeit for fear they kept silence. Ruggieri was not a little disconcerted by the fall, but, finding that thereby the chest was come open, he judged that, happen what might, he would be better out of it than in it; and not knowing where he was, and being otherwise at his wits' end, he began to grope about the house, if haply he might find a stair or door whereby he might take himself off.

Hearing him thus groping his way, the alarmed women gave tongue with: — "Who is there?"

Ruggieri, not knowing the voice, made no answer: wherefore the women fell to calling the two young men, who, having had a long day, were fast asleep, and heard nought of what went on. Which served to increase the fright of the women, who rose and got them to divers windows, and raised the cry: — "Take thief, take thief!"

At which summons there came running from divers quarters not a few of the neighbours, who got into the house by the roof or otherwise as each best might: likewise the young men, aroused by the din, got up; and Ruggieri being now all but beside himself for sheer amazement, and knowing not whither to turn him to escape them, they took him and delivered him to the officers of the Governor of the city, who, hearing the uproar, had hasted to the spot. And so he was brought before the Governor, who, knowing him to be held of all a most arrant evildoer, put him forthwith to the torture, and, upon his confessing that he had entered the house of the usurers with intent to rob, was minded to make short work of it, and have him hanged by the neck.

In the morning 'twas bruited throughout all Salerno that Ruggieri had been taken a thieving in the house of the usurers. Whereat the lady and her maid were all amazement and bewilderment, insomuch that they were within an ace of persuading themselves that what they had done the night before they had not done, but had only dreamed it; besides which, the peril in which Ruggieri stood caused the lady such anxiety as brought her to the verge of madness. Shortly after half tierce the leech, being returned from Amalfi, and minded now to treat his patient, called for his water, and finding the bottle empty made a great commotion, protesting that nought in his house could be let alone.

The lady, having other cause of annoy, lost temper, and said:— "What would you say, Master, of an important matter, when you raise such a din because a bottle of water has been upset? Is there never another to be found in the world?"

"Madam," replied the leech, "thou takest this to have been mere water: 'twas no such thing, but an artificial water of a soporiferous virtue"; and he told her for what purpose he had made it. Which the lady no sooner heard, than, guessing that Ruggieri had drunk it, and so had seemed to them to be dead, she said:—

"Master, we knew it not; wherefore make you another."

And so the leech, seeing that there was no help for it, had another made. Not long after, the maid, who by the lady's command had gone to find out what folk said of Ruggieri, returned, saying:—"Madam, of Ruggieri they say nought but evil, nor, by what I have been able to discover, has he friend or kinsman that has or will come to his aid; and 'tis held for certain that to-morrow the Stadic[1] will have him hanged. Besides which, I have that to tell you which will surprise you; for, methinks, I have found out how he came into the usurers' house. List, then, how it was: you know the carpenter in front of whose shop stood the chest we put Ruggieri into: he had to-day the most violent altercation in the world with one to whom it would seem the chest belongs, by whom he was required to make good the value of the chest, to which he made answer that he had not sold it, but that it had been stolen from him in the night. 'Not so,' said the other; 'thou soldst it to the two young usurers, as they themselves told me last night, when I saw it in their house at the time Ruggieri was taken.' 'They lie,' replied the carpenter. 'I never sold it them, but they must have stolen it from me last night; go we to them.' So with one accord off they went to the usurers' house, and I came back here. And so, you see, I make out that 'twas on such

[1]The Neapolitan term for the chief of police.

wise that Ruggieri was brought where he was found; but how he came to life again, I am at a loss to conjecture."

The lady now understood exactly how things were, and accordingly told the maid what she had learned from the leech, and besought her to aid her to get Ruggieri off, for so she might, if she would, and at the same time preserve her honour.

"Madam," said the maid, "do but shew me how; and glad shall I be to do just as you wish."

Whereupon the lady, to whom necessity taught invention, formed her plan on the spur of the moment, and expounded it in detail to the maid; who (as the first step) hied her to the leech, and, weeping, thus addressed him: — "Sir, it behoves me to ask your pardon of a great wrong that I have done you."

"And what may that be?" inquired the leech.

"Sir," said the maid, who ceased not to weep, "you know what manner of man is Ruggieri da Jeroli. Now he took a fancy to me, and partly for fear, partly for love, I this year agreed to be his mistress; and knowing yestereve that you were from home, he coaxed me into bringing him into your house to sleep with me in my room. Now he was athirst, and I, having no mind to be seen by your lady, who was in the hall, and knowing not whither I might sooner betake me for wine or water, bethought me that I had seen a bottle of water in your room, and ran and fetched it, and gave it him to drink, and then put the bottle back in the place whence I had taken it; touching which I find that you have made a great stir in the house. Verily I confess that I did wrong; but who is there that does not wrong sometimes? Sorry indeed am I to have so done, but 'tis not for such a cause and that which ensued thereon that Ruggieri should lose his life. Wherefore, I do most earnestly beseech you, pardon me, and suffer me to go help him as best I may be able."

Wroth though he was at what he heard, the leech replied in a bantering tone: — "Thy pardon thou hast by thine own deed; for, whereas thou didst last night think to have with thee a gallant that would thoroughly dust thy pelisse for thee, he was but a sleepy-head; wherefore get thee gone, and do what thou mayst for the deliverance of thy lover, and for the future look thou bring him not into the house; else I will pay thee for that turn and this to boot." The maid, deeming that she had come off well in the first brush, hied her with all speed to the prison where Ruggieri lay, and by her cajoleries prevailed upon the warders to let her speak with him; and having told him how he must answer the Stadic if he would get off, she succeeded in obtaining preaudience of the Stadic; who, seeing that the baggage was lusty and mettlesome, was minded before he heard her to grapple her with the hook, to which she was by no means averse, knowing that such a preliminary would secure her a better hearing.

When she had undergone the operation and was risen: — "Sir," said she, "you have here Ruggieri da Jeroli, apprehended on a charge of theft; which charge is false."

Whereupon she told him the whole story from beginning to end, how she, being Ruggieri's mistress, had brought him into the leech's house and had given him the opiate, not knowing it for such, and taking him to be dead, had put him in the chest; and then recounting what she had heard pass between the carpenter and the owner of the chest, she shewed him how Ruggieri came into the house of the usurers.

Seeing that 'twas easy enough to find out whether the story were true, the Stadic began by questioning the leech as to the water, and found that 'twas as she had said: he then summoned the carpenter, the owner of the chest and the usurers, and after much further parley ascertained that the usurers had stolen the chest during the night, and brought it into their house: finally he sent for Ruggieri, and asked him where he had lodged that night, to which Ruggieri answered that where he had lodged he knew not, but he well remembered going to pass the night with Master Mazzeo's maid, in whose room he had drunk some water by reason of a great thirst that he had; but what happened to him afterwards, except that, when he awoke, he found himself in a chest in the house of the usurers, he knew not.

All which matters the Stadic heard with great interest, and caused the maid and Ruggieri and the carpenter and the usurers to rehearse them several times. In the end, seeing that Ruggieri was innocent, he released him, and mulcted the usurers in fifteen ounces for the theft of the chest. How glad Ruggieri was thus to escape, it boots not to ask; and glad beyond measure was his lady. And so, many a time did they laugh and make merry together over the affair, she and he and the dear maid that had proposed to give him a taste of the knife; and remaining constant in their love, they had ever better and better solace thereof. The like whereof befall me, sans the being put in the chest.

Heartsore as the gentle ladies had been made by the preceding stories, this last of Dioneo provoked them to such merriment, more especially the passage about the Stadic and the hook, that they lacked not relief of the piteous mood engendered by the others. But the king observing that the sun was now taking a yellowish tinge, and that the end of his sovereignty was come, in terms most courtly made his excuse to the fair ladies, that he had made so direful a theme as lovers' infelicity the topic of their discourse; after which, he rose, took the laurel wreath from his head, and, while the ladies watched to see to whom he would give it, set it graciously upon the blond head of Fiammetta, saying: — "Herewith

I crown thee, as deeming that thou, better than any other, wilt know how to make to-morrow console our fair companions for the rude trials of to-day."

Fiammetta, whose wavy tresses fell in a flood of gold over her white and delicate shoulders, whose softly rounded face was all radiant with the very tints of the white lily blended with the red of the rose, who carried two eyes in her head that matched those of a peregrine falcon, while her tiny sweet mouth shewed a pair of lips that shone as rubies, replied with a smile: — "And gladly take I the wreath, Filostrato, and that thou mayst more truly understand what thou hast done, 'tis my present will and pleasure that each make ready to discourse to-morrow of good fortune befalling lovers after divers direful or disastrous adventures."

The theme propounded was approved by all; whereupon the queen called the seneschal, and having made with him all meet arrangements, rose and gaily dismissed all the company until the supper hour; wherefore, some straying about the garden, the beauties of which were not such as soon to pall, others bending their steps towards the mills that were grinding without, each, as and where it seemed best, they took meanwhile their several pleasures. The supper hour come, they all gathered, in their wonted order, by the fair fountain, and in the gayest of spirits and well served they supped. Then rising they addressed them, as was their wont, to dance and song, and while Filomena led the dance: — "Filostrato," said the queen, "being minded to follow in the footsteps of our predecessors, and that, as by their, so by our command a song be sung; and well witting that thy songs are even as thy stories, to the end that no day but this be vexed with thy misfortunes, we ordain that thou give us one of them, whichever thou mayst prefer."

Filostrato answered that he would gladly do so; and without delay began to sing on this wise: —

> Full well my tears attest,
>   O traitor Love, with what just cause the heart,
>   With which thou once hast broken faith, doth smart.
>
> Love, when thou first didst in my heart enshrine
>   Her for whom still I sigh, alas! in vain,
>   Nor any hope do know,
>   A damsel so complete thou didst me shew,
>   That light as air I counted every pain,
>   Wherewith behest of thine
>   Condemned my soul to pine.
>   Ah! but I gravely erred; the which to know
>   Too late, alas! doth but enhance my woe.

The cheat I knew not ere she did me leave,
  She, she, in whom alone my hopes were placed:
  For 'twas when I did most
  Flatter myself with hope, and proudly boast
  Myself her vassal lowliest and most graced,
  Nor thought Love might bereave,
  Nor dreamed he e'er might grieve,
  'Twas then I found that she another's worth
Into her heart had ta'en, and me cast forth.

A plant of pain, alas! my heart did bear,
  What time my hapless self cast forth I knew;
  And there it doth remain;
  And day and hour I curse and curse again,
  When first that front of love shone on my view
  That front so queenly fair,
  And bright beyond compare!
  Wherefore at once my faith, my hope, my fire
My soul doth imprecate, ere she expire.

My lord, thou knowest how comfortless my woe,
  Thou, Love, my lord, whom thus I supplicate
  With many a piteous moan,
  Telling thee how in anguish sore I groan,
  Yearning for death my pain to mitigate.
  Come death, and with one blow
  Cut short my span, and so
  With my curst life me of my frenzy ease;
For wheresoe'er I go, 'twill sure decrease.

Save death no way of comfort doth remain:
  No anodyne beside for this sore smart.
  The boon, then, Love bestow;
  And presently by death annul my woe,
  And from this abject life release my heart.
  Since from me joy is ta'en,
  And every solace, deign
  My prayer to grant, and let my death the cheer
Complete, that she now hath of her new fere.

Song, it may be that no one shall thee learn:
  Nor do I care; for none I wot, so well
  As I may chant thee; so,
  This one behest I lay upon thee, go
  Hie thee to Love, and him in secret tell,

How I my life do spurn,
My bitter life, and yearn,
That to a better harbourage he bring
Me, of all might and grace that own him king.

Full well my tears attest, etc.

Filostrato's mood and its cause were made abundantly manifest by the words of this song; and perchance they had been made still more so by the looks of a lady that was among the dancers, had not the shades of night, which had now overtaken them, concealed the blush that suffused her face. Other songs followed until the hour for slumber arrived: whereupon at the behest of the queen all the ladies sought their several chambers.

FIFTH DAY

STORY IV.

Ricciardo Manardi is found by Messer Lizio da Valbona with his daughter, whom he marries, and remains at peace with her father.

Know then, noble ladies, that 'tis no long time since there dwelt in Romagna a right worthy and courteous knight, Messer Lizio da Valbona by name, who was already verging upon old age, when, as it happened, there was born to him of his wife, Madonna Giacomina, a daughter, who, as she grew up, became the fairest and most debonair of all the girls of those parts, and, for that she was the only daughter left to them, was most dearly loved and cherished by her father and mother, who guarded her with most jealous care, thinking to arrange some great match for her. Now there was frequently in Messer Lizio's house, and much in his company, a fine, lusty young man, one Ricciardo de' Manardi da Brettinoro, whom Messer Lizio and his wife would as little have thought of mistrusting as if he had been their own son: who, now and again taking note of the damsel, that she was very fair and graceful, and in bearing and behaviour most commendable, and of marriageable age, fell vehemently in love with her, which love he was very careful to conceal.

The damsel detected it, however, and in like manner plunged headlong into love with him, to Ricciardo's no small satisfaction. Again and again he was on the point of speaking to her, but refrained for fear; at length, however, he summoned up his courage, and seizing his opportunity, thus addressed her: — "Caterina, I implore thee, suffer me not to die for love of thee."

Whereto the damsel forthwith responded: — "Nay, God grant that it be not rather that I die for love of thee."

Greatly exhilarated and encouraged, Ricciardo made answer: — "'Twill never be by default of mine that thou lackest aught that may pleasure thee; but it rests with thee to find the means to save thy life and mine."

Then said the damsel: — "Thou seest, Ricciardo, how closely watched

102

I am, insomuch that I see not how 'twere possible for thee to come to me; but if thou seest aught that I may do without dishonour, speak the word, and I will do it."

Ricciardo was silent a while, pondering many matters: then, of a sudden, he said:—"Sweet my Caterina, there is but one way that I can see, to wit, that thou shouldst sleep either on or where thou mightst have access to the terrace by thy father's garden, where, so I but knew that thou wouldst be there at night, I would without fail contrive to meet thee, albeit 'tis very high."

"As for my sleeping there," replied Caterina, "I doubt not that it may be managed, if thou art sure that thou canst join me."

Ricciardo answered in the affirmative. Whereupon they exchanged a furtive kiss, and parted.

On the morrow, it being now towards the close of May, the damsel began complaining to her mother that by reason of the excessive heat she had not been able to get any sleep during the night. "Daughter," said the lady, "what heat was there? Nay, there was no heat at all."

"Had you said, 'to my thinking,' mother," rejoined Caterina, "you would perhaps have said sooth; but you should bethink you how much more heat girls have in them than ladies that are advanced in years."

"True, my daughter," returned the lady, "but I cannot order that it shall be hot and cold, as thou perchance wouldst like; we must take the weather as we find it, and as the seasons provide it: perchance to-night it will be cooler, and thou wilt sleep better."

"God grant it be so," said Caterina, "but 'tis not wonted for the nights to grow cooler as the summer comes on."

"What then," said the lady, "wouldst thou have me do?"

"With your leave and my father's," answered Caterina, "I should like to have a little bed made up on the terrace by his room and over his garden, where, hearing the nightingales sing, and being in a much cooler place, I should sleep much better than in your room."

Whereupon:—"Daughter, be of good cheer," said the mother; "I will speak to thy father, and we will do as he shall decide."

So the lady told Messer Lizio what had passed between her and the damsel; but he, being old and perhaps for that reason a little morose, said:—"What nightingale is this, to whose chant she would fain sleep? I will see to it that the cicalas shall yet lull her to sleep."

Which speech, coming to Caterina's ears, gave her such offence, that for anger, rather than by reason of the heat, she not only slept not herself that night, but suffered not her mother to sleep, keeping up a perpetual complaint of the great heat.

Wherefore her mother hied her in the morning to Messer Lizio, and said to him:—"Sir, you hold your daughter none too dear; what difference can it make to you that she lie on the terrace? She has tossed about all night long by reason of the heat; and besides, can you wonder that she, girl that she is, loves to hear the nightingale sing? Young folk naturally affect their likes."

Whereto Messer Lizio made answer:—"Go, make her a bed there to your liking, and set a curtain round it, and let her sleep there, and hear the nightingale sing to her heart's content."

Which the damsel no sooner learned, than she had a bed made there with intent to sleep there that same night; wherefore she watched until she saw Ricciardo, whom by a concerted sign she gave to understand what he was to do. Messer Lizio, as soon as he had heard the damsel go to bed, locked a door that led from his room to the terrace, and went to sleep himself.

When all was quiet, Ricciardo with the help of a ladder got upon a wall, and standing thereon laid hold of certain toothings of another wall, and not without great exertion and risk, had he fallen, clambered up on to the terrace, where the damsel received him quietly with the heartiest of cheer. Many a kiss they exchanged; and then got them to bed, where well-nigh all night long they had solace and joyance of one another, and made the nightingale sing not a few times. But, brief being the night and great their pleasure, towards dawn, albeit they wist it not, they fell asleep, Caterina's right arm encircling Ricciardo's neck, while with her left hand she held him by that part of his person which your modesty, my ladies, is most averse to name in the company of men. So, peacefully they slept, and were still asleep when day broke and Messer Lizio rose; and calling to mind that his daughter slept on the terrace, softly opened the door, saying to himself:—Let me see what sort of night's rest the nightingale has afforded our Caterina? And having entered, he gently raised the curtain that screened the bed, and saw Ricciardo asleep with her and in her embrace as described, both being quite naked and uncovered; and having taken note of Ricciardo, he went away, and hied him to his lady's room, and called her, saying:— "Up, up, wife, come and see; for thy daughter has fancied the nightingale to such purpose that she has caught him, and holds him in her hand."

"How can this be?" said the lady.

"Come quickly, and thou shalt see," replied Messer Lizio.

So the lady huddled on her clothes, and silently followed Messer Lizio, and when they were come to the bed, and had raised the curtain, Madonna Giacomina saw plainly enough how her daughter had caught, and did hold the nightingale, whose song she had so longed to hear.

Whereat the lady, deeming that Ricciardo had played her a cruel trick, would have cried out and upbraided him; but Messer Lizio said to her: — "Wife, as thou valuest my love, say not a word; for in good sooth, seeing that she has caught him, he shall be hers. Ricciardo is a gentleman and wealthy; an alliance with him cannot but be to our advantage: if he would part from me on good terms, he must first marry her, so that the nightingale shall prove to have been put in his own cage and not in that of another."

Whereby the lady was reassured, seeing that her husband took the affair so quietly, and that her daughter had had a good night, and was rested, and had caught the nightingale. So she kept silence; nor had they long to wait before Ricciardo awoke; and, seeing that 'twas broad day, deemed that 'twas as much as his life was worth, and aroused Caterina, saying: — "Alas! my soul, what shall we do, now that day has come and surprised me here?"

Which question Messer Lizio answered by coming forward, and saying: "We shall do well."

At sight of him Ricciardo felt as if his heart were torn out of his body, and sate up in bed, and said: — "My lord, I cry you mercy for God's sake. I wot that my disloyalty and delinquency have merited death; wherefore deal with me even as it may seem best to you: however, I pray you, if so it may be, to spare my life, that I die not."

"Ricciardo," replied Messer Lizio, "the love I bore thee, and the faith I reposed in thee, merited a better return; but still, as so it is, and youth has seduced thee into such a transgression, redeem thy life, and preserve my honour, by making Caterina thy lawful spouse, that thine, as she has been for this past night, she may remain for the rest of her life. In this way thou mayst secure my peace and thy safety; otherwise commend thy soul to God."

Pending this colloquy, Caterina let go the nightingale, and having covered herself, began with many a tear to implore her father to forgive Ricciardo, and Ricciardo to do as Messer Lizio required, that thereby they might securely count upon a long continuance of such nights of delight. But there needed not much supplication; for, what with remorse for the wrong done, and the wish to make amends, and the fear of death, and the desire to escape it, and above all ardent love, and the craving to possess the beloved one, Ricciardo lost no time in making frank avowal of his readiness to do as Messer Lizio would have him. Wherefore Messer Lizio, having borrowed a ring from Madonna Giacomina, Ricciardo did there and then in their presence wed Caterina.

Which done, Messer Lizio and the lady took their leave, saying: — "Now rest ye a while; for so perchance 'twere better for you than if ye rose."

And so they left the young folks, who forthwith embraced, and not having travelled more than six miles during the night, went two miles further before they rose, and so concluded their first day. When they were risen, Ricciardo and Messer Lizio discussed the matter with more formality; and some days afterwards Ricciardo, as was meet, married the damsel anew in presence of their friends and kinsfolk, and brought her home with great pomp, and celebrated his nuptials with due dignity and splendour. And so for many a year thereafter he lived with her in peace and happiness, and snared the nightingales day and night to his heart's content.

STORY IX.

Federigo degli Alberighi loves and is not loved in return: he wastes his substance by lavishness until nought is left but a single falcon, which, his lady being come to see him at his house, he gives her to eat: she, knowing his case, changes her mind, takes him to husband and makes him rich.

You are then to know, that Coppo di Borghese Domenichi, a man that in our day was, and perchance still is, had in respect and great reverence in our city, being not only by reason of his noble lineage, but, and yet more, for manners and merit most illustrious and worthy of eternal renown, was in his old age not seldom wont to amuse himself by discoursing of things past with his neighbours and other folk; wherein he had not his match for accuracy and compass of memory and concinnity of speech. Among other good stories, he would tell, how that there was of yore in Florence a gallant named Federigo di Messer Filippo Alberighi, who for feats of arms and courtesy had not his peer in Tuscany; who, as is the common lot of gentlemen, became enamoured of a lady named Monna Giovanna, who in her day held rank among the fairest and most elegant ladies of Florence; to gain whose love he jousted, tilted, gave entertainments, scattered largess, and in short set no bounds to his expenditure. However the lady, no less virtuous than fair, cared not a jot for what he did for her sake, nor yet for him.

Spending thus greatly beyond his means, and making nothing, Federigo could hardly fail to come to lack, and was at length reduced to such poverty that he had nothing left but a little estate, on the rents of which he lived very straitly, and a single falcon, the best in the world. The estate was at Campi, and thither, deeming it no longer possible for him to live in the city as he desired, he repaired, more in love than ever before; and there, in complete seclusion, diverting himself with hawking, he bore his poverty as patiently as he might.

Now, Federigo being thus reduced to extreme poverty, it so happened that one day Monna Giovanna's husband, who was very rich, fell ill, and, seeing that he was nearing his end, made his will, whereby he left his estate to his son, who was now growing up, and in the event of

107

his death without lawful heir named Monna Giovanna, whom he dearly loved, heir in his stead; and having made these dispositions he died.

Monna Giovanna, being thus left a widow, did as our ladies are wont, and repaired in the summer to one of her estates in the country which lay very near to that of Federigo. And so it befell that the urchin began to make friends with Federigo, and to shew a fondness for hawks and dogs, and having seen Federigo's falcon fly not a few times, took a singular fancy to him, and greatly longed to have him for his own, but still did not dare to ask him of Federigo, knowing that Federigo prized him so much. So the matter stood when by chance the boy fell sick; whereby the mother was sore distressed, for he was her only son, and she loved him as much as might be, insomuch that all day long she was beside him, and ceased not to comfort him, and again and again asked him if there were aught that he wished for, imploring him to say the word, and, if it might by any means be had, she would assuredly do her utmost to procure it for him.

Thus repeatedly exhorted, the boy said:—"Mother mine, do but get me Federigo's falcon, and I doubt not I shall soon be well."

Whereupon the lady was silent a while, bethinking her what she should do. She knew that Federigo had long loved her, and had never had so much as a single kind look from her: wherefore she said to herself:—How can I send or go to beg of him this falcon, which by what I hear is the best that ever flew, and moreover is his sole comfort? And how could I be so unfeeling as to seek to deprive a gentleman of the one solace that is now left him? And so, albeit she very well knew that she might have the falcon for the asking, she was perplexed, and knew not what to say, and gave her son no answer. At length, however, the love she bore the boy carried the day, and she made up her mind, for his contentment, come what might, not to send, but to go herself and fetch him the falcon. So:—"Be of good cheer, my son," she said, "and doubt not thou wilt soon be well; for I promise thee that the very first thing that I shall do to-morrow morning will be to go and fetch thee the falcon." Whereat the child was so pleased that he began to mend that very day.

On the morrow the lady, as if for pleasure, hied her with another lady to Federigo's little house, and asked to see him. 'Twas still, as for some days past, no weather for hawking, and Federigo was in his garden, busy about some small matters which needed to be set right there. When he heard that Monna Giovanna was at the door, asking to see him, he was not a little surprised and pleased, and hied him to her with all speed.

As soon as she saw him, she came forward to meet him with womanly grace, and having received his respectful salutation, said to him:— "Good morrow, Federigo," and continued:—"I am come to requite thee for what thou hast lost by loving me more than thou shouldst: which compensation is this, that I and this lady that accompanies me will breakfast with thee without ceremony this morning."

"Madam," Federigo replied with all humility, "I mind not ever to have lost aught by loving you, but rather to have been so much profited that, if I ever deserved well in aught, 'twas to your merit that I owed it, and to the love that I bore you. And of a surety had I still as much to spend as I have spent in the past, I should not prize it so much as this visit you so frankly pay me, come as you are to one who can afford you but a sorry sort of hospitality."

Which said, with some confusion, he bade her welcome to his house, and then led her into his garden, where, having none else to present to her by way of companion, he said:—"Madam, as there is none other here, this good woman, wife of this husbandman, will bear you company, while I go to have the table set."

Now, albeit his poverty was extreme, yet he had not known as yet how sore was the need to which his extravagance had reduced him; but this morning 'twas brought home to him, for that he could find nought wherewith to do honour to the lady, for love of whom he had done the honours of his house to men without number: wherefore, distressed beyond measure, and inwardly cursing his evil fortune, he sped hither and thither like one beside himself, but never a coin found he, nor yet aught to pledge. Meanwhile it grew late, and sorely he longed that the lady might not leave his house altogether unhonoured, and yet to crave help of his own husbandman was more than his pride could brook.

In these desperate straits his glance happened to fall on his brave falcon on his perch in his little parlour. And so, as a last resource, he took him, and finding him plump, deemed that he would make a dish meet for such a lady. Wherefore, without thinking twice about it, he wrung the bird's neck, and caused his maid forthwith pluck him and set him on a spit, and roast him carefully; and having still some spotless table-linen, he had the table laid therewith, and with a cheerful countenance hied him back to his lady in the garden, and told her that such breakfast as he could give her was ready. So the lady and her companion rose and came to table, and there, with Federigo, who waited on them most faithfully, ate the brave falcon, knowing not what they ate.

When they were risen from table, and had dallied a while in gay converse with him, the lady deemed it time to tell the reason of her visit: wherefore, graciously addressing Federigo, thus began she:—

"Federigo, by what thou rememberest of thy past life and my virtue, which, perchance, thou hast deemed harshness and cruelty, I doubt not thou must marvel at my presumption, when thou hearest the main purpose of my visit; but if thou hadst sons, or hadst had them, so that thou mightest know the full force of the love that is borne them, I should make no doubt that thou wouldst hold me in part excused. Nor, having a son, may I, for that thou hast none, claim exemption from the laws to which all other mothers are subject, and, being thus bound to own their sway, I must, though fain were I not, and though 'tis neither meet nor right, crave of thee that which I know thou dost of all things and with justice prize most highly, seeing that this extremity of thy adverse fortune has left thee nought else wherewith to delight, divert and console thee; which gift is no other than thy falcon, on which my boy has so set his heart that, if I bring him it not, I fear lest he grow so much worse of the malady that he has, that thereby it may come to pass that I lose him. And so, not for the love which thou dost bear me, and which may nowise bind thee, but for that nobleness of temper, whereof in courtesy more conspicuously than in aught else thou hast given proof, I implore thee that thou be pleased to give me the bird, that thereby I may say that I have kept my son alive, and thus made him for aye thy debtor."

No sooner had Federigo apprehended what the lady wanted, than, for grief that 'twas not in his power to serve her, because he had given her the falcon to eat, he fell a weeping in her presence, before he could so much as utter a word. At first the lady supposed that 'twas only because he was loath to part with the brave falcon that he wept, and as good as made up her mind that he would refuse her: however, she awaited with patience Federigo's answer, which was on this wise:—

"Madam, since it pleased God that I should set my affections upon you there have been matters not a few, in which to my sorrow I have deemed Fortune adverse to me; but they have all been trifles in comparison of the trick that she now plays me: the which I shall never forgive her, seeing that you are come here to my poor house, where, while I was rich, you deigned not to come, and ask a trifling favour of me, which she has put it out of my power to grant: how 'tis so, I will briefly tell you. When I learned that you, of your grace, were minded to breakfast with me, having respect to your high dignity and desert, I deemed it due and seemly that in your honour I should regale you, to the best of my power, with fare of a more excellent quality than is commonly set before others; and, calling to mind the falcon which you now ask of me, and his excellence, I judged him meet food for you, and so you have had him roasted on the trencher this morning; and well indeed I thought I had bestowed him; but, as now I see that you would fain have had him in another guise, so mortified am I that I am not able to serve you, that I doubt I shall never know peace of mind more."

In witness whereof he had the feathers and feet and beak of the bird brought in and laid before her.

The first thing the lady did, when she had heard Federigo's story, and seen the relics of the bird, was to chide him that he had killed so fine a falcon to furnish a woman with a breakfast; after which the magnanimity of her host, which poverty had been and was powerless to impair, elicited no small share of inward commendation. Then, frustrate of her hope of possessing the falcon, and doubting of her son's recovery, she took her leave with the heaviest of hearts, and hied her back to the boy: who, whether for fretting, that he might not have the falcon, or by the unaided energy of his disorder, departed this life not many days after, to the exceeding great grief of his mother.

For a while she would do nought but weep and bitterly bewail herself; but being still young, and left very wealthy, she was often urged by her brothers to marry again, and though she would rather have not done so, yet being importuned, and remembering Federigo's high desert, and the magnificent generosity with which he had finally killed his falcon to do her honour, she said to her brothers: — "Gladly, with your consent, would I remain a widow, but if you will not be satisfied except I take a husband, rest assured that none other will I ever take save Federigo degli Alberighi."

Whereupon her brothers derided her, saying: — "Foolish woman, what is't thou sayst? How shouldst thou want Federigo, who has not a thing in the world?"

To whom she answered: — "My brothers, well wot I that 'tis as you say; but I had rather have a man without wealth than wealth without a man."

The brothers, perceiving that her mind was made up, and knowing Federigo for a good man and true, poor though he was, gave her to him with all her wealth. And so Federigo, being mated with such a wife, and one that he had so much loved, and being very wealthy to boot, lived happily, keeping more exact accounts, to the end of his days.

SIXTH DAY

STORY IV.

Chichibio, cook to Currado Gianfigliazzi, owes his safety to a ready answer, whereby he converts Currado's wrath into laughter, and evades the evil fate with which Currado had threatened him.

Albeit, loving ladies, ready wit not seldom ministers words apt and excellent and congruous with the circumstances of the speakers, 'tis also true that Fortune at times comes to the aid of the timid, and unexpectedly sets words upon the tongue, which in a quiet hour the speaker could never have found for himself: the which 'tis my purpose to shew you by my story.

Currado Gianfigliazzi, as the eyes and ears of each of you may bear witness, has ever been a noble citizen of our city, open-handed and magnificent, and one that lived as a gentleman should with hounds and hawks, in which, to say nothing at present of more important matters, he found unfailing delight. Now, having one day hard by Peretola despatched a crane with one of his falcons, finding it young and plump, he sent it to his excellent cook, a Venetian, Chichibio by name, bidding him roast it for supper and make a dainty dish of it. Chichibio, who looked, as he was, a very green-head, had dressed the crane, and set it to the fire and was cooking it carefully, when, the bird being all but roasted, and the fumes of the cooking very strong, it so chanced that a girl, Brunetta by name, that lived in the same street, and of whom Chichibio was greatly enamoured, came into the kitchen, and perceiving the smell and seeing the bird, began coaxing Chichibio to give her a thigh. By way of answer Chichibio fell a singing:—"You get it not from me, Madam Brunetta, you get it not from me."

Whereat Madam Brunetta was offended, and said to him:—"By God, if thou givest it me not, thou shalt never have aught from me to pleasure thee."

112

In short there was not a little altercation; and in the end Chichibio, fain not to vex his mistress, cut off one of the crane's thighs, and gave it to her. So the bird was set before Currado and some strangers that he had at table with him, and Currado, observing that it had but one thigh, was surprised, and sent for Chichibio, and demanded of him what was become of the missing thigh.

Whereto the mendacious Venetian answered readily:—"The crane, Sir, has but one thigh and one leg."

"What the devil?" rejoined Currado in a rage: "so the crane has but one thigh and one leg? thinkst thou I never saw crane before this?"

But Chichibio continued:—"'Tis even so as I say, Sir; and, so please you, I will shew you that so it is in the living bird."

Currado had too much respect for his guests to pursue the topic; he only said:—"Since thou promisest to shew me in the living bird what I have never seen or heard tell of, I bid thee do so to-morrow, and I shall be satisfied, but if thou fail, I swear to thee by the body of Christ that I will serve thee so that thou shalt ruefully remember my name for the rest of thy days."

No more was said of the matter that evening, but on the morrow, at daybreak, Currado, who had by no means slept off his wrath, got up still swelling therewith, and ordered his horses, mounted Chichibio on a hackney, and saying to him:—"We shall soon see which of us lied yesternight, thou or I," set off with him for a place where there was much water, beside which there were always cranes to be seen about dawn.

Chichibio, observing that Currado's ire was unabated, and knowing not how to bolster up his lie, rode by Currado's side in a state of the utmost trepidation, and would gladly, had he been able, have taken to flight; but, as he might not, he glanced, now ahead, now aback, now aside, and saw everywhere nought but cranes standing on two feet. However, as they approached the river, the very first thing they saw upon the bank was a round dozen of cranes standing each and all on one foot, as is their wont, when asleep. Which Chichibio presently pointed out to Currado, saying:—"Now may you see well enough, Sir, that 'tis true as I said yesternight, that the crane has but one thigh and one leg; mark but how they stand over there."

Whereupon Currado:—"Wait," quoth he, "and I will shew thee that they have each thighs and legs twain."

So, having drawn a little nigher to them, he ejaculated, "Oho!" Which caused the cranes to bring each the other foot to the ground, and, after hopping a step or two, to take flight.

Currado then turned to Chichibio, saying:—"How now, rogue? art satisfied that the bird has thighs and legs twain?"

Whereto Chichibio, all but beside himself with fear, made answer:—

"Ay, Sir; but you cried not, oho! to our crane of yestereve: had you done so, it would have popped its other thigh and foot forth, as these have done."

Which answer Currado so much relished, that, all his wrath changed to jollity and laughter:—"Chichibio," quoth he, "thou art right, indeed I ought to have so done."

Thus did Chichibio by his ready and jocund retort arrest impending evil, and make his peace with his master.

STORY X.

Fra Cipolla promises to shew certain country-folk a feather of the Angel Gabriel, in lieu of which he finds coals, which he avers to be of those with which St. Lawrence was roasted.

Certaldo, as perchance you may have heard, is a town of Val d'Elsa within our country-side, which, small though it is, had in it aforetime people of rank and wealth. Thither, for that there he found good pasture 'twas long the wont of one of the Friars of St. Antony to resort once every year, to collect the alms that fools gave them. Fra Cipolla[1] — so hight the friar — met with a hearty welcome, no less, perchance, by reason of his name than for other cause, the onions produced in that district being famous throughout Tuscany. He was little of person, red-haired, jolly-visaged, and the very best of good fellows; and therewithal, though learning he had none, he was so excellent and ready a speaker that whoso knew him not would not only have esteemed him a great rhetorician, but would have pronounced him Tully himself or, perchance, Quintilian; and in all the country-side there was scarce a soul to whom he was not either gossip or friend or lover.

Being thus wont from time to time to visit Certaldo, the friar came there once upon a time in the month of August, and on a Sunday morning, all the good folk of the neighbouring farms being come to mass in the parish church, he took occasion to come forward and say: —

"Ladies and gentlemen, you wot 'tis your custom to send year by year to the poor of Baron Master St. Antony somewhat of your wheat and oats, more or less, according to the ability and the devoutness of each, that blessed St. Antony may save your oxen and asses and pigs and sheep from harm; and you are also accustomed, and especially those whose names are on the books of our confraternity, to pay your trifling annual dues. To collect which offerings, I am hither sent by my superior, to wit, Master Abbot; wherefore, with the blessing of God, after

---

[1]Onion.

nones, when you hear the bells ring, you will come out of the church
to the place where in the usual way I shall deliver you my sermon, and
you will kiss the cross; and therewithal, knowing, as I do, that you are
one and all most devoted to Baron Master St. Antony, I will by way of
especial grace shew you a most holy and goodly relic, which I brought
myself from the Holy Land overseas, which is none other than one of
the feathers of the Angel Gabriel, which he left behind him in the
room of the Virgin Mary, when he came to make her the annunciation
in Nazareth."

And having said thus much, he ceased, and went on with the mass.
Now among the many that were in the church, while Fra Cipolla made
this speech, were two very wily young wags, the one Giovanni del
Bragoniera by name, the other Biagio Pizzini; who, albeit they were on
the best of terms with Fra Cipolla and much in his company, had a sly
laugh together over the relic, and resolved to make game of him and
his feather. So, having learned that Fra Cipolla was to breakfast that
morning in the town with one of his friends, as soon as they knew that
he was at table, down they hied them into the street, and to the inn
where the friar lodged, having complotted that Biagio should keep the
friar's servant in play, while Giovanni made search among the friar's
goods and chattels for this feather, whatever it might be, to carry it off,
that they might see how the friar would afterwards explain the matter
to the people. Now Fra Cipolla had for servant one Guccio,[1] whom
some called by way of addition Balena,[2] others Imbratta,[3] others again
Porco,[4] and who was such a rascallion that sure it is that Lippo Topo[5]
himself never painted his like.

Concerning whom Fra Cipolla would ofttimes make merry with his
familiars, saying: — "My servant has nine qualities, any one of which in
Solomon, Aristotle, or Seneca, would have been enough to spoil all
their virtue, wisdom and holiness. Consider, then, what sort of a man
he must be that has these nine qualities, and yet never a spark of either
virtue or wisdom or holiness."

And being asked upon divers occasions what these nine qualities
might be, he strung them together in rhyme, and answered: — "I will
tell you. Lazy and uncleanly and a liar he is, Negligent, disobedient
and foul-mouthed, iwis, And reckless and witless and mannerless: and
therewithal he has some other petty vices, which 'twere best to pass

---

[1]Diminutive of Arriguccio.
[2]Whale.
[3]Filth.
[4]Hog.
[5]The works of this painter seem to be lost.

over. And the most amusing thing about him is, that, wherever he goes, he is for taking a wife and renting a house, and on the strength of a big, black, greasy beard he deems himself so very handsome a fellow and seductive, that he takes all the women that see him to be in love with him, and, if he were left alone, he would slip his girdle and run after them all. True it is that he is of great use to me, for that, be any minded to speak with me never so secretly, he must still have his share of the audience; and, if perchance aught is demanded of me, such is his fear lest I should be at a loss what answer to make, that he presently replies, ay or no, as he deems meet."

Now, when he left this knave at the inn, Fra Cipolla had strictly enjoined him on no account to suffer any one to touch aught of his, at least of all his wallet, because it contained the holy things. But Guccio Imbratta, who was fonder of the kitchen than any nightingale of the green boughs, and most particularly if he espied there a maid, and in the host's kitchen had caught sight of a coarse fat woman, short and misshapen, with a pair of breasts that shewed as two buckets of muck and a face that might have belonged to one of the Baronci, all reeking with sweat and grease and smoke, left Fra Cipolla's room and all his things to take care of themselves, and like a vulture swooping down upon the carrion, was in the kitchen in a trice. Where, though 'twas August, he sat him down by the fire, and fell a gossiping with Nuta—such was the maid's name—and told her that he was a gentleman by procuration,[1] and had more florins than could be reckoned, besides those that he had to give away, which were rather more than less, and that he could do and say such things as never were or might be seen or heard forever, good Lord! and a day. And all heedless of his cowl, which had as much grease upon it as would have furnished forth the caldron of Altopascio,[2] and of his rent and patched doublet, inlaid with filth about the neck and under the armpits, and so stained that it shewed hues more various than ever did silk from Tartary or the Indies, and of his shoes that were all to pieces, and of his hose that were all in tatters, he told her in a tone that would have become the Sieur de Châtillon, that he was minded to rehabit her and put her in trim and raise her from her abject condition, and place her where, though she would not have much to call her own, at any rate she would have hope of better things, with much more to the like effect; which professions, though made with every appearance of good will, proved, like most of his schemes, insubstantial as air, and came to nothing.

Finding Guccio Porco thus occupied with Nuta, the two young men

---

[1] One of the humorous ineptitudes of which Boccaccio is fond.
[2] An abbey near Lucca famous for its doles of broth.

gleefully accounted their work half done, and, none gainsaying them, entered Fra Cipolla's room, which was open, and lit at once upon the wallet, in which was the feather. The wallet opened, they found, wrapt up in many folds of taffeta, a little casket, on opening which they discovered one of the tail-feathers of a parrot, which they deemed must be that which the friar had promised to shew the good folk of Certaldo. And in sooth he might well have so imposed upon them, for in those days the luxuries of Egypt had scarce been introduced into Tuscany, though they have since been brought over in prodigious abundance, to the grave hurt of all Italy. And though some conversance with them there was, yet in those parts folk knew next to nothing of them; but, adhering to the honest, simple ways of their forefathers, had not seen, nay for the most part had not so much as heard tell of, a parrot.

So the young men, having found the feather, took it out with great glee; and looking around for something to replace it, they espied in a corner of the room some pieces of coal, wherewith they filled the casket; which they then closed, and having set the room in order exactly as they had found it, they quitted it unperceived, and hied them merrily off with the feather, and posted themselves where they might hear what Fra Cipolla would say when he found the coals in its stead. Mass said, the simple folk that were in the church went home with the tidings that the feather of the Angel Gabriel was to be seen after none; and this goodman telling his neighbour, and that goodwife her gossip, by the time every one had breakfasted, the town could scarce hold the multitude of men and women that flocked thither all agog to see this feather.

Fra Cipolla, having made a hearty breakfast and had a little nap, got up shortly after none, and marking the great concourse of country-folk that were come to see the feather, sent word to Guccio Imbratta to go up there with the bells, and bring with him the wallet. Guccio, though 'twas with difficulty that he tore himself away from the kitchen and Nuta, hied him up with the things required; and though, when he got up, he was winded, for he was corpulent with drinking nought but water, he did Fra Cipolla's bidding by going to the church door and ringing the bells amain. When all the people were gathered about the door, Fra Cipolla, all unwitting that aught of his was missing, began his sermon, and after much said in glorification of himself, caused the confiteor to be recited with great solemnity, and two torches to be lit by way of preliminary to the shewing of the feather of the Angel Gabriel: he then bared his head, carefully unfolded the taffeta, and took out the casket, which, after a few prefatory words in praise and laudation of the Angel Gabriel and his relic, he opened. When he saw that it contained nought but coals, he did not suspect Guccio Balena of playing the trick, for he knew that he was not clever enough, nor did he curse him, that his carelessness had allowed another to play it, but he inly imprecated himself, that he had committed his things to the keeping of one whom he knew to be "negligent and disobedient, reckless and witless."

Nevertheless, he changed not colour, but with face and hands upturned to heaven, he said in a voice that all might hear: — "Oh God, blessed be Thy might for ever and ever."

Then, closing the casket, and turning to the people: — "Ladies and gentlemen," he said, "you are to know, that when I was yet a very young man, I was sent by my superior into those parts where the sun rises, and I was expressly bidden to search until I should find the Privileges of Porcellana, which, though they cost nothing to seal, are of much more use to others than to us. On which errand I set forth, taking my depar-ture from Venice, and traversing the Borgo de' Greci,[1] and thence on horseback the realm of Algarve,[2] and so by Baldacca[3] I came to Parione,[4] whence, somewhat athirst, I after a while got on to Sardinia.[5] But wherefore go I about to enumerate all the lands in which I pursued my quest? Having passed the straits of San Giorgio, I arrived at Truffia[6] and Buffia,[7] countries thickly populated and with great nations, whence I pursued my journey to Menzogna,[8] where I met with many of our own brethren, and of other religious not a few, intent one and all on eschewing hardship for the love of God, making little account of others' toil, so they might ensue their own advantage, and paying in nought but unminted coin[9] throughout the length and breadth of the country; and so I came to the land of Abruzzi, where the men and women go in pattens on the mountains, and clothe the hogs with their own entrails;[10] and a little farther on I found folk that carried bread in staves and wine in sacks.[11] And leaving them, I arrived at the mountains of the Bachi,[12] where all the waters run downwards.

---

[1]Perhaps part of the "sesto" of Florence known as the Borgo, as the tradition of the commentators that the friar's itinerary is wholly Florentine is not to be lightly set aside.

[2]Il-Garbo, a quarter or street in Florence, doubtless so called because the wares of Algarve were there sold. Rer. Ital. Script. (Muratori: Suppl. Tartini) ii. 119. Villani, Istorie Fiorentine, iv. 12, xii. 18.

[3]A famous tavern in Florence. Florio, Vocab. Ital. e Ingl., ed Torriano, 1659.

[4]A "borgo" in Florence. Villani, Istorie Fiorentine, iv. 7.

[5]A suburb of Florence on the Arno, ib. ix. 256.

[6]The land of Cajolery.

[7]The land of Drollery.

[8]The land of Lies.

[9]I.e. in false promises: suggested by Dante's Pagando di moneta senza conio. Parad. xxix. 126.

[10]A reference to sausage-making.

[11]I.e. cakes fashioned in a hollow ring, and wines in leathern bottles.

[12]Grubs.

"In short I penetrated so far that I came at last to India Pastinaca,[1] where I swear to you by the habit that I wear, that I saw pruning-hooks[2] fly: a thing that none would believe that had not seen it. Whereof be my witness that I lie not Maso del Saggio, that great merchant, whom I found there cracking nuts, and selling the shells by retail! However, not being able to find that whereof I was in quest, because from thence one must travel by water, I turned back, and so came at length to the Holy Land, where in summer cold bread costs four deniers, and hot bread is to be had for nothing. And there I found the venerable father Nonmiblasmetesevoipiace,[3] the most worshipful Patriarch of Jerusalem; who out of respect for the habit that I have ever worn, to wit, that of Baron Master St. Antony, was pleased to let me see all the holy relics that he had by him, which were so many, that, were I to enumerate them all, I should not come to the end of them in some miles. However, not to disappoint you, I will tell you a few of them.

"In the first place, then, he shewed me the finger of the Holy Spirit, as whole and entire as it ever was, and the tuft of the Seraph that appeared to St. Francis, and one of the nails of the Cherubim, and one of the ribs of the Verbum Caro hie thee to the casement,[4] and some of the vestments of the Holy Catholic Faith, and some of the rays of the star that appeared to the Magi in the East, and a phial of the sweat of St. Michael a battling with the Devil and the jaws of death of St. Lazarus, and other relics. And for that I gave him a liberal supply of the acclivities[5] of Monte Morello in the vulgar and some chapters of Caprezio, of which he had long been in quest, he was pleased to let me participate in his holy relics, and gave me one of the teeth of the Holy Cross, and in a small phial a bit of the sound of the bells of Solomon's temple, and this feather of the Angel Gabriel, whereof I have told you, and one of the pattens of San Gherardo da Villa Magna, which, not long ago, I gave at Florence to Gherardo di Bonsi, who holds him in prodigious veneration. He also gave me some of the coals with which the most blessed martyr, St. Lawrence, was roasted.

"All which things I devoutly brought thence, and have them all safe. True it is that my superior has not hitherto permitted me to shew them, until he should be certified that they are genuine. However, now that this is avouched by certain miracles wrought by them, of which we

---

[1]In allusion to the shapeless fish, so called, which was proverbially taken as a type of the outlandish.
[2]A *jeu de mots*, "pennati," pruning-hooks, signifying also *feathered*, though "pennuti" is more common in that sense.
[3]Takemenottotaskanitlikeyou.
[4]*fatti alle finestre*, a subterfuge for *factum est*.
[5]*piagge*, jocularly for *pagine*: doubtless some mighty tome of school divinity is meant.

have tidings by letter from the Patriarch, he has given me leave to shew them. But, fearing to trust them to another, I always carry them with me; and to tell you the truth I carry the feather of the Angel Gabriel, lest it should get spoiled, in a casket, and the coals, with which St. Lawrence was roasted, in another casket; which caskets are so like the one to the other, that not seldom I mistake one for the other, which has befallen me on this occasion; for, whereas I thought to have brought with me the casket wherein is the feather, I have brought instead that which contains the coals. Nor deem I this a mischance; nay, methinks, 'tis by interposition of God, and that He Himself put the casket of coals in my hand, for I mind me that the feast of St. Lawrence falls but two days hence. Wherefore God, being minded that by shew-ing you the coals, with which he was roasted, I should rekindle in your souls the devotion that you ought to feel towards him, guided my hand, not to the feather which I meant to take, but to the blessed coals that were extinguished by the humours that exuded from that most holy body. And so, blessed children, bare your heads and devoutly draw nigh to see them. But first of all I would have you know, that whoso has the sign of the cross made upon him with these coals, may live secure for the whole of the ensuing year, that fire shall not touch him, that he feel it not."

Having so said, the friar, chanting a hymn in praise of St. Lawrence, opened the casket, and shewed the coals. Whereon the foolish crowd gazed a while in awe and reverent wonder, and then came pressing forward in a mighty throng about Fra Cipolla with offerings beyond their wont, each and all praying him to touch them with the coals. Wherefore Fra Cipolla took the coals in his hand, and set about making on their white blouses, and on their doublets, and on the veils of the women crosses as big as might be, averring the while that whatever the coals might thus lose would be made good to them again in the casket, as he had often proved. On this wise, to his exceeding great profit, he marked all the folk of Certaldo with the cross, and, thanks to his ready wit and resource, had his laugh at those, who by robbing him of the feather thought to make a laughing-stock of him. They, indeed, being among his hearers, and marking his novel expedient, and now voluble he was, and what a long story he made of it, laughed till they thought their jaws would break; and, when the congregation was dispersed, they went up to him, and never so merrily told him what they had done, and returned him his feather; which next year proved no less lucrative to him than that day the coals had been.

Immense was the delight and diversion which this story afforded to all the company alike, and great and general was the laughter over Fra Cipolla, and more especially at his pilgrimage, and the relics, as well

those that he had but seen as those that he had brought back with him.
Which being ended, the queen, taking note that therewith the close of
her sovereignty was come, stood up, took off the crown, and set it on
Dioneo's head, saying with a laugh:—"'Tis time, Dioneo, that thou
prove the weight of the burden of having ladies to govern and guide. Be
thou king then; and let thy rule be such that, when 'tis ended, we may
have cause to commend it."

Dioneo took the crown, and laughingly answered:—"Kings worthier
far than I you may well have seen many a time ere now—I speak of the
kings in chess; but let me have of you that obedience which is due to a
true king, and of a surety I will give you to taste of that solace, without
which perfection of joy there may not be in any festivity. But enough
of this: I will govern as best I may."

Then, as was the wont, he sent for the seneschal, and gave him
particular instruction how to order matters during the term of his sovereignty; which done, he said:—"Noble ladies, such and so diverse has
been our discourse of the ways of men and their various fortunes, that
but for the visit that we had a while ago from Madam Licisca, who by
what she said has furnished me with matter of discourse for to-morrow,
I doubt I had been not a little put to it to find a theme. You heard how
she said that there was not a woman in her neighbourhood whose
husband had her virginity; adding that well she knew how many and
what manner of tricks they, after marriage, played their husbands. The
first count we may well leave to the girls whom it concerns; the second,
methinks, should prove a diverting topic: wherefore I ordain that, taking
our cue from Madam Licisca, we discourse to-morrow of the tricks that,
either for love or for their deliverance from peril, ladies have heretofore
played their husbands, and whether they were by the said husbands
detected or no."

To discourse of such a topic some of the ladies deemed unmeet for
them, and besought the king to find another theme. But the king
made answer:—

"Ladies, what manner of theme I have prescribed I know as well as
you, nor was I to be diverted from prescribing it by that which you now
think to declare unto me, for I wot the times are such that, so only men
and women have a care to do nought that is unseemly, 'tis allowable to
them to discourse of what they please. For in sooth, as you must know, so
out of joint are the times that the judges have deserted the judgment-seat,
the laws are silent, and ample licence to preserve his life as best he may
is accorded to each and all. Wherefore, if you are somewhat less strict
of speech than is your wont, not that aught unseemly in act may follow,
but that you may afford solace to yourselves and others, I see not how
you can be open to reasonable censure on the part of any. Furthermore,

nought that has been said from the first day to the present moment has, methinks, in any degree sullied the immaculate honour of your company, nor, God helping us, shall aught ever sully it. Besides, who is there that knows not the quality of your honour? which were proof, I make no doubt, against not only the seductive influence of diverting discourse, but even the terror of death. And, to tell you the truth, whoso wist that you refused to discourse of these light matters for a while, would be apt to suspect that 'twas but for that you had yourselves erred in like sort. And truly a goodly honour would you confer upon me, obedient as I have ever been to you, if after making me your king and your lawgiver, you were to refuse to discourse of the theme which I prescribe. Away, then, with this scruple fitter for low minds than yours, and let each study how she may give us a goodly story, and Fortune prosper her therein."

So spake the king, and the ladies, hearkening, said that, even as he would, so it should be: whereupon he gave all leave to do as they might be severally minded until the supper-hour. The sun was still quite high in the heaven, for they had not enlarged in their discourse: wherefore, Dioneo with the other gallants being set to play at dice, Elisa called the other ladies apart, and said: — "There is a nook hard by this place, where I think none of you has ever been: 'tis called the Ladies' Vale: whither, ever since we have been here, I have desired to take you, but time meet I have not found until to-day, when the sun is still so high: if, then, you are minded to visit it, I have no manner of doubt that, when you are there, you will be very glad you came."

The ladies answered that they were ready, and so, saying nought to the young men, they summoned one of their maids, and set forth; nor had they gone much more than a mile, when they arrived at the Vale of Ladies. They entered it by a very strait gorge, through which there issued a rivulet, clear as crystal, and a sight, than which nought more fair and pleasant, especially at that time when the heat was great, could be imagined, met their eyes. Within the valley, as one of them afterwards told me, was a plain about half-a-mile in circumference, and so exactly circular that it might have been fashioned according to the compass, though it seemed a work of Nature's art, not man's: 'twas girdled about by six hills of no great height, each crowned with a palace that shewed as a goodly little castle.

The slopes of the hills were graduated from summit to base after the manner of the successive tiers, ever abridging their circle, that we see in our theatres; and as many as fronted the southern rays were all planted so close with vines, olives, almond-trees, cherry-trees, fig-trees and other fruit-bearing trees not a few, that there was not a hand's-breadth of vacant space. Those that fronted the north were in like manner covered with

copses of oak saplings, ashes and other trees, as green and straight as
might be. Besides which, the plain, which was shut in on all sides save
that on which the ladies had entered, was full of firs, cypresses, and bay-
trees, with here and there a pine, in order and symmetry so meet and
excellent as had they been planted by an artist, the best that might be
found in that kind; wherethrough, even when the sun was in the
zenith, scarce a ray of light might reach the ground, which was all one
lawn of the finest turf, pranked with the hyacinth and divers other flowers.
Add to which—nor was there aught there more delightsome—a rivulet
that, issuing from one of the gorges between two of the hills, descended
over ledges of living rock, making, as it fell, a murmur most gratifying
to the ear, and, seen from a distance, shewed as a spray of finest, pow-
dered quick-silver, and no sooner reached the little plain, than 'twas
gathered into a tiny channel, by which it sped with great velocity to the
middle of the plain, where it formed a diminutive lake, like the fish-
ponds that townsfolk sometimes make in their gardens, when they have
occasion for them.

The lake was not so deep but that a man might stand therein with
his breast above the water; and so clear, so pellucid was the water that
the bottom, which was of the finest gravel, shewed so distinct, that
one, had he wished, who had nought better to do, might have counted
the stones. Nor was it only the bottom that was to be seen, but such a
multitude of fishes, glancing to and fro, as was at once a delight and a
marvel to behold. Bank it had none, but its margin was the lawn, to
which it imparted a goodlier freshness. So much of the water as it
might not contain was received by another tiny channel, through
which, issuing from the vale, it glided swiftly to the plain below.

To which pleasaunce the damsels being come surveyed it with roving
glance, and finding it commendable, and marking the lake in front of
them, did, as 'twas very hot, and they deemed themselves secure from
observation, resolve to take a bath. So, having bidden their maid wait
and keep watch over the access to the vale, and give them warning, if
haply any should approach it, they all seven undressed and got into the
water, which to the whiteness of their flesh was even such a veil as fine
glass is to the vermeil of the rose. They, being thus in the water, the
clearness of which was thereby in no wise affected, did presently begin
to go hither and thither after the fish, which had much ado where to
bestow themselves so as to escape out of their hands. In which diversion
they spent some time, and caught a few, and then they hied them out
of the water and dressed them again, and bethinking them that 'twas
time to return to the palace, they began slowly sauntering thither,
dilating much as they went upon the beauty of the place, albeit they
could not extol it more than they had already done.

'Twas still quite early when they reached the palace, so that they found the gallants yet at play where they had left them. To whom quoth Pampinea with a smile:—"We have stolen a march upon you to-day."

"So," replied Dioneo, "'tis with you do first and say after?"

"Ay, my lord," returned Pampinea, and told him at large whence they came, and what the place was like, and how far 'twas off, and what they had done. What she said of the beauty of the spot begat in the king a desire to see it: wherefore he straightway ordered supper, whereof when all had gaily partaken, the three gallants parted from the ladies and hied them with their servants to the vale, where none of them had ever been before, and, having marked all its beauties, extolled it as scarce to be matched in all the world. Then, as the hour was very late, they did but bathe, and as soon as they had resumed their clothes, returned to the ladies, whom they found dancing a carol to an air that Fiammetta sang, which done, they conversed of the Ladies' Vale, waxing eloquent in praise thereof: insomuch that the king called the seneschal, and bade him have some beds made ready and carried thither on the morrow, that any that were so minded might there take their siesta.

He then had lights and wine and comfits brought; and when they had taken a slight refection, he bade all address them to the dance. So at his behest Pamfilo led a dance, and then the king, turning with gracious mien to Elisa:—"Fair damsel," quoth he, "'twas thou to-day didst me this honour of the crown; and 'tis my will that thine to-night be the honour of the song; wherefore sing us whatsoever thou hast most lief."

"That gladly will I," replied Elisa smiling; and thus with dulcet voice began:—

> If of thy talons, Love, be quit I may,
>   I deem it scarce can be
>   But other fangs I may elude for aye.
>
> Service I took with thee, a tender maid,
>   In thy war thinking perfect peace to find,
>   And all my arms upon the ground I laid,
>   Yielding myself to thee with trustful mind:
>   Thou, harpy-tyrant, whom no faith may bind,
>   Eftsoons didst swoop on me,
>   And with thy cruel claws mad'st me thy prey.
>
> Then thy poor captive, bound with many a chain,
>   Thou tookst, and gav'st to him, whom fate did call
>   Hither my death to be; for that in pain

And bitter tears I waste away, his thrall:
Nor heave I e'er a sigh, or tear let fall,
So harsh a lord is he,
That him inclines a jot my grief to allay.

My prayers upon the idle air are spent:
He hears not, will not hear; wherefore in vain
The more each hour my soul doth her torment;
Nor may I die, albeit to die were gain.
Ah! Lord, have pity of my bitter pain!
Help have I none but thee;
Then take and bind and at my feet him lay.

But if thou wilt not, do my soul but loose
From hope, that her still binds with triple chain.
Sure, O my lord, this prayer thou'lt not refuse:
The which so thou to grant me do but deign,
I look my wonted beauty to regain,
And banish misery
With roses white and red bedecked and gay.

So with a most piteous sigh ended Elisa her song, whereat all wondered exceedingly, nor might any conjecture wherefore she so sang. But the king, who was in a jolly humour, sent for Tindaro, and bade him out with his cornemuse, and caused them tread many a measure thereto, until, no small part of the night being thus spent, he gave leave to all to betake them to rest.

SEVENTH DAY

STORY VI.

Madonna Isabella has with her Leonetto, her accepted lover, when she is surprised by one Messer Lambertuccio, by whom she is beloved: her husband coming home about the same time, she sends Messer Lambertuccio forth of the house drawn sword in hand, and the husband afterwards escorts Leonetto home.

In our city, rich in all manner of good things, there dwelt a young gentlewoman, fair exceedingly, and wedded to a most worthy and excellent gentleman. And as it not seldom happens that one cannot keep ever to the same diet, but would fain at times vary it, so this lady, finding her husband not altogether to her mind, became enamoured of a gallant, Leonetto by name, who, though of no high rank, was not a little debonair and courteous, and he in like manner fell in love with her; and (as you know that 'tis seldom that what is mutually desired fails to come about) 'twas not long before they had fruition of their love. Now the lady being, as I said, fair and winsome, it so befell that a gentleman, Messer Lambertuccio by name, grew mightily enamoured of her, but so tiresome and odious did she find him, that for the world she could not bring herself to love him. So, growing tired of fruitlessly soliciting her favour by ambassage, Messer Lambertuccio, who was a powerful signior, sent her at last another sort of message in which he threatened to defame her if she complied not with his wishes. Wherefore the lady, knowing her man, was terrified, and disposed herself to pleasure him.

Now it so chanced that Madonna Isabella, for such was the lady's name, being gone, as is our Florentine custom in the summer, to spend some time on a very goodly estate that she had in the contado, one morning finding herself alone, for her husband had ridden off to tarry some days elsewhere, she sent for Leonetto to come and keep her company; and Leonetto came forthwith in high glee. But while they were together, Messer Lambertuccio, who, having got wind that the husband

127

was away, had mounted his horse and ridden thither quite alone, knocked at the door. Whereupon the lady's maid hied her forthwith to her mistress, who was alone with Leonetto, and called her, saying:— "Madam, Messer Lambertuccio is here below, quite alone."

Whereat the lady was vexed beyond measure; and being also not a little dismayed, she said to Leonetto:— "Prithee, let it not irk thee to withdraw behind the curtain, and there keep close until Messer Lambertuccio be gone."

Leonetto, who stood in no less fear of Messer Lambertuccio than did the lady, got into his hiding-place; and the lady bade the maid go open to Messer Lambertuccio: she did so; and having dismounted and fastened his palfrey to a pin, he ascended the stairs; at the head of which the lady received him with a smile and as gladsome a greeting as she could find words for, and asked him on what errand he was come. The gentleman embraced and kissed her, saying:— "My soul, I am informed that your husband is not here, and therefore I am come to stay a while with you." Which said, they went into the room, and locked them in, and Messer Lambertuccio fell a toying with her.

Now, while thus he sped the time with her, it befell that the lady's husband, albeit she nowise expected him, came home, and, as he drew nigh the palace, was observed by the maid, who forthwith ran to the lady's chamber, and said:— "Madam, the master will be here anon; I doubt he is already in the courtyard."

Whereupon, for that she had two men in the house, and the knight's palfrey, that was in the courtyard, made it impossible to hide him, the lady gave herself up for dead. Nevertheless she made up her mind on the spur of the moment, and springing out of bed:— "Sir," quoth she to Messer Lambertuccio, "if you have any regard for me, and would save my life, you will do as I bid you: that is to say, you will draw your blade, and put on a fell and wrathful countenance, and hie you downstairs, saying:— 'By God, he shall not escape me elsewhere.' And if my husband would stop you, or ask you aught, say nought but what I have told you, and get you on horseback and tarry with him on no account."

"To hear is to obey," quoth Messer Lambertuccio, who, with the flush of his recent exertion and the rage that he felt at the husband's return still on his face, and drawn sword in hand, did as she bade him.

The lady's husband, being now dismounted in the courtyard, and not a little surprised to see the palfrey there, was about to go up the stairs, when he saw Messer Lambertuccio coming down them, and marvelling both at his words and at his mien:— "What means this, Sir?" quoth he.

But Messer Lambertuccio clapped foot in stirrup, and mounted, saying nought but:— "Zounds, but I will meet him elsewhere"; and so he rode off.

The gentleman then ascended the stairs, at the head of which he found his lady distraught with terror, to whom he said: — "What manner of thing is this? After whom goes Messer Lambertuccio, so wrathful and menacing?"

Whereto the lady, drawing nigher the room, that Leonetto might hear her, made answer: — "Never, Sir, had I such a fright as this. There came running in here a young man, who to me is quite a stranger, and at his heels Messer Lambertuccio with a drawn sword in his hand; and as it happened the young man found the door of this room open, and trembling in every limb, cried out: — 'Madam, your succour, for God's sake, that I die not in your arms.' So up I got, and would have asked him who he was, and how bested, when up came Messer Lambertuccio, exclaiming: — 'Where art thou, traitor?' I planted myself in the doorway, and kept him from entering, and seeing that I was not minded to give him admittance, he was courteous enough, after not a little parley, to take himself off, as you saw."

Whereupon: — "Wife," quoth the husband, "thou didst very right. Great indeed had been the scandal, had some one been slain here, and 'twas a gross affront on Messer Lambertuccio's part to pursue a fugitive within the house."

He then asked where the young man was. Whereto the lady answered: — "Nay, where he may be hiding, Sir, I wot not."

So: — "Where art thou?" quoth the knight. "Fear not to shew thyself." Then forth of his hiding-place, all of a tremble, for in truth he had been thoroughly terrified, crept Leonetto, who had heard all that had passed. To whom: — "What hast thou to do with Messer Lambertuccio?" quoth the knight.

"Nothing in the world," replied the young man: "wherefore, I doubt he must either be out of his mind, or have mistaken me for another; for no sooner had he sight of me in the street hard by the palace, than he laid his hand on his sword, and exclaimed: — 'Traitor, thou art a dead man.' Whereupon I sought not to know why, but fled with all speed, and got me here, and so, thanks to God and this gentlewoman, I escaped his hands."

"Now away with thy fears," quoth the knight; "I will see thee home safe and sound; and then 'twill be for thee to determine how thou shalt deal with him."

And so, when they had supped, he set him on horseback, and escorted him to Florence, and left him not until he was safe in his own house. And the very same evening, following the lady's instructions, Leonetto spoke privily with Messer Lambertuccio, and so composed the affair with him, that, though it occasioned not a little talk, the knight never wist how he had been tricked by his wife.

STORY IX.

Lydia, wife of Nicostratus, loves Pyrrhus, who to assure himself thereof, asks three things of her, all of which she does, and therewithal enjoys him in presence of Nicostratus, and makes Nicostratus believe that what he saw was not real.

In Argos, that most ancient city of Achaia, the fame of whose kings of old time is out of all proportion to its size, there dwelt of yore Nicostratus, a nobleman, to whom, when he was already verging on old age, Fortune gave to wife a great lady, Lydia by name, whose courage matched her charms. Nicostratus, as suited with his rank and wealth, kept not a few retainers and hounds and hawks, and was mightily addicted to the chase. Among his dependants was a young man named Pyrrhus, a gallant of no mean accomplishment, and goodly of person and beloved and trusted by Nicostratus above all other. Of whom Lydia grew mighty enamoured, insomuch that neither by day nor by night might her thoughts stray from him: but, whether it was that Pyrrhus wist not her love, or would have none of it, he gave no sign of recognition; whereby the lady's suffering waxing more than she could bear, she made up her mind to declare her love to him; and having a chambermaid, Lusca by name, in whom she placed great trust, she called her, and said:—

"Lusca, tokens thou hast had from me of my regard that should ensure thy obedience and loyalty; wherefore have a care that what I shall now tell thee reach the ears of none but him to whom I shall bid thee impart it. Thou seest, Lusca, that I am in the prime of my youth and lustihead, and have neither lack nor stint of all such things as folk desire, save only, to be brief, that I have one cause to repine, to wit, that my husband's years so far outnumber my own. Wherefore with that wherein young ladies take most pleasure I am but ill provided, and, as my desire is no less than theirs, 'tis now some while since I determined that, if Fortune has shewn herself so little friendly to me by giving me a husband so advanced in years, at least I will not be mine own enemy by sparing to devise the means whereby my happiness and health may

130

be assured; and that herein, as in all other matters, my joy may be complete, I have chosen, thereto to minister by his embraces, our Pyrrhus, deeming him more worthy than any other man, and have so set my heart upon him that I am ever ill at ease save when he is present either to my sight or to my mind, insomuch that, unless I forgather with him without delay, I doubt not that 'twill be the death of me. And so, if thou holdest my life dear, thou wilt shew him my love on such wise as thou mayst deem best, and make my suit to him that he be pleased to come to me, when thou shalt go to fetch him."

"That gladly will I," replied the chambermaid; and as soon as she found convenient time and place, she drew Pyrrhus apart, and, as best she knew how, conveyed her lady's message to him.

Which Pyrrhus found passing strange to hear, for 'twas in truth a complete surprise to him, and he doubted the lady did but mean to try him. Wherefore he presently, and with some asperity, answered thus:— "Lusca, believe I cannot that this message comes from my lady: have a care, therefore, what thou sayst, and if, perchance, it does come from her, I doubt she does not mean it; and if, perchance, she does mean it, why, then I am honoured by my lord above what I deserve, and I would not for my life do him such a wrong: so have a care never to speak of such matters to me again."

Lusca, nowise disconcerted by his uncompliant tone, rejoined:—"I shall speak to thee, Pyrrhus, of these and all other matters, wherewith I may be commissioned by my lady, as often as she shall bid me, whether it pleases or irks thee; but thou art a blockhead."

So, somewhat chafed, Lusca bore Pyrrhus' answer back to her lady, who would fain have died, when she heard it, and some days afterwards resumed the topic, saying:—"Thou knowest, Lusca, that 'tis not the first stroke that fells the oak; wherefore, methinks, thou wert best go back to this strange man, who is minded to evince his loyalty at my expense, and choosing a convenient time, declare to him all my passion, and do thy best endeavour that the affair be carried through; for if it should thus lapse, 'twould be the death of me; besides which, he would think we had but trifled with him, and, whereas 'tis his love we would have, we should earn his hatred."

So, after comforting the lady, the maid hied her in quest of Pyrrhus, whom she found in a gladsome and propitious mood, and thus addressed:—

"'Tis not many days, Pyrrhus, since I declared to thee how ardent is the flame with which thy lady and mine is consumed for love of thee, and now again I do thee to wit thereof, and that, if thou shalt not relent of the harshness that thou didst manifest the other day, thou mayst rest assured that her life will be short: wherefore I pray thee to be pleased to give her solace of her desire, and shouldst thou persist in thy obduracy, I, that gave thee credit for not a little sense, shall deem thee a great fool. How flattered thou shouldst be to know thyself beloved above all else by a lady so beauteous and high-born! And how indebted shouldst thou feel thyself to Fortune, seeing that she has in store for thee a boon so great and so suited to the cravings of thy youth, ay, and so like to be of service to thee upon occasion of need! Bethink thee, if there be any of thine equals whose life is ordered more agreeably than thine will be if thou but be wise. Which of them wilt thou find so well furnished with arms and horses, clothes and money as thou shalt be, if thou but give my lady thy love? Receive, then, my words with open mind; be thyself again; bethink thee that 'tis Fortune's way to confront a man but once with smiling mien and open lap, and, if he then accept not her bounty, he has but himself to blame, if afterward he find himself in want, in beggary. Besides which, no such loyalty is demanded between servants and their masters as between friends and kinsfolk; rather 'tis for servants, so far as they may, to behave towards their masters as their masters behave towards them. Thinkest thou, that, if thou hadst a fair wife or mother or daughter or sister that found favour in Nicostratus' eyes, he would be so scrupulous on the point of loyalty as thou art disposed to be in regard of his lady? Thou art a fool, if so thou dost believe. Hold it for certain, that, if blandishments and supplications did not suffice, he would, whatever thou mightest think of it, have recourse to force. Observe we, then, towards them and theirs the same rule which they observe towards us and ours. Take the boon that Fortune offers thee; repulse her not; rather go thou to meet her, and hail her advance; for be sure that, if thou do not so, to say nought of thy lady's death, which will certainly ensue, thou thyself wilt repent thee thereof so often that thou wilt be fain of death."

Since he had last seen Lusca, Pyrrhus had repeatedly pondered what she had said to him, and had made his mind up that, should she come again, he would answer her in another sort, and comply in all respects with the lady's desires, provided he might be assured that she was not merely putting him to the proof; wherefore he now made answer:—

"Lo, now, Lusca, I acknowledge the truth of all that thou sayst; but, on the other hand, I know that my lord is not a little wise and wary, and, as he has committed all his affairs to my charge, I sorely misdoubt me that 'tis with his approbation, and by his advice, and but to prove me, that Lydia does this: wherefore let her do three things which I shall demand of her for my assurance, and then there is nought that she shall crave of me, but I will certainly render her prompt obedience. Which three things are these:—first, let her in Nicostratus' presence kill his fine sparrow-hawk: then she must send me a lock of Nicostratus' beard, and lastly one of his best teeth."

Hard seemed these terms to Lusca, and hard beyond measure to the lady, but Love, that great fautor of enterprise, and master of stratagem, gave her resolution to address herself to their performance: wherefore through the chambermaid she sent him word that what he required of her she would do, and that without either reservation or delay; and therewithal she told him, that, as he deemed Nicostratus so wise, she would contrive that they should enjoy one another in Nicostratus' presence, and that Nicostratus should believe that 'twas a mere show. Pyrrhus, therefore, anxiously expected what the lady would do. Some days thus passed, and then Nicostratus gave a great breakfast, as was his frequent wont, to certain gentlemen, and when the tables were removed, the lady, robed in green samite, and richly adorned, came forth of her chamber into the hall wherein they sate, and before the eyes of Pyrrhus and all the rest of the company hied her to the perch, on which stood the sparrow-hawk that Nicostratus so much prized, and loosed him, and, as if she were minded to carry him on her hand, took him by the jesses and dashed him against the wall so that he died.

Whereupon:—"Alas! my lady, what has thou done?" exclaimed Nicostratus: but she vouchsafed no answer, save that, turning to the gentlemen that had sate at meat with him, she said:—

"My lords, ill fitted were I to take vengeance on a king that had done me despite, if I lacked the courage to be avenged on a sparrow-hawk. You are to know that by this bird I have long been cheated of all the time that ought to be devoted by gentlemen to pleasuring their ladies; for with the first streaks of dawn Nicostratus has been up and got him to horse, and hawk on hand hied him to the champaign to see him fly, leaving me, such as you see me, alone and ill content abed. For which cause I have oftentimes been minded to do that which I have now done, and have only refrained therefrom, that, biding my time, I might do it in the presence of men that should judge my cause justly, as I trust you will do."

Which hearing, the gentlemen, who deemed her affections no less fixed on Nicostratus than her words imported, broke with one accord into a laugh, and turning to Nicostratus, who was sore displeased, fell a saying:—"Now well done of the lady to avenge her wrongs by the death of the sparrow-hawk!" and so, the lady being withdrawn to her chamber, they passed the affair off with divers pleasantries, turning the wrath of Nicostratus to laughter.

Pyrrhus, who had witnessed what had passed, said to himself:—Nobly indeed has my lady begun, and on such wise as promises well for the felicity of my love. God grant that she so continue. And even so Lydia did: for not many days after she had killed the sparrow-hawk, she, being with Nicostratus in her chamber, from caressing passed to toying and trifling with him, and he, sportively pulling her by the hair, gave her occasion to fulfil, the second of Pyrrhus' demands; which she did by nimbly laying hold of one of the lesser tufts of his beard, and, laughing the while, plucking it so hard that she tore it out of his chin.

Which Nicostratus somewhat resenting:—"Now what cause hast thou," quoth he, "to make such a wry face? 'Tis but that I have plucked some half-dozen hairs from thy beard. Thou didst not feel it as much as did I but now thy tugging of my hair."

And so they continued jesting and sporting with one another, the lady jealously guarding the tuft that she had torn from the beard, which the very same day she sent to her cherished lover. The third demand caused the lady more thought; but, being amply endowed with wit, and powerfully seconded by Love, she failed not to hit upon an apt expedient.

Nicostratus had in his service two lads, who, being of gentle birth, had been placed with him by their kinsfolk, that they might learn manners, one of whom, when Nicostratus sate at meat, carved before him, while the other gave him to drink. Both lads Lydia called to her, and gave them to understand that their breath smelt, and admonished them that, when they waited on Nicostratus, they should hold their heads as far back as possible, saying never a word of the matter to any. The lads believing her, did as she bade them. Whereupon she took occasion to say to Nicostratus:—"Hast thou marked what these lads do when they wait upon thee?"

"Troth, that have I," replied Nicostratus; "indeed I have often had it in mind to ask them why they do so."

"Nay," rejoined the lady, "spare thyself the pains; for I can tell thee the reason, which I have for some time kept close, lest it should vex thee; but as I now see that others begin to be ware of it, it need no longer be withheld from thee. 'Tis for that thy breath stinks shrewdly that they thus avert their heads from thee: 'twas not wont to be so, nor know I why it should be so; and 'tis most offensive when thou art in converse with gentlemen; and therefore 'twould be well to find some way of curing it."

"I wonder what it could be," returned Nicostratus; "is it perchance that I have a decayed tooth in my jaw?"

"That may well be," quoth Lydia: and taking him to a window, she caused him open his mouth, and after regarding it on this side and that:— "Oh! Nicostratus," quoth she, "how couldst thou have endured it so long? Thou hast a tooth here, which, by what I see, is not only decayed, but actually rotten throughout; and beyond all manner of doubt, if thou let it remain long in thy head, 'twill infect its neighbours; so 'tis my advice that thou out with it before the matter grows worse."

"My judgment jumps with thine," quoth Nicostratus; "wherefore send without delay for a chirurgeon to draw it."

"God forbid," returned the lady, "that chirurgeon come hither for such a purpose; methinks, the case is such that I can very well dispense with him, and draw the tooth myself. Besides which, these chirurgeons do these things in such a cruel way, that I could never endure to see thee or know thee under the hands of any of them: wherefore my mind is quite made up to do it myself, that, at least, if thou shalt suffer too much, I may give it over at once, as a chirurgeon would not do."

And so she caused the instruments that are used on such occasions to be brought her, and having dismissed all other attendants save Lusca from the chamber, and locked the door, made Nicostratus lie down on a table, set the pincers in his mouth, and clapped them on one of his teeth, which, while Lusca held him, so that, albeit he roared for pain, he might not move, she wrenched by main force from his jaw, and keeping it close, took from Lusca's hand another and horribly decayed tooth, which she shewed him, suffering and half dead as he was, saying:—"See what thou hadst in thy jaw; mark how far gone it is."

Believing what she said, and deeming that, now the tooth was out, his breath would no more be offensive, and being somewhat eased of the pain, which had been extreme, and still remained, so that he murmured not little, by divers comforting applications, he quitted the chamber: whereupon the lady forthwith sent the tooth to her lover, who, having now full assurance of her love, placed himself entirely at her service. But the lady being minded to make his assurance yet more sure, and deeming each hour a thousand till she might be with him, now saw fit, for the more ready performance of the promise she had given him, to feign sickness; and Nicostratus, coming to see her one day after breakfast, attended only by Pyrrhus, she besought him for her better solacement, to help her down to the garden.

Wherefore Nicostratus on one side, and Pyrrhus on the other, took her and bore her down to the garden, and set her on a lawn at the foot of a beautiful pear-tree: and after they had sate there a while, the lady, who had already given Pyrrhus to understand what he must do, said to him:—"Pyrrhus, I should greatly like to have some of those pears; get thee up the tree, and shake some of them down."

Pyrrhus climbed the tree in a trice, and began to shake down the pears, and while he did so:—"Fie! Sir," quoth he, "what is this you do? And you, Madam, have you no shame, that you suffer him to do so in my presence? Think you that I am blind? 'Twas but now that you were gravely indisposed. Your cure has been speedy indeed to permit of your so behaving: and as for such a purpose you have so many goodly chambers, why betake you not yourselves to one of them, if you must needs so disport yourselves? 'Twould be much more decent than to do so in my presence."

Whereupon the lady, turning to her husband: — "Now what can Pyrrhus mean?" said she. "Is he mad?"

"Nay, Madam," quoth Pyrrhus; "mad am not I. Think you I see you not?"

Whereat Nicostratus marvelled not a little; and: — "Pyrrhus," quoth he, "I verily believe thou dreamest."

"Nay, my lord," replied Pyrrhus, "not a whit do I dream; neither do you; rather you wag it with such vigour, that, if this pear-tree did the like, there would be never a pear left on it."

Then the lady: — "What can this mean?" quoth she: "can it be that it really seems to him to be as he says? Upon my hope of salvation, were I but in my former health, I would get me up there to judge for myself what these wonders are which he professes to see."

Whereupon, as Pyrrhus in the pear-tree continued talking in the same strange strain: — "Come down," quoth Nicostratus; and when he was down: — "Now, what," said Nicostratus, "is it thou sayst thou seest up there?"

"I suppose," replied Pyrrhus, "that you take me to be deluded or dreaming: but as I must needs tell you the truth, I saw you lying upon your wife, and then, when I came down, I saw you get up and sit you down here where you now are."

"Therein," said Nicostratus, "thou wast certainly deluded, for, since thou clombest the pear-tree, we have not budged a jot, save as thou seest."

Then said Pyrrhus: — "Why make more words about the matter? See you I certainly did; and, seeing you, I saw you lying upon your own."

Nicostratus' wonder now waxed momentarily, insomuch that he said: — "I am minded to see if this pear-tree be enchanted, so that whoso is in it sees marvels"; and so he got him up into it.

Whereupon the lady and Pyrrhus fell to disporting them, and Nicostratus, seeing what they were about, exclaimed: — "Ah! lewd woman, what is this thou doest? And thou, Pyrrhus, in whom I so much trusted!"

And so saying, he began to climb down. Meanwhile the lady and Pyrrhus had made answer: — "We are sitting here": and seeing him descending, they placed themselves as they had been when he had left them, whom Nicostratus, being come down, no sooner saw, than he fell a rating them.

Then quoth Pyrrhus: — "Verily, Nicostratus, I now acknowledge, that, as you said a while ago, what I saw when I was in the pear-tree was but a false show, albeit I had never understood that so it was but that I now see and know that thou hast also seen a false show. And that I speak truth, you may sufficiently assure yourself, if you but reflect whether 'tis likely that your wife, who for virtue and discretion has not her peer among women, would, if she were minded so to dishonour you, see fit to do so before your very eyes. Of myself I say nought, albeit I had liefer be hewn in pieces than that I should so much as think of such a thing, much less do it in your presence. Wherefore 'tis evident that 'tis some illusion of sight that is propagated from the pear-tree; for nought in the world would have made me believe that I saw not you lying there in carnal intercourse with your wife, had I not heard you say that you saw me doing that which most assuredly, so far from doing, I never so much as thought of."

The lady then started up with a most resentful mien, and burst out with: — "Foul fall thee, if thou knowest so little of me as to suppose that, if I were minded to do thee such foul dishonour as thou sayst thou didst see me do, I would come hither to do it before thine eyes! Rest assured that for such a purpose, were it ever mine, I should deem one of our chambers more meet, and it should go hard but I would so order the matter that thou shouldst never know aught of it."

Nicostratus, having heard both, and deeming that what they both averred must be true, to wit, that they would never have ventured upon such an act in his presence, passed from chiding to talk of the singularity of the thing, and how marvellous it was that the vision should reshape itself for every one that clomb the tree. The lady, however, made a show of being distressed that Nicostratus should so have thought of her, and: — "Verily," quoth she, "no woman, neither I nor another, shall again suffer loss of honour by his pear-tree: run, Pyrrhus, and bring hither an axe, and at one and the same time vindicate thy honour and mine by felling it, albeit 'twere better far Nicostratus' skull should feel the weight of the axe, seeing that in utter heedlessness he so readily suffered the eyes of his mind to be blinded; for, albeit this vision was seen by the bodily eye, yet ought the understanding by no means to have entertained and affirmed it as real."

So Pyrrhus presently hied him to fetch the axe, and returning therewith felled the pear; whereupon the lady, turning towards Nicostratus: — "Now that this foe of my honour is fallen," quoth she, "my wrath is gone from me." Nicostratus then craving her pardon, she graciously granted it him, bidding him never again to suffer himself to be betrayed into thinking such a thing of her, who loved him more dearly than herself. So the poor duped husband went back with her and her lover to the palace, where not seldom in time to come Pyrrhus and Lydia took their pastime together more at ease. God grant us the like.

EIGHTH DAY

STORY I.

Gulfardo borrows moneys of Guasparruolo, which he has agreed to give Guasparruolo's wife, that he may lie with her. He gives them to her, and in her presence tells Guasparruolo that he has done so, and she acknowledges that 'tis true.

Know, then, that there was once at Milan a Germany mercenary, Gulfardo by name, a doughty man, and very loyal to those with whom he took service; a quality most uncommon in Germans. And as he was wont to be most faithful in repaying whatever moneys he borrowed, he would have had no difficulty in finding a merchant to advance him any amount of money at a low rate of interest. Now, tarrying thus at Milan, Gulfardo fixed his affection on a very fine woman, named Madonna Ambruogia, the wife of a wealthy merchant, one Guasparruolo Cagastraccio, with whom he was well acquainted and on friendly terms: which amour he managed with such discretion that neither the husband nor any one else wist aught of it. So one day he sent her a message, beseeching her of her courtesy to gratify his passion, and assuring her that he on his part was ready to obey her every behest.

The lady made a great many words about the affair, the upshot of which was that she would do as Gulfardo desired upon the following terms: to wit, that, in the first place, he should never discover the matter to a soul, and, secondly, that, as for some purpose or another she required two hundred florins of gold, he out of his abundance should supply her necessity; these conditions being satisfied she would be ever at his service. Offended by such base sordidness in one whom he had supposed to be an honourable woman, Gulfardo passed from ardent love to something very like hatred, and cast about how he might flout her. So he sent her word that he would right gladly pleasure her in this and in any other matter that might be in his power; let her but say when he was to come to see her, and he would bring the moneys with him, and none should

138

know of the matter except a comrade of his, in whom he placed much trust, and who was privy to all that he did. The lady, if she should not rather be called the punk, gleefully made answer that in the course of a few days her husband, Guasparruolo, was to go to Genoa on business, and that, when he was gone, she would let Gulfardo know, and appoint a time for him to visit her.

Gulfardo thereupon chose a convenient time, and hied him to Guasparruolo, to whom: — "I am come," quoth he, "about a little matter of business which I have on hand, for which I require two hundred florins of gold, and I should be glad if thou wouldst lend me at the rate of interest which thou art wont to charge me."

"That gladly will I," replied Guasparruolo, and told out the money at once.

A few days later Guasparruolo being gone to Genoa, as the lady had said, she sent word to Gulfardo that he should bring her the two hundred florins of gold. So Gulfardo hied him with his comrade to the lady's house, where he found her expecting him, and lost no time in handing her the two hundred florins of gold in his comrade's presence, saying: — "You will keep the money, Madam, and give it to your husband when he returns."

Witting not why Gulfardo so said, but thinking that 'twas but to conceal from his comrade that it was given by way of price, the lady made answer: — "That will I gladly; but I must first see whether the amount is right"; whereupon she told the florins out upon a table, and when she found that the two hundred were there, she put them away in high glee, and turning to Gulfardo, took him into her chamber, where, not on that night only but on many another night, while her husband was away, he had of her all that he craved.

On Guasparruolo's return Gulfardo presently paid him a visit, having first made sure that the lady would be with him, and so in her presence: — "Guasparruolo," quoth he, "I had after all no occasion for the money, to wit, the two hundred florins of gold that thou didst lend me the other day, being unable to carry through the transaction for which I borrowed them, and so I took an early opportunity of bringing them to thy wife, and gave them to her: thou wilt therefore cancel the account."

Whereupon Guasparruolo turned to the lady, and asked her if she had had them. She, not daring to deny the fact in presence of the witness, answered: — "Why, yes, I had them, and quite forgot to tell thee."

"Good," quoth then Guasparruolo, "we are quits, Gulfardo; make thy mind easy; I will see that thy account is set right."

Gulfardo then withdrew, leaving the flouted lady to hand over her ill-gotten gains to her husband; and so the astute lover had his pleasure of his greedy mistress for nothing.

STORY II.

The priest of Varlungo lies with Monna Belcolore: he leaves with her his cloak by way of pledge, and receives from her a mortar. He returns the mortar, and demands of her the cloak that he had left in pledge, which the good lady returns him with a gibe.

I say then, that at Varlungo, a village hard by here, as all of you, my ladies, should wot either of your own knowledge or by report, there dwelt a worthy priest, and doughty of body in the service of the ladies: who, albeit he was none too quick at his book, had no lack of precious and blessed solecisms to edify his flock withal of a Sunday under the elm. And when the men were out of doors, he would visit their wives as never a priest had done before him, bringing them feast-day gowns and holy water, and now and again a bit of candle, and giving them his blessing.

Now it so befell that among those of his fair parishioners whom he most affected the first place was at length taken by one Monna Belcolore, the wife of a husbandman that called himself Bentivegna del Mazzo. And in good sooth she was a winsome and lusty country lass, brown as a berry and buxom enough, and fitter than e'er another for his mill. Moreover she had not her match in playing the tabret and singing: — The borage is full sappy,[1] and in leading a brawl or a

---

[1] For this folk-song see *Cantilene e Ballate, Strambotti e Madrigali*, ed. Carducci (1871), p. 60. The fragment there printed may be freely rendered as follows: —

> The borage is full sappy,
>   And clusters red we see,
> And my love would make me happy;
>   So that maiden give to me.
>
> Ill set I find this dance,
>   And better might it be:
> So, comrade mine, advance,
>   And, changing place with me,
> Stand thou thy love beside.

breakdown, no matter who might be next her, with a fair and dainty kerchief in her hand. Which spells so wrought upon Master Priest, that for love of her he grew distracted, and did nought all day long but loiter about the village on the chance of catching sight of her. And if of a Sunday morning he espied her in church, he strove might and main to acquit himself of his Kyrie and Sanctus in the style of a great singer, albeit his performance was liken to the braying of an ass: whereas, if he saw her not, he scarce exerted himself at all. However, he managed with such discretion that neither Bentivegna del Mazzo nor any of the neighbours wist aught of his love. And hoping thereby to ingratiate himself with Monna Belcolore, he from time to time would send her presents, now a clove of fresh garlic, the best in all the country-side, from his own garden, which he tilled with his own hands, and anon a basket of beans or a bunch of chives or shallots; and, when he thought it might serve his turn, he would give her a sly glance, and follow it up with a little amorous mocking and mowing, which she, with rustic awkwardness, feigned not to understand, and ever maintained her reserve, so that Master Priest made no headway.

Now it so befell that one day, when the priest at high noon was aimlessly gadding about the village, he encountered Bentivegna del Mazzo at the tail of a well laden ass, and greeted him, asking him whither he was going. "T'faith, Sir," quoth Bentivegna, "for sure 'tis to town I go, having an affair or two to attend to there; and I am taking these things to Ser Buonaccorri da Ginestreto, to get him to stand by me in I wot not what matter, whereof the justice o' th' coram has by his provoker served me with a pertrumpery summons to appear before him."

Whereupon:—"'Tis well, my son," quoth the priest, overjoyed, "my blessing go with thee: good luck to thee and a speedy return; and harkye, shouldst thou see Lapuccio or Naldino, do not forget to tell them to send me those thongs for my flails."

"It shall be done," quoth Bentivegna, and jogged on towards Florence, while the priest, thinking that now was his time to hie him to Belcolore and try his fortune, put his best leg forward, and stayed not till he was at the house, which entering, he said:—"God be gracious to us! Who is within?"

Belcolore, who was up in the loft, made answer:—"Welcome, Sir; but what dost thou, gadding about in the heat?"

"Why, as I hope for God's blessing," quoth he, "I am just come to stay with thee a while, having met thy husband on his way to town."

Whereupon down came Belcolore, took a seat, and began sifting cabbage-seed that her husband had lately threshed. By and by the priest began:—"So, Belcolore, wilt thou keep me ever a dying thus?"

Whereat Belcolore tittered, and said:—"Why, what is't I do to you?"

"Truly, nothing at all," replied the priest: "but thou sufferest me not to do to thee that which I had lief, and which God commands."

"Now away with you!" returned Belcolore, "do priests do that sort of thing?"

"Indeed we do," quoth the priest, "and to better purpose than others: why not? I tell you our grinding is far better; and wouldst thou know why? 'tis because 'tis intermittent. And in truth 'twill be well worth thy while to keep thine own counsel, and let me do it."

"Worthy my while!" ejaculated Belcolore. "How may that be? There is never a one of you but would overreach the very Devil."

"'Tis not for me to say," returned the priest; "say but what thou wouldst have: shall it be a pair of dainty shoes? Or wouldst thou prefer a fillet? Or perchance a gay riband? What's thy will?"

"Marry, no lack have I," quoth Belcolore, "of such things as these. But, if you wish me so well, why do me not a service? and I would then be at your command."

"Name but the service," returned the priest, "and gladly will I do it."

Quoth then Belcolore:—"On Saturday I have to go to Florence to deliver some wool that I have spun, and to get my spinning-wheel put in order: lend me but five pounds—I know you have them—and I will redeem my perse petticoat from the pawnshop, and also the girdle that I wear on saints' days, and that I had when I was married—you see that without them I cannot go to church or anywhere else, and then I will do just as you wish thenceforth and forever."

Whereupon:—"So God give me a good year," quoth he, "as I have not the money with me: but never fear that I will see that thou hast it before Saturday with all the pleasure in life."

"Ay, ay," rejoined Belcolore, "you all make great promises, but then you never keep them. Think you to serve me as you served Biliuzza, whom you left in the lurch at last? God's faith, you do not so. To think that she turned woman of the world just for that! If you have not the money with you, why, go and get it."

"Prithee," returned the priest, "send me not home just now. For, seest thou, 'tis the very nick of time with me, and the coast is clear, and perchance it might not be so on my return, and in short I know not when it would be likely to go so well as now."

Whereto she did but rejoin:—"Good; if you are minded to go, get you gone; if not, stay where you are."

The priest, therefore, seeing that she was not disposed to give him what he wanted, as he was fain, to wit, on his own terms, but was bent upon having a *quid pro quo*, changed his tone; and:—"Lo, now," quoth he, "thou doubtest I will not bring thee the money; so to set thy mind at rest, I will leave thee this cloak—thou seest 'tis good sky-blue silk—in pledge."

So raising her head and glancing at the cloak:—"And what may the cloak be worth?" quoth Belcolore.

"Worth!" ejaculated the priest: "I would have thee know that 'tis all Douai, not to say Trouai, make: nay, there are some of our folk here that say 'tis Quadrouai; and 'tis not a fortnight since I bought it of Lotto, the second-hand dealer, for seven good pounds, and then had it five good soldi under value, by what I hear from Buglietto, who, thou knowest, is an excellent judge of these articles."

"Oh! say you so?" exclaimed Belcolore. "So help me God, I should not have thought it; however, let me look at it."

So Master Priest, being ready for action, doffed the cloak and handed it to her. And she, having put it in a safe place, said to him:—"Now, Sir, we will away to the hut; there is never a soul goes there"; and so they did. And there Master Priest, giving her many a mighty buss and straining her to his sacred person, solaced himself with her no little while.

Which done, he hied him away in his cassock, as if he were come from officiating at a wedding; but, when he was back in his holy quarters, he bethought him that not all the candles that he received by way of offering in the course of an entire year would amount to the half of five pounds, and saw that he had made a bad bargain, and repented him that he had left the cloak in pledge, and cast about how he might recover it without paying anything. And as he did not lack cunning, he hit upon an excellent expedient, by which he compassed his end. So on the morrow, being a saint's day, he sent a neighbour's lad to Monna Belcolore with a request that she would be so good as to lend him her stone mortar, for that Binguccio dal Poggio and Nuto Buglietti were to breakfast with him that morning, and he therefore wished to make a sauce.

Belcolore having sent the mortar, the priest, about breakfast time, reckoning that Bentivegna del Mazzo and Belcolore would be at their meal, called his clerk, and said to him:—"Take the mortar back to Belcolore, and say:—'My master thanks you very kindly, and bids you return the cloak that the lad left with you in pledge.'"

The clerk took the mortar to Belcolore's house, where, finding her at table with Bentivegna, he set the mortar down and delivered the priest's message. Whereto Belcolore would fain have demurred; but Bentivegna gave her a threatening glance, saying:—"So, then, thou takest a pledge from Master Priest? By Christ, I vow, I have half a mind to give thee a great clout o' the chin. Go, give it back at once, a murrain on thee! And look to it that whatever he may have a mind to, were it our very ass, he be never denied."

So, with a very bad grace, Belcolore got up, and went to the wardrobe, and took out the cloak, and gave it to the clerk, saying:—

"Tell thy master from me:—Would to God he may never ply pestle in my mortar again, such honour has he done me for this turn!"

So the clerk returned with the cloak, and delivered the message to Master Priest; who, laughing, made answer:—"Tell her, when thou next seest her, that, so she lend us not the mortar, I will not lend her the pestle: be it tit for tat."

Bentivegna made no account of his wife's words, deeming that 'twas but his chiding that had provoked them. But Belcolore was not a little displeased with Master Priest, and had never a word to say to him till the vintage; after which, what with the salutary fear in which she stood of the mouth of Lucifer the Great, to which he threatened to consign her, and the must and roast chestnuts that he sent her, she made it up with him, and many a jolly time they had together. And though she got not the five pounds from him, he put a new skin on her tabret, and fitted it with a little bell, wherewith she was satisfied.

NINTH DAY

STORY II.

An abbess rises in haste and in the dark, with intent to surprise an accused nun abed with her lover: thinking to put on her veil, she puts on instead the breeches of a priest that she has with her: the nun, espying her headgear, and doing her to wit thereof, is acquitted, and thenceforth finds it easier to forgather with her lover.

You are to know, then, that in a convent in Lombardy of very great repute for strict and holy living there was, among other ladies that there wore the veil, a young woman of noble family, and extraordinary beauty. Now Isabetta—for such was her name—having speech one day of one of her kinsmen at the grate, became enamoured of a fine young gallant that was with him; who, seeing her to be very fair, and reading her passion in her eyes, was kindled with a like flame for her: which mutual and unsolaced love they bore a great while not without great suffering to both. But at length, both being intent thereon, the gallant discovered a way by which he might with all secrecy visit his nun; and she approving, he paid her not one visit only, but many, to their no small mutual solace. But, while thus they continued their intercourse, it so befell that one night one of the sisters observed him take his leave of Isabetta and depart, albeit neither he nor she was ware that they had thus been discovered. The sister imparted what she had seen to several others.

At first they were minded to denounce her to the abbess, one Madonna Usimbalda, who was reputed by the nuns, and indeed by all that knew her, to be a good and holy woman; but on second thoughts they deemed it expedient, that there might be no room for denial, to cause the abbess to take her and the gallant in the act. So they held their peace, and arranged between them to keep her in watch and close espial, that they might catch her unawares. Of which practice Isabetta recking, witting nought, it so befell that one night, when she had her lover to see her, the sisters that were on the watch were soon ware of it,

145

and at what they deemed the nick of time parted into two companies, of which one mounted guard at the threshold of Isabetta's cell, while the other hasted to the abbess's chamber, and knocking at the door, roused her, and as soon as they heard her voice, said:—"Up, Madam, without delay: we have discovered that Isabetta has a young man with her in her cell."

Now that night the abbess had with her a priest whom she used not seldom to have conveyed to her in a chest; and the report of the sisters making her apprehensive lest for excess of zeal and hurry they should force the door open, she rose in a trice; and huddling on her clothes as best she might in the dark, instead of the veil that they wear, which they call the psalter, she caught up the priest's breeches, and having clapped them on her head, hied her forth, and locked the door behind her, saying:—"Where is this woman accursed of God?"

And so, guided by the sisters, all so agog to catch Isabetta a sinning that they perceived not what manner of headgear the abbess wore, she made her way to the cell, and with their aid broke open the door; and entering they found the two lovers abed in one another's arms; who, as it were, thunderstruck to be thus surprised, lay there, witting not what to do. The sisters took the young nun forthwith, and by command of the abbess brought her to the chapter-house. The gallant, left behind in the cell, put on his clothes and waited to see how the affair would end, being minded to make as many nuns as he might come at pay dearly for any despite that might be done his mistress, and to bring her off with him. The abbess, seated in the chapter-house with all her nuns about her, and all eyes bent upon the culprit, began giving her the severest reprimand that ever woman got, for that by her disgraceful and abominable conduct, should it get wind, she had sullied the fair fame of the convent; whereto she added menaces most dire.

Shamefast and timorous, the culprit essayed no defence, and her silence begat pity of her in the rest; but, while the abbess waxed more and more voluble, it chanced that the girl raised her head and espied the abbess's headgear, and the points that hung down on this side and that. The significance whereof being by no means lost upon her, she quite plucked up heart, and:—"Madam," quoth she, "so help you God, tie up your coif, and then you may say what you will to me."

Whereto the abbess, not understanding her, replied:—"What coif, lewd woman? So thou has the effrontery to jest! Think'st thou that what thou hast done is a matter meet for jests?"

Whereupon:—"Madam," quoth the girl again, "I pray you, tie up your coif, and then you may say to me whatever you please."

Which occasioned not a few of the nuns to look up at the abbess's head, and the abbess herself to raise her hands thereto, and so she and they at one and the same time apprehended Isabetta's meaning. Wherefore the abbess, finding herself detected by all in the same sin, and that no disguise was possible, changed her tone, and held quite another sort of language than before, the upshot of which was that 'twas impossible to withstand the assaults of the flesh, and that, accordingly, observing due secrecy as theretofore, all might give themselves a good time, as they had opportunity. So, having dismissed Isabetta to rejoin her lover in her cell, she herself returned to lie with her priest. And many a time thereafter, in spite of the envious, Isabetta had her gallant to see her, the others, that lacked lovers, doing in secret the best they might to push their fortunes.

TENTH DAY

STORY III.

Mitridanes, holding Nathan in despite by reason of his courtesy, journeys with intent to kill him, and falling in with him unawares, is advised by him how to compass his end. Following his advice, he finds him in a copse, and recognizing him, is shame-stricken and becomes his friend.

Beyond all question, if we may believe the report of certain Genoese, and other folk that have been in those regions, there dwelt of yore in the parts of Cathay one Nathan, a man of noble lineage and incomparable wealth. Who, having a seat hard by a road, by which whoso would travel from the West eastward, or from the East westward, must needs pass, and being magnanimous and liberal, and zealous to approve himself such in act, did set on work cunning artificers not a few, and cause one of the finest and largest and most luxurious palaces that ever were seen, to be there builded and furnished in the goodliest manner with all things meet for the reception and honourable entertainment of gentlemen. And so, keeping a great array of excellent servants, he courteously and hospitably did the honours of his house to whoso came and went: in which laudable way of life he persevered, until not only the East, but well-nigh all the West had heard his fame; which thus, what time he was well-stricken in years, albeit not for that cause grown weary of shewing courtesy, reached the ears of one Mitridanes, a young man of a country not far distant. Who, knowing himself to be no less wealthy than Nathan, grew envious of the renown that he had of his good deeds, and resolved to obliterate, or at least to obscure it, by a yet greater liberality. So he had built for himself a palace like that of Nathan, of which he did the honours with a lavish courtesy that none had ever equalled, to whoso came or went that way; and verily in a short while he became famous enough.

Now it so befell that on a day when the young man was all alone in the courtyard of the palace, there came in by one of the gates a poor

148

woman, who asked of him an alms, and had it; but, not content therewith, came again to him by the second gate, and asked another alms,
and had it, and after the like sort did even unto the twelfth time; but,
she returning for the thirteenth time:—"My good woman," quoth
Mitridanes, "thou art not a little pertinacious in thy begging": howbeit
he gave her an alms.

Whereupon:—"Ah! the wondrous liberality of Nathan!" quoth the
beldam: "thirty-two gates are there to his palace, by every one of which
I have entered, and asking alms of him, was never—for aught he
shewed—recognized, or refused, and here, though I have entered as
yet by but thirteen gates, I am recognized and reprimanded." And
therewith she departed, and returned no more.

Mitridanes, who accounted the mention of Nathan's fame an abate-
ment of his own, was kindled by her words with a frenzy of wrath, and
began thus to commune with himself:—Alas! when shall I attain to the
grandeur of Nathan's liberality, to say nought of transcending it, as I
would fain, seeing that in the veriest trifles I cannot approach him? Of a
surety my labour is in vain, if I rid not the earth of him: which, since old
age relieves me not of him, I must forthwith do with mine own hands.

And in the flush of his despite up he started, and giving none to
know of his purpose, got to horse with a small company, and after three
days arrived at the place where Nathan abode; and having enjoined
his comrades to make as if they were none of his, and knew him not,
and to go quarter themselves as best they might until they had his further orders, he, being thus alone, towards evening came upon Nathan,
also alone, at no great distance from his splendid palace. Nathan
was recreating himself by a walk, and was very simply clad; so that
Mitridanes, knowing him not, asked him if he could shew him where
Nathan dwelt.

"My son," replied Nathan gladsomely, "that can none in these parts
better than I; wherefore, so it please thee, I will bring thee thither."

The young man replied that 'twould be mighty agreeable to him,
but that, if so it might be, he had a mind to be neither known nor seen
by Nathan.

"And herein also," returned Nathan, "since 'tis thy pleasure, I will
gratify thee."

Whereupon Mitridanes dismounted, and with Nathan, who soon
engaged him in delightsome discourse, walked to the goodly palace.
Arrived there Nathan caused one of his servants take the young man's
horse, and drawing close to him, bade him in a whisper to see to it without delay that none in the house should tell the young man that he was
Nathan: and so 'twas done.

Being come into the palace, Nathan quartered Mitridanes in a most goodly chamber, where none saw him but those whom he had appointed to wait upon him; and he himself kept him company, doing him all possible honour. Of whom Mitridanes, albeit he reverenced him as a father, yet, being thus with him, forbore not to ask who he was.

Whereto Nathan made answer:—"I am a petty servant of Nathan: old as I am, I have been with him since my childhood, and never has he advanced me to higher office than this wherein thou seest me: wherefore, howsoever other folk may praise him, little cause have I to do so."

Which words afforded Mitridanes some hope of carrying his wicked purpose into effect with more of plan and less of risk than had otherwise been possible. By and by Nathan very courteously asked him who he was, and what business brought him thither; offering him such counsel and aid as he might be able to afford him.

Mitridanes hesitated a while to reply: but at last he resolved to trust him, and when with no little circumlocution he had demanded of him fidelity, counsel and aid, he fully discovered to him who he was, and the purpose and motive of his coming thither.

Now, albeit to hear Mitridanes thus unfold his horrid design caused Nathan no small inward commotion, yet 'twas not long before courageously and composedly he thus made answer:—"Noble was thy father, Mitridanes, and thou art minded to shew thyself not unworthy of him by this lofty emprise of thine, to wit, of being liberal to all comers: and for that thou art envious of Nathan's merit I greatly commend thee; for were many envious for a like cause, the world, from being a most wretched, would soon become a happy place. Doubt not that I shall keep secret the design which thou hast confided to me, for the furtherance whereof 'tis good advice rather than substantial aid that I have to offer thee. Which advice is this. Hence, perhaps half a mile off, thou mayst see a copse, in which almost every morning Nathan is wont to walk, taking his pleasure, for quite a long while: 'twill be an easy matter for thee to find him there, and deal with him as thou mayst be minded. Now, shouldst thou slay him, thou wilt get thee home with less risk of let, if thou take not the path by which thou camest hither, but that which thou seest issue from the copse on the left, for, though 'tis somewhat more rough, it leads more directly to thy house, and will be safer for thee."

Possessed of this information, Mitridanes, when Nathan had left him, privily apprised his comrades, who were likewise lodged in the palace, of the place where they were to await him on the ensuing day; which being come, Nathan, inflexibly determined to act in all respects according to the advice which he had given Mitridanes, hied him forth to the copse unattended, to meet his death.

Mitridanes, being risen, took his bow and sword, for other arms he had none with him, mounted his horse, and rode to the copse, through which, while he was yet some way off, he saw Nathan passing, quite alone. And being minded, before he fell upon him, to see his face and hear the sound of his voice, as, riding at a smart pace, he came up with him, he laid hold of him by his head-gear, exclaiming: — "Greybeard, thou art a dead man."

Whereto Nathan answered nought but: — "Then 'tis but my desert."

But Mitridanes, hearing the voice, and scanning the face, forthwith knew him for the same man that had welcomed him heartily, consorted with him familiarly, and counselled him faithfully; whereby his wrath presently subsided, and gave place to shame. Wherefore, casting away the sword that he held drawn in act to strike, he sprang from his horse, and weeping, threw himself at Nathan's feet, saying: — "Your liberality, dearest father, I acknowledge to be beyond all question, seeing with what craft you did plot your coming hither to yield me your life, for which, by mine own avowal, you knew that I, albeit cause I had none, did thirst. But God, more regardful of my duty than I myself, has now, in this moment of supreme stress, opened the eyes of my mind, that wretched envy had fast sealed. The prompter was your compliance, the greater is the debt of penitence that I owe you for my fault; wherefore wreak even such vengeance upon me as you may deem answerable to my transgression."

But Nathan raised Mitridanes to his feet, and tenderly embraced him, saying: — "My son, thy enterprise, howsoever thou mayst denote it, whether evil or otherwise, was not such that thou shouldst crave, or I give, pardon thereof; for 'twas not in malice but in that thou wouldst fain have been reputed better than I that thou ensuedst it. Doubt then no more of me; nay, rest assured that none that lives bears thee such love as I, who know the loftiness of thy spirit, bent not to heap up wealth, as do the caitiffs, but to dispense in bounty thine accumulated store. Think it no shame that to enhance thy reputation thou wouldst have slain me; nor deem that I marvel thereat. To slay not one man, as thou wast minded, but countless multitudes, to waste whole countries with fire, and to raze cities to the ground has been well-nigh the sole art, by which the mightiest emperors and the greatest kings have extended their dominions, and by consequence their fame. Wherefore, if thou, to increase thy fame, wouldst fain have slain me, 'twas nothing marvellous or strange, but wonted."

Whereto Mitridanes made answer, not to excuse his wicked design, but to commend the seemly excuse found for it by Nathan, whom at length he told how beyond measure he marvelled that Nathan had not only been consenting to the enterprise, but had aided him therein by his counsel.

But Nathan answered:—"Liefer had I, Mitridanes, that thou didst not marvel either at my consent or at my counsel, for that, since I was my own master and of a mind to that emprise whereon thou art also bent, never a soul came to my house, but, so far as in me lay, I gave him all that he asked of me. Thou camest, lusting for my life; and so, when I heard thee crave it of me, I forthwith, that thou mightst not be the only guest to depart hence ill content, resolved to give it thee; and to that end I gave thee such counsel as I deemed would serve thee both to the taking of my life and the preservation of thine own.

"Wherefore yet again I bid thee, nay, I entreat thee, if so thou art minded, to take it for thy satisfaction: I know not how I could better bestow it. I have had the use of it now for some eighty years, and pleasure and solace thereof; and I know that, by the course of Nature and the common lot of man and all things mundane, it can continue to be mine for but a little while; and so I deem that 'twere much better to bestow it, as I have ever bestowed and dispensed my wealth, than to keep it, until, against my will, it be reft from me by Nature. 'Twere but a trifle, though 'twere a hundred years: how insignificant, then, the six or eight years that are all I have to give! Take it, then, if thou hadst lief, take it, I pray thee; for, long as I have lived here, none have I found but thee to desire it; nor know I when I may find another, if thou take it not, to demand it of me. And if, peradventure, I should find one such, yet I know that the longer I keep it, the less its worth will be; wherefore, ere it be thus cheapened, take it, I implore thee."

Sore shame-stricken, Mitridanes made answer:—"Now God forefend that I should so much as harbour, as but now I did, such a thought, not to say do such a deed, as to wrest from you a thing so precious as your life, the years whereof, so far from abridging, I would gladly supplement with mine own."

"So then," rejoined Nathan promptly, "thou wouldst, if thou couldst, add thy years to mine, and cause me to serve thee as I never yet served any man, to wit, to take from thee that which is thine, I that never took aught from a soul!"

"Ay, that would I," returned Mitridanes.

"Then," quoth Nathan, "do as I shall bid thee. Thou art young: tarry here in my house, and call thyself Nathan; and I will get me to thy house, and ever call myself Mitridanes."

Whereto Mitridanes made answer:—"Were I but able to discharge this trust, as you have been and are, scarce would I hesitate to accept your offer; but, as too sure am I that aught that I might do would but serve to lower Nathan's fame, and I am not minded to mar that in another which I cannot mend in myself, accept it I will not."

After which and the like interchange of delectable discourse, Nathan and Mitridanes, by Nathan's desire, returned to the palace; where Nathan for some days honourably entreated Mitridanes, and by his sage counsel confirmed and encouraged him in his high and noble resolve; after which, Mitridanes, being minded to return home with his company, took his leave of Nathan, fully persuaded that 'twas not possible to surpass him in liberality.

STORY VI.

King Charles the Old, being conqueror, falls in love with a young maiden, and afterward growing ashamed of his folly bestows her and her sister honourably in marriage.

There is none of you but may not seldom have heard tell of King Charles the Old, or the First, by whose magnificent emprise, and the ensuing victory gained over King Manfred, the Ghibellines were driven forth of Florence, and the Guelfs returned thither. For which cause a knight, Messer Neri degli Uberti by name, departing Florence with his household and not a little money, resolved to fix his abode under no other sway than that of King Charles. And being fain of a lonely place in which to end his days in peace, he betook him to Castello da Mare di Stabia; and there, perchance a cross-bow-shot from the other houses of the place, amid the olives and hazels and chestnuts that abound in those parts, he bought an estate, on which he built a goodly house and commodious, with a pleasant garden beside it, in the midst of which, having no lack of running water, he set, after our Florentine fashion, a pond fair and clear, and speedily filled it with fish.

And while thus he lived, daily occupying himself with nought else but how to make his garden more fair, it befell that King Charles in the hot season betook him to Castello da Mare to refresh himself a while, and hearing of the beauty of Messer Neri's garden, was desirous to view it. And having learned to whom it belonged, he bethought him that, as the knight was an adherent of the party opposed to him, he would use more familiarity towards him than he would otherwise have done; and so he sent him word that he and four comrades would sup privily with him in his garden on the ensuing evening. Messer Neri felt himself much honoured; and having made his preparations with magnificence, and arranged the order of the ceremonies with his household, did all he could and knew to make the King cordially welcome to his fair garden.

When the King had viewed the garden throughout, as also Messer Neri's house, and commended them, he washed, and seated himself at one of the tables, which were set beside the pond, and bade Count

154

Guy de Montfort, who was one of his companions, sit on one side of him, and Messer Neri on the other, and the other three to serve, as they should be directed by Messer Neri. The dishes that were set before them were dainty, the wines excellent and rare, the order of the repast very fair and commendable, without the least noise or aught else that might distress; whereon the King bestowed no stinted praise.

As thus he gaily supped, well-pleased with the lovely spot, there came into the garden two young maidens, each perhaps fifteen years old, blonde both, their golden tresses falling all in ringlets about them, and crowned with a dainty garland of periwinkle-flowers; and so delicate and fair of face were they that they shewed liker to angels than aught else, each clad in a robe of finest linen, white as snow upon their flesh, close-fitting as might be from the waist up, but below the waist ample, like a pavilion to the feet. She that was foremost bore on her shoulders a pair of nets, which she held with her left hand, carrying in her right a long pole. Her companion followed, bearing on her left shoulder a frying-pan, under her left arm a bundle of faggots, and in her left hand a tripod, while in the other hand she carried a cruse of oil and a lighted taper. At sight of whom the King marvelled, and gazed intent to learn what it might import. The two young maidens came forward with becoming modesty, and did obeisance to the King; which done they hied them to the place of ingress to the pond, and she that had the frying-pan, having set it down, and afterward the other things, took the pole that the other carried, and so they both went down into the pond, being covered by its waters to their breasts.

Whereupon one of Messer Neri's servants, having forthwith lit a fire, and set the tripod on the faggots and oil therein, addressed himself to wait, until some fish should be thrown to him by the girls. Who, the one searching with the pole in those parts where she knew the fish lay hid, while the other made ready the nets, did in a brief space of time, to the exceeding great delight of the King, who watched them attentively, catch fish not a few, which they tossed to the servant, who set them, before the life was well out of them, in the frying-pan. After which, the maidens, as pre-arranged, addressed them to catch some of the finest fish, and cast them on to the table before the King, and Count Guy, and their father. The fish wriggled about the table to the prodigious delight of the King, who in like manner took some of them, and courteously returned them to the girls; with which sport they diverted them, until the servant had cooked the fish that had been given him: which, by Messer Neri's command, were set before the King rather as a side-dish than as aught very rare or delicious.

When the girls saw that all the fish were cooked, and that there was no occasion for them to catch any more, they came forth of the pond, their fine white garments cleaving everywhere close to their flesh so as to hide scarce any part of their delicate persons, took up again the things that they had brought, and passing modestly before the King, returned to the house. The King, and the Count, and the other gentlemen that waited, had regarded the maidens with no little attention, and had, one and all, inly bestowed on them no little praise, as being fair and shapely, and therewithal sweet and debonair; but 'twas in the King's eyes that they especially found favour. Indeed, as they came forth of the water, the King had scanned each part of their bodies so intently that, had one then pricked him, he would not have felt it, and his thoughts afterwards dwelling upon them, though he knew not who they were, nor how they came to be there, he felt stir within his heart a most ardent desire to pleasure them, whereby he knew very well that, if he took not care, he would grow enamoured; howbeit he knew not whether of the twain pleased him the more, so like was each to the other.

Having thus brooded a while, he turned to Messer Neri, and asked who the two damsels were. Whereto:—"Sire," replied Messer Neri, "they are my twin daughters, and they are called, the one, Ginevra the Fair, and the other, Isotta the Blonde."

Whereupon the King was loud in praise of them, and exhorted Messer Neri to bestow them in marriage. To which Messer Neri demurred, for that he no longer had the means. And nought of the supper now remaining to serve, save the fruit, in came the two young damsels in gowns of taffeta very fine, bearing in their hands two vast silver salvers full of divers fruits, such as the season yielded, and set them on the table before the King. Which done, they withdrew a little space and fell a singing to music a ditty, of which the opening words were as follows:—

Love, many words would not suffice
There where I am come to tell.

And so dulcet and and delightsome was the strain that to the King, his eyes and ears alike charmed, it seemed as if all the nine orders of angels were descended there to sing. The song ended, they knelt and respectfully craved the King's leave to depart; which, though sorely against his will, he gave them with a forced gaiety.

Supper ended, the King and his companions, having remounted their horses, took leave of Messer Neri, and conversing of divers matters, returned to the royal quarters; where the King, still harbouring his secret passion, nor, despite affairs of state that supervened, being able to forget the beauty and sweetness of Ginevra the Fair, for whose sake he likewise loved her twin sister, was so limed by Love that he could scarce think of aught else. So, feigning other reasons, he consorted familiarly with Messer Neri, and did much frequent his garden, that he might see Ginevra. And at length, being unable to endure his suffering any longer, and being minded, for that he could devise no other expedient, to despoil their father not only of the one but of the other damsel also, he discovered both his love and his project to Count Guy; who, being a good man and true, thus made answer:—

"Sire, your tale causes me not a little astonishment, and that more especially because of your conversation from your childhood to this very day, I have, methinks, known more than any other man. And as no such passion did I ever mark in you, even in your youth, when Love should more readily have fixed you with his fangs, as now I discern, when you are already on the verge of old age, 'tis to me so strange, so surprising that you should veritably love, that I deem it little short of a miracle. And were it meet for me to reprove you, well wot I the language I should hold to you, considering that you are yet in arms in a realm but lately won, among a people as yet unknown to you, and wily and treacherous in the extreme, and that the gravest anxieties and matters of high policy engross your mind, so that you are not as yet able to sit you down, and nevertheless amid all these weighty concerns you have given harbourage to false, flattering Love.

"This is not the wisdom of a great king, but the folly of a feather-pated boy. And moreover, what is far worse, you say that you are resolved to despoil this poor knight of his two daughters, whom, entertaining you in his house, and honouring you to the best of his power, he brought into your presence all but naked, testifying thereby, how great is his faith in you, and how assured he is that you are a king, and not a devouring wolf. Have you so soon forgotten that 'twas Manfred's outrageous usage of his subjects that opened you the way into this realm? What treachery was he ever guilty of that better merited eternal torment, than 'twould be in you to wrest from one that honourably entreats you at once his hope and his consolation? What would be said of you if so you should do? Perchance you deem that 'twould suffice to say:—'I did it because he is a Ghibelline.' Is it then consistent with the justice of a king that those, be they who they may, who seek his protection, as this man has sought yours, should be entreated after this sort?

"King, I bid you remember that exceeding great as is your glory to have vanquished Manfred, yet to conquer oneself is a still greater glory: wherefore you, to whom belongs the correction of others, see to it that you conquer yourself, and refrain this unruly passion; and let not such a blot mar the splendour of your achievements."

Sore stricken at heart by the Count's words, and the more mortified that he acknowledged their truth, the King heaved a fervent sigh or two, and then:—"Count," quoth he, "that enemy there is none, however mighty, but to the practised warrior is weak enough and easy to conquer in comparison of his own appetite, I make no doubt; but, great though the struggle will be and immeasurable the force that it demands, so shrewdly galled am I by your words, that not many days will have gone by before I shall without fail have done enough to shew you that I, that am the conqueror of others, am no less able to gain the victory over myself."

And indeed but a few days thereafter, the King, on his return to Naples, being minded at once to leave himself no excuse for dishonourable conduct, and to recompense the knight for his honourable entreatment of him, did, albeit 'twas hard for him to endow another with that which he had most ardently desired for himself, none the less resolve to bestow the two damsels in marriage, and that not as Messer Neri's daughters, but as his own. Wherefore, Messer Neri consenting, he provided both with magnificent dowries, and gave Ginevra the Fair to Messer Maffeo da Palizzi, and Isotta the Blonde to Messer Guglielmo della Magna, noble knights and great barons both; which done, sad at heart beyond measure, he betook him to Apulia, and by incessant travail did so mortify his vehement appetite that he snapped and broke in pieces the fetters of Love, and for the rest of his days was no more vexed by such passion.

Perchance there will be those who say that 'tis but a trifle for a king to bestow two girls in marriage; nor shall I dispute it: but say we that a king in love bestowed in marriage her whom he loved, neither having taken nor taking, of his love, leaf or flower or fruit; then this I say was a feat great indeed, nay, as great as might be.

After such a sort then did this magnificent King, at once generously rewarding the noble knight, commendably honouring the damsels that he loved, and stoutly subduing himself.

STORY X.

The Marquis of Saluzzo, overborne by the entreaties of his vassals, con-
sents to take a wife, but, being minded to please himself in the choice of
her, takes a husbandman's daughter. He has two children by her, both of
whom he makes her believe that he has put to death. Afterward, feigning
to be tired of her, and to have taken another wife, he turns her out of
doors in her shift, and brings his daughter into the house in guise of his
bride; but, finding her patient under it all, he brings her home again, and
shews her her children, now grown up, and honours her, and causes her
to be honoured, as Marchioness.

There was in olden days a certain Marquis of Saluzzo, Gualtieri by
name, a young man, but head of the house, who, having neither wife
nor child, passed his time in nought else but in hawking and hunting,
and of taking a wife and begetting children had no thought; wherein
he should have been accounted very wise: but his vassals, brooking it
ill, did oftentimes entreat him to take a wife, that he might not die without an heir, and they be left without a lord; offering to find him one of
such a pattern, and of such parentage, that he might marry with good
hope, and be well content with the sequel.

To whom:— "My friends," replied Gualtieri, "you enforce me to that
which I had resolved never to do, seeing how hard it is to find a wife,
whose ways accord well with one's own, and how plentiful is the supply
of such as run counter thereto, and how grievous a life he leads who
chances upon a lady that matches ill with him. And to say that you
think to know the daughters by the qualities of their fathers and mothers,
and thereby—so you would argue—to provide me with a wife to my
liking, is but folly; for I wot not how you may penetrate the secrets of
their mothers so as to know their fathers; and granted that you do know
them, daughters oftentimes resemble neither of their parents. However,
as you are minded to rivet these fetters upon me, I am content that so
it be; and that I may have no cause to reproach any but myself, should
it turn out ill, I am resolved that my wife shall be of my own choosing;
but of this rest assured, that, no matter whom I choose, if she receive

not from you the honour due to a lady, you shall prove to your great cost, how sorely I resent being thus constrained by your importunity to take a wife against my will."

The worthy men replied that they were well content, so only he would marry without more ado. And Gualtieri, who had long noted with approval the mien of a poor girl that dwelt on a farm hard by his house, and found her fair enough, deemed that with her he might pass a tolerably happy life. Wherefore he sought no further, but forthwith resolved to marry her; and having sent for her father, who was a very poor man, he contracted with him to take her to wife.

Which done, Gualtieri assembled all the friends he had in those parts, and:—"My friends," quoth he, "you were and are minded that I should take a wife, and rather to comply with your wishes, than for any desire that I had to marry, I have made up my mind to do so. You remember the promise you gave me, to wit, that, whomsoever I should take, you would pay her the honour due to a lady. Which promise I now require you to keep, the time being come when I am to keep mine. I have found hard by here a maiden after mine own heart, whom I purpose to take to wife, and to bring hither to my house in the course of a few days. Wherefore bethink you, how you may make the nuptial feast splendid, and welcome her with all honour; that I may confess myself satisfied with your observance of your promise, as you will be with my observance of mine."

The worthy men, one and all, answered with alacrity that they were well content, and that, whoever she might be, they would entreat her as a lady, and pay her all due honour as such. After which, they all addressed them to make goodly and grand and gladsome celebration of the event, as did also Gualtieri. He arranged for a wedding most stately and fair, and bade thereto a goodly number of his friends and kinsfolk, and great gentlemen, and others, of the neighbourhood; and therewithal he caused many a fine and costly robe to be cut and fashioned to the figure of a girl who seemed to him of the like proportions as the girl that he purposed to wed; and laid in store, besides, of girdles and rings, with a costly and beautiful crown, and all the other paraphernalia of a bride.

The day that he had appointed for the wedding being come, about half tierce he got him to horse with as many as had come to do him honour, and having made all needful dispositions:—"Gentlemen," quoth he, "'tis time to go bring home the bride."

And so away he rode with his company to the village; where, being come to the house of the girl's father, they found her returning from the spring with a bucket of water, making all the haste she could, that she might afterwards go with the other women to see Gualtieri's bride come by. Whom Gualtieri no sooner saw, than he called her by her name, to wit, Griselda, and asked her where her father was.

To whom she modestly made answer:—"My lord, he is in the house."

Whereupon Gualtieri dismounted, and having bidden the rest await him without, entered the cottage alone; and meeting her father, whose name was Giannucolo:—"I am come," quoth he, "to wed Griselda, but first of all there are some matters I would learn from her own lips in thy presence."

He then asked her, whether, if he took her to wife, she would study to comply with his wishes, and be not wroth, no matter what he might say or do, and be obedient, with not a few other questions of a like sort: to all which she answered, ay. Whereupon Gualtieri took her by the hand, led her forth, and before the eyes of all his company, and as many other folk as were there, caused her to strip naked, and let bring the garments that he had had fashioned for her, and had her forthwith arrayed therein, and upon her unkempt head let set a crown; and then, while all wondered:—"Gentlemen," quoth he, "this is she whom I purpose to make my wife, so she be minded to have me for husband."

Then, she standing abashed and astonied, he turned to her, saying:— "Griselda, wilt thou have me for thy husband?"

To whom:—"Ay, my lord," answered she.

"And I will have thee to wife," said he, and married her before them all. And having set her upon a palfrey, he brought her home with pomp.

The wedding was fair and stately, and had he married a daughter of the King of France, the feast could not have been more splendid. It seemed as if, with the change of her garb, the bride had acquired a new dignity of mind and mien. She was, as we have said, fair of form and feature; and therewithal she was now grown so engaging and gracious and debonair, that she shewed no longer as the shepherdess, and the daughter of Giannucolo, but as the daughter of some noble lord, insomuch that she caused as many as had known her before to marvel. Moreover, she was so obedient and devoted to her husband, that he deemed himself the happiest and luckiest man in the world. And likewise so gracious and kindly was she to her husband's vassals, that there was none of them but loved her more dearly than himself, and was zealous to do her honour, and prayed for her welfare and prosperity and aggrandisement, and instead of, as erstwhile, saying that Gualtieri had done foolishly to take her to wife, now averred that he had not his like in the world for wisdom and discernment, for that, save to him, her noble qualities would ever have remained hidden under her sorry apparel and the garb of the peasant girl. And in short she so comported herself as in no long time to bring it to pass that, not only in the marquisate, but far and wide besides, her virtues and her admirable conversation were matter of common talk, and, if aught had been said to the disadvantage of her husband, when he married her, the judgment was now altogether to the contrary effect.

She had not been long with Gualtieri before she conceived; and in due time she was delivered of a girl; whereat Gualtieri made great cheer. But, soon after, a strange humour took possession of him, to wit, to put her patience to the proof by prolonged and intolerable hard usage; wherefore he began by afflicting her with his gibes, putting on a vexed air, and telling her that his vassals were most sorely dissatisfied with her by reason of her base condition, and all the more so since they saw that she was a mother, and that they did nought but most ruefully murmur at the birth of a daughter.

Whereto Griselda, without the least change of countenance or sign of discomposure, made answer:—"My lord, do with me as thou mayst deem best for thine own honour and comfort, for well I wot that I am of less account than they, and unworthy of this honourable estate to which of thy courtesy thou hast advanced me."

By which answer Gualtieri was well pleased, witting that she was in no degree puffed up with pride by his, or any other's, honourable entreatment of her. A while afterwards, having in general terms given his wife to understand that the vassals could not endure her daughter, he sent her a message by a servant. So the servant came, and:—"Madam," quoth he with a most dolorous mien, "so I value my life, I must needs do my lord's bidding. He has bidden me take your daughter and . . . "

He said no more, but the lady by what she heard, and read in his face, and remembered of her husband's words, understood that he was bidden to put the child to death. Whereupon she presently took the child from the cradle, and having kissed and blessed her, albeit she was very sore at heart, she changed not countenance, but placed it in the servant's arms, saying:—

"See that thou leave nought undone that my lord and thine has charged thee to do, but leave her not so that the beasts and the birds devour her, unless he have so bidden thee." So the servant took the child, and told Gualtieri what the lady had said; and Gualtieri, marvelling at her constancy, sent him with the child to Bologna, to one of his kinswomen, whom he besought to rear and educate the child with all care, but never to let it be known whose child she was.

Soon after it befell that the lady again conceived, and in due time was delivered of a son, whereat Gualtieri was overjoyed. But, not content with what he had done, he now even more poignantly afflicted the lady; and one day with a ruffled mien:—"Wife," quoth he, "since thou gavest birth to this boy, I may on no wise live in peace with my vassals, so bitterly do they reproach me that a grandson of Giannucolo is to succeed me as their lord; and therefore I fear that, so I be not minded to be sent a packing hence, I must even do herein as I did before, and in the end put thee away, and take another wife."

The lady heard him patiently, and answered only:—"My lord, study how thou mayst content thee and best please thyself, and waste no thought upon me, for there is nought I desire save in so far as I know that 'tis thy pleasure."

Not many days after, Gualtieri, in like manner as he had sent for the daughter, sent for the son, and having made a shew of putting him to death, provided for his, as for the girl's, nurture at Bologna. Whereat the lady shewed no more discomposure of countenance or speech than at the loss of her daughter: which Gualtieri found passing strange, and inly affirmed that there was never another woman in the world that would have so done. And but that he had marked that she was most tenderly affectionate towards her children, while 'twas well pleasing to him, he had supposed that she was tired of them, whereas he knew that 'twas of her discretion that she so did. His vassals, who believed that he had put the children to death, held him mightily to blame for his cruelty, and felt the utmost compassion for the lady. She, however, said never aught to the ladies that condoled with her on the death of her children, but that the pleasure of him that had begotten them was her pleasure likewise.

Years not a few had passed since the girl's birth, when Gualtieri at length deemed the time come to put his wife's patience to the final proof. Accordingly, in the presence of a great company of his vassals he declared that on no wise might he longer brook to have Griselda to wife, that he confessed that in taking her he had done a sorry thing and the act of a stripling, and that he therefore meant to do what he could to procure the Pope's dispensation to put Griselda away, and take another wife: for which cause being much upbraided by many worthy men, he made no other answer but only that needs must it so be. Whereof the lady being apprised, and now deeming that she must look to go back to her father's house, and perchance tend the sheep, as she had aforetime, and see him, to whom she was utterly devoted, engrossed by another woman, did inly bewail herself right sorely: but still with the same composed mien with which she had borne Fortune's former buffets, she set herself to endure this last outrage. Nor was it long before Gualtieri by counterfeit letters, which he caused to be sent to him from Rome, made his vassals believe that the Pope had thereby given him a dispensation to put Griselda away, and take another wife.

Wherefore, having caused her to be brought before him, he said to her in the presence of not a few:—"Wife, by license granted me by the Pope, I am now free to put thee away, and take another wife; and, for that my forbears have always been great gentlemen and lords of these parts, whereas thine have ever been husbandmen, I purpose that thou go back to Giannucolo's house with the dowry that thou broughtest me; whereupon I shall bring home a lady that I have found, and who is meet to be my wife."

'Twas not without travail most grievous that the lady, as she heard this announcement, got the better of her woman's nature, and suppressing her tears, made answer:—

"My lord, I ever knew that my low degree was on no wise congruous with your nobility, and acknowledged that the rank I had with you was of your and God's bestowal, nor did I ever make as if it were mine by gift, or so esteem it, but still accounted it as a loan. 'Tis your pleasure to recall it, and therefore it should be, and is, my pleasure to render it up to you. So, here is your ring, with which you espoused me; take it back. You bid me take with me the dowry that I brought you; which to do will require neither paymaster on your part nor purse nor pack-horse on mine; for I am not unmindful that naked was I when you first had me. And if you deem it seemly that that body in which I have borne children, by you begotten, be beheld of all, naked will I depart; but yet, I pray you, be pleased, in guerdon of the virginity that I brought you and take not away, to suffer me to bear hence upon my back a single shift—I crave no more—besides my dowry."

There was nought of which Gualtieri was so fain as to weep; but yet, setting his face as a flint, he made answer:—"I allow thee a shift to thy back; so get thee hence."

All that stood by besought him to give her a robe, that she, who had been his wife for thirteen years and more, might not be seen to quit his house in so sorry and shameful a plight, having nought on her but a shift. But their entreaties went for nothing: the lady in her shift, and barefoot and bareheaded, having bade them adieu, departed the house, and went back to her father amid the tears and lamentations of all that saw her. Giannucolo, who had ever deemed it a thing incredible that Gualtieri should keep his daughter to wife, and had looked for this to happen every day, and had kept the clothes that she had put off on the morning that Gualtieri had wedded her, now brought them to her; and she, having resumed them, applied herself to the petty drudgery of her father's house, as she had been wont, enduring with fortitude this cruel visitation of adverse Fortune.

Now no sooner had Gualtieri dismissed Griselda, than he gave his vassals to understand that he had taken to wife a daughter of one of the Counts of Panago. He accordingly made great preparations as for the nuptials, during which he sent for Griselda. To whom, being come, quoth he:—

"I am bringing hither my new bride, and in this her first home-coming I purpose to shew her honour; and thou knowest that women I have none in the house that know how to set chambers in due order, or attend to the many other matters that so joyful an event requires; wherefore do thou, that understandest these things better than another, see to all that needs be done, and bid hither such ladies as thou mayst see fit, and receive them, as if thou wert the lady of the house, and then, when the nuptials are ended, thou mayst go back to thy cottage."

Albeit each of these words pierced Griselda's heart like a knife, for that, in resigning her good fortune, she had not been able to renounce the love she bore Gualtieri, nevertheless:—"My lord," she made answer, "I am ready and prompt to do your pleasure."

And so, clad in her sorry garments of coarse romagnole, she entered the house, which, but a little before, she had quitted in her shift, and addressed her to sweep the chambers, and arrange arras and cushions in the halls, and make ready the kitchen, and set her hand to everything, as if she had been a paltry serving-wench: nor did she rest until she had brought all into such meet and seemly trim as the occasion demanded. This done, she invited in Gualtieri's name all the ladies of those parts to be present at his nuptials, and awaited the event. The day being come, still wearing her sorry weeds, but in heart and soul and mien the lady, she received the ladies as they came, and gave each a gladsome greeting.

Now Gualtieri, as we said, had caused his children to be carefully nurtured and brought up by a kinswoman of his at Bologna, which kinswoman was married into the family of the Counts of Panago; and, the girl being now twelve years old, and the loveliest creature that ever was seen, and the boy being about six years old, he had sent word to his kinswoman's husband at Bologna, praying him to be pleased to come with this girl and boy of his to Saluzzo, and to see that he brought a goodly and honourable company with him, and to give all to understand that he brought the girl to him to wife, and on no wise to disclose to any, who she really was.

The gentlemen did as the Marquis bade him, and within a few days of his setting forth arrived at Saluzzo about breakfast-time with the girl, and her brother, and a noble company, and found all the folk of those parts, and much people besides, gathered there in expectation of Gualtieri's new bride. Who, being received by the ladies, was no sooner come into the hall, where the tables were set, than Griselda advanced to meet her, saying with hearty cheer:—"Welcome, my lady."

So the ladies, who had with much instance, but in vain, besought Gualtieri, either to let Griselda keep in another room, or at any rate to furnish her with one of the robes that had been hers, that she might not present herself in such a sorry guise before the strangers, sate down to table; and the service being begun, the eyes of all were set on the girl, and every one said that Gualtieri had made a good exchange, and Griselda joined with the rest in greatly commending her, and also her little brother.

And now Gualtieri, sated at last with all that he had seen of his wife's patience, marking that this new and strange turn made not the least alteration in her demeanour, and being well assured that 'twas not due to apathy, for he knew her to be of excellent understanding, deemed it time to relieve her of the suffering which he judged her to dissemble under a resolute front; and so, having called her to him in presence of them all, he said with a smile:—"And what thinkst thou of our bride?"

"My lord," replied Griselda, "I think mighty well of her; and if she be but as discreet as she is fair—and so I deem her—I make no doubt but you may reckon to lead with her a life of incomparable felicity; but with all earnestness I entreat you, that you spare her those tribulations which you did once inflict upon another that was yours, for I scarce think she would be able to bear them, as well because she is younger, as for that she has been delicately nurtured, whereas that other had known no respite of hardship since she was but a little child."

Marking that she made no doubt but that the girl was to be his wife, and yet spoke never a whit the less sweetly, Gualtieri caused her to sit down beside him, and:—"Griselda," said he, "'tis now time that thou see the reward of thy long patience, and that those, who have deemed me cruel and unjust and insensate, should know that what I did was done of purpose aforethought, for that I was minded to give both thee and them a lesson, that thou mightst learn to be a wife, and they in like manner might learn how to take and keep a wife, and that I might beget me perpetual peace with thee for the rest of my life; whereof being in great fear, when I came to take a wife, lest I should be disappointed, I therefore, to put the matter to the proof, did, and how sorely thou knowest, harass and afflict thee. And since I never knew thee either by deed or by word to deviate from my will, I now, deeming myself to have of thee that assurance of happiness which I desired, am minded to restore to thee at once all that, step by step, I took from thee, and by extremity of joy to compensate the tribulations that I inflicted on thee. Receive, then, this girl, whom thou supposest to be my bride, and her brother, with glad heart, as thy children and mine. These are they, whom by thee and many another it has long been supposed that I did ruthlessly to death, and I am thy husband, that loves thee more dearly than aught else, deeming that other there is none that has the like good cause to be well content with his wife."

Which said, he embraced and kissed her; and then, while she wept for joy, they rose and hied them there where sate the daughter, all astonied to hear the news, whom, as also her brother, they tenderly embraced, and explained to them, and many others that stood by, the whole mystery. Whereat the ladies, transported with delight, rose from table and betook

them with Griselda to a chamber, and, with better omen, divested her
of her sorry garb, and arrayed her in one of her own robes of state; and
so, in guise of a lady (howbeit in her rags she had shewed as no less)
they led her back into the hall. Wondrous was the cheer which there
they made with the children; and, all overjoyed at the event, they
revelled and made merry amain, and prolonged the festivities for several
days; and very discreet they pronounced Gualtieri, albeit they censured
as intolerably harsh the probation to which he had subjected Griselda,
and most discreet beyond all compare they accounted Griselda.

Some days after, the Count of Panago returned to Bologna, and
Gualtieri took Giannucolo from his husbandry, and established him in
honour as his father-in-law, wherein to his great solace he lived for
the rest of his days. Gualtieri himself, having mated his daughter with
a husband of high degree, lived long and happily thereafter with Griselda,
to whom he ever paid all honour.

Now what shall we say in this case but that even into the cots of the
poor the heavens let fall at times spirits divine, as into the palaces of
kings souls that are fitter to tend hogs than to exercise lordship over
men? Who but Griselda had been able, with a countenance not only
tearless, but cheerful, to endure the heard and unheard-of trials to
which Gualtieri subjected her? Who perhaps might have deemed himself to have made no bad investment, had he chanced upon one, who,
having been turned out of his house in her shift, had found means so
to dust the pelisse of another as to get herself thereby a fine robe.

So ended Dioneo's story, whereof the ladies, diversely inclining, one
to censure where another found matter for commendation, had discoursed not a little, when the king, having glanced at the sky, and marked
that the sun was now low, insomuch that 'twas nigh the vesper hour,
still keeping his seat, thus began:—

"Exquisite my ladies, as, methinks, you wot, 'tis not only in minding
them of the past and apprehending the present that the wit of mortals
consists; but by one means or the other to be able to foresee the future
is by the sages accounted the height of wisdom. Now, to-morrow, as you
know, 'twill be fifteen days since, in quest of recreation and for the con-
servation of our health and life, we, shunning the dismal and dolorous
and afflicting spectacles that have ceased not in our city since this season
of pestilence began, took our departure from Florence. Wherein, to my
thinking, we have done nought that was not seemly; for, if I have duly
used my powers of observation, albeit some gay stories, and of a kind to
stimulate concupiscence, have here been told, and we have daily
known no lack of dainty dishes and good wine, nor yet of music and
song, things, one and all, apt to incite weak minds to that which is not

seemly, neither on your part, nor on ours, have I marked deed or word, or aught of any kind, that called for reprehension; but, by what I have seen and heard, seemliness and the sweet intimacy of brothers and sisters have ever reigned among us. Which, assuredly, for the honour and advantage which you and I have had thereof, is most grateful to me.

"Wherefore, lest too long continuance in this way of life might beget some occasion of weariness, and that no man may be able to misconstrue our too long abidance here, and as we have all of us had our day's share of the honour which still remains in me, I should deem it meet, so you be of like mind, that we now go back whence we came: and that the rather that our company, the bruit whereof has already reached divers others that are in our neighbourhood, might be so increased that all our pleasure would be destroyed. And so, if my counsel meet with your approval, I will keep the crown I have received of you until our departure, which, I purpose, shall be to-morrow morning. Should you decide otherwise, I have already determined whom to crown for the ensuing day."

Much debate ensued among the ladies and young men; but in the end they approved the king's proposal as expedient and seemly; and resolved to do even as he had said. The king therefore summoned the seneschal; and having conferred with him of the order he was to observe on the morrow, he dismissed the company until supper-time. So, the king being risen, the ladies and the rest likewise rose, and betook them, as they were wont, to their several diversions. Supper-time being come, they supped with exceeding great delight. Which done, they addressed them to song and music and dancing; and, while Lauretta was leading a dance, the king bade Fiammetta give them a song; whereupon Fiammetta right debonairly sang on this wise: —

> So came but Love, and brought no jealousy,
>   So blithe, I wot, as I,
>   Dame were there none, be she whoe'er she be.
>
> If youth's fresh, lusty pride
>   May lady of her lover well content,
>   Or valour's just renown,
>   Hardihood, prowess tried,
>   Wit, noble mien, discourse most excellent,
>   And of all grace the crown;
>   That she am I, who, fain for love to swoun,
>   There where my hope doth lie
>   These several virtues all conjoined do see.

But, for that I less wise
 Than me no whit do other dames discern,
 Trembling with sore dismay,
 I still the worst surmise,
 Deeming their hearts with the same flame to burn
 That of mine maketh prey:
 Wherefore of him that is my hope's one stay
 Disconsolate I sigh,
 Yea mightily, and daily do me dree.

If but my lord as true
 As worthy to be loved I might approve,
 I were not jealous then:
 But, for that charmer new
 Doth all too often gallant lure to love,
 Forsworn I hold all men,
 And sick at heart I am, of death full fain;
 Nor lady doth him eye,
 But I do quake, lest she him wrest from me.

'Fore God, then, let each she
 List to my prayer, nor e'er in my despite
 Such grievous wrong essay;
 For should there any be
 That by or speech or mien's allurements light
 Of him to rob me may
 Study or plot, I, witting, shall find way,
 My beauty it aby!
 To cause her sore lament such frenesie.

As soon as Fiammetta had ended her song, Dioneo, who was beside her, said with a laugh:—"Madam, 'twould be a great courtesy on your part to do all ladies to wit, who he is, that he be not stolen from you in ignorance, seeing that you threaten such dire resentment."

Several other songs followed; and it being then nigh upon midnight, all, as the king was pleased to order, betook them to rest. With the first light of the new day they rose, and, the seneschal having already conveyed thence all their chattels, they, following the lead of their discreet king, hied them back to Florence; and in Santa Maria Novella, whence they had set forth, the three young men took leave of the seven ladies, and departed to find other diversions elsewhere, while the ladies in due time repaired to their homes.

DOVER·THRIFT·EDITIONS

POETRY

"MINIVER CHEEVY" AND OTHER POEMS, Edwin Arlington Robinson. 64pp. 28756-4 $1.00

EARLY POEMS, Ezra Pound. 80pp. (Available in U.S. only) 28745-9 $1.00

EARLY POEMS, William Carlos Williams. 64pp. (Available in U.S. only) 29294-0 $1.00

"THE WASTE LAND" AND OTHER POEMS, T. S. Eliot. 64pp. (Available in U.S. only) 40061-1 $1.00

RENASCENCE AND OTHER POEMS, Edna St. Vincent Millay. 64pp. (Available in U.S. only) 26873-X $1.00

SELECTED POEMS, John Milton. 128pp. 27554-X $1.50

SELECTED CANTERBURY TALES, Geoffrey Chaucer. 144pp. 28241-4 $1.00

GREAT SONNETS, Paul Negri (ed.). 96pp. 28052-7 $1.00

CIVIL WAR POETRY: An Anthology, Paul Negri. 128pp. 29883-3 $1.50

WAR IS KIND AND OTHER POEMS, Stephen Crane. 64pp. 40424-2 $1.00

THE RAVEN AND OTHER FAVORITE POEMS, Edgar Allan Poe. 64pp. 26685-0 $1.00

ESSAY ON MAN AND OTHER POEMS, Alexander Pope. 128pp. 28053-5 $1.50

GOBLIN MARKET AND OTHER POEMS, Christina Rossetti. 64pp. 28055-1 $1.00

CHICAGO POEMS, Carl Sandburg. 80pp. 28057-8 $1.00

THE SHOOTING OF DAN MCGREW AND OTHER POEMS, Robert Service. 96pp. (Available in U.S. only) 27556-6 $1.00

COMPLETE SONNETS, William Shakespeare. 80pp. 26686-9 $1.00

SELECTED POEMS, Percy Bysshe Shelley. 128pp. 27558-2 $1.50

100 BEST-LOVED POEMS, Philip Smith (ed.). 96pp. 28553-7 $1.00

101 GREAT AMERICAN POEMS, The American Poetry & Literacy Project (ed.). (Available in U.S. only) 40158-8 $1.00

NATIVE AMERICAN SONGS AND POEMS: An Anthology, Brian Swann (ed.). 64pp. 29450-1 $1.00

SELECTED POEMS, Alfred Lord Tennyson. 112pp. 27282-6 $1.00

LITTLE ORPHANT ANNIE AND OTHER POEMS, James Whitcomb Riley. 80pp. 28260-0 $1.00

CHRISTMAS CAROLS: COMPLETE VERSES, Shane Weller (ed.). 64pp. 27397-0 $1.00

GREAT LOVE POEMS, Shane Weller (ed.). 128pp. 27284-2 $1.00

LOVE: A Book of Quotations, Herb Galewitz (ed.). 64pp. 40004-2 $1.00

EVANGELINE AND OTHER POEMS, Henry Wadsworth Longfellow. 64pp. 28255-4 $1.00

CIVIL WAR POETRY AND PROSE, Walt Whitman. 96pp. 28507-3 $1.00

SELECTED POEMS, Walt Whitman. 128pp. 26878-0 $1.00

THE BALLAD OF READING GAOL AND OTHER POEMS, Oscar Wilde. 64pp. 27072-6 $1.00

FAVORITE POEMS, William Wordsworth. 80pp. 27073-4 $1.00

WORLD WAR ONE BRITISH POETS: Brooke, Owen, Sassoon, Rosenberg and Others, Candace Ward (ed.). (Available in U.S. only) 29568-0 $1.00

THE CAVALIER POETS: An Anthology, Thomas Crofts (ed.). 80pp. 28766-1 $1.00

ENGLISH ROMANTIC POETRY: An Anthology, Stanley Appelbaum (ed.). 256pp. 29282-7 $2.00

EARLY POEMS, William Butler Yeats. 128pp. 27808-5 $1.50

"EASTER, 1916" AND OTHER POEMS, William Butler Yeats. 80pp. (Available in U.S. only) 29771-3 $1.00

DOVER · THRIFT · EDITIONS

FICTION

FLATLAND: A ROMANCE OF MANY DIMENSIONS, Edwin A. Abbott. 96pp. 27263-X $1.00

PERSUASION, Jane Austen. 224pp. 29555-9 $2.00

PRIDE AND PREJUDICE, Jane Austen. 272pp. 28473-5 $2.00

SENSE AND SENSIBILITY, Jane Austen. 272pp. 29049-2 $2.00

WUTHERING HEIGHTS, Emily Brontë. 256pp. 29256-8 $2.00

BEOWULF, Beowulf (trans. by R. K. Gordon). 64pp. 27264-8 $1.00

CIVIL WAR STORIES, Ambrose Bierce. 128pp. 28038-1 $1.00

THE AUTOBIOGRAPHY OF AN EX-COLORED MAN, James Weldon Johnson. 112pp. 28512-X $1.00

TARZAN OF THE APES, Edgar Rice Burroughs. 224pp. (Available in U.S. only) 29570-2 $2.00

ALICE'S ADVENTURES IN WONDERLAND, Lewis Carroll. 96pp. 27543-4 $1.00

O PIONEERS!, Willa Cather. 128pp. 27785-2 $1.00

MY ÁNTONIA, Willa Cather. 176pp. 28240-6 $2.00

PAUL'S CASE AND OTHER STORIES, Willa Cather. 64pp. 29057-3 $1.00

IN A GERMAN PENSION: 13 Stories, Katherine Mansfield. 112pp. 28719-X $1.50

THE STORY OF AN AFRICAN FARM, Olive Schreiner. 256pp. 40165-0 $2.00

"THE YELLOW WALLPAPER" AND OTHER STORIES, Charlotte Perkins Gilman. 80pp. 29857-4 $1.00

HERLAND, Charlotte Perkins Gilman. 128pp. 40429-3 $1.50

FIVE GREAT SHORT STORIES, Anton Chekhov. 96pp. 26463-7 $1.00

"THE FIDDLER OF THE REELS" AND OTHER SHORT STORIES, Thomas Hardy. 80pp. 29960-0 $1.50

FAVORITE FATHER BROWN STORIES, G. K. Chesterton. 96pp. 27545-0 $1.00

THE WARDEN, Anthony Trollope. 176pp. 40076-X $2.00

THE COUNTRY OF THE POINTED FIRS, Sarah Orne Jewett. 96pp. 28196-5 $1.00

GREAT SHORT STORIES BY AMERICAN WOMEN, Candace Ward (ed.). 192pp. 28776-9 $2.00

SHORT STORIES, Louisa May Alcott. 64pp. 29063-8 $1.00

THE AWAKENING, Kate Chopin. 128pp. 27786-0 $1.00

A PAIR OF SILK STOCKINGS AND OTHER STORIES, Kate Chopin. 64pp. 29264-9 $1.00

THE REVOLT OF "MOTHER" AND OTHER STORIES, Mary E. Wilkins Freeman. 128pp. 40428-5 $1.50

HEART OF DARKNESS, Joseph Conrad. 80pp. 26464-5 $1.00

THE SECRET SHARER AND OTHER STORIES, Joseph Conrad. 128pp. 27546-9 $1.00

THE "LITTLE REGIMENT" AND OTHER CIVIL WAR STORIES, Stephen Crane. 80pp. 29557-5 $1.00

THE OPEN BOAT AND OTHER STORIES, Stephen Crane. 128pp. 27547-7 $1.50

THE RED BADGE OF COURAGE, Stephen Crane. 112pp. 26465-3 $1.00

A CHRISTMAS CAROL, Charles Dickens. 80pp. 26865-9 $1.00

THE CRICKET ON THE HEARTH AND OTHER CHRISTMAS STORIES, Charles Dickens. 128pp. 28039-X $1.00

THE DOUBLE, Fyodor Dostoyevsky. 128pp. 29572-9 $1.50

NOTES FROM THE UNDERGROUND, Fyodor Dostoyevsky. 96pp. 27053-X $1.00

THE GAMBLER, Fyodor Dostoyevsky. 112pp. 29081-6 $1.50

THE ADVENTURE OF THE DANCING MEN AND OTHER STORIES, Sir Arthur Conan Doyle. 80pp. 29558-3 $1.00

THE HOUND OF THE BASKERVILLES, Arthur Conan Doyle. 128pp. 28214-7 $1.00

SIX GREAT SHERLOCK HOLMES STORIES, Sir Arthur Conan Doyle. 112pp. 27055-6 $1.00

SILAS MARNER, George Eliot. 160pp. 29246-0 $1.50

DOVER·THRIFT·EDITIONS

FICTION

MADAME BOVARY, Gustave Flaubert. 256pp. 29257-6 $2.00

WHERE ANGELS FEAR TO TREAD, E. M. Forster. 128pp. (Available in U.S. only) 27791-7 $1.50

A ROOM WITH A VIEW, E. M. Forster. 176pp. (Available in U.S. only) 28467-0 $2.00

THE OVERCOAT AND OTHER STORIES, Nikolai Gogol. 112pp. 27057-2 $1.50

GREAT GHOST STORIES, John Grafton (ed.). 112pp. 27270-2 $1.00

"THE MOONLIT ROAD" AND OTHER GHOST AND HORROR STORIES, Ambrose Bierce (John Grafton, ed.). 96pp. 40056-5 $1.00

THE MABINOGION, Lady Charlotte E. Guest. 192pp. 29541-9 $2.00

WINESBURG, OHIO, Sherwood Anderson. 160pp. 28269-4 $2.00

THE LUCK OF ROARING CAMP AND OTHER STORIES, Bret Harte. 96pp. 27271-0 $1.00

THIS SIDE OF PARADISE, F. Scott Fitzgerald. 208pp. 28999-0 $2.00

"THE DIAMOND AS BIG AS THE RITZ" AND OTHER STORIES, F. Scott Fitzgerald. 29991-0 $2.00

THE SCARLET LETTER, Nathaniel Hawthorne. 192pp. 28048-9 $2.00

YOUNG GOODMAN BROWN AND OTHER STORIES, Nathaniel Hawthorne. 128pp. 27060-2 $1.00

THE GIFT OF THE MAGI AND OTHER SHORT STORIES, O. Henry. 96pp. 27061-0 $1.00

THE NUTCRACKER AND THE GOLDEN POT, E. T. A. Hoffmann. 128pp. 27806-9 $1.00

THE BEAST IN THE JUNGLE AND OTHER STORIES, Henry James. 128pp. 27552-3 $1.00

DAISY MILLER, Henry James. 64pp. 28773-4 $1.00

WASHINGTON SQUARE, Henry James. 176pp. 40431-5 $2.00

THE TURN OF THE SCREW, Henry James. 96pp. 26684-2 $1.00

DUBLINERS, James Joyce. 160pp. 26870-5 $1.00

A PORTRAIT OF THE ARTIST AS A YOUNG MAN, James Joyce. 192pp. 28050-0 $2.00

DEATH IN VENICE, Thomas Mann. 96pp. (Available in U.S. only) 28714-9 $1.00

THE METAMORPHOSIS AND OTHER STORIES, Franz Kafka. 96pp. 29030-1 $1.50

THE MAN WHO WOULD BE KING AND OTHER STORIES, Rudyard Kipling. 128pp. 28051-9 $1.50

SREDNI VASHTAR AND OTHER STORIES, Saki (H. H. Munro). 96pp. 28521-9 $1.00

THE OIL JAR AND OTHER STORIES, Luigi Pirandello. 96pp. 28459-X $1.00

SELECTED SHORT STORIES, D. H. Lawrence. 128pp. 27794-1 $1.00

GREEN TEA AND OTHER GHOST STORIES, J. Sheridan LeFanu. 96pp. 27795-X $1.00

SHORT STORIES, Theodore Dreiser. 112pp. 28215-5 $1.50

THE CALL OF THE WILD, Jack London. 64pp. 26472-6 $1.00

FIVE GREAT SHORT STORIES, Jack London. 96pp. 27063-7 $1.00

WHITE FANG, Jack London. 160pp. 26968-X $1.00

THE NECKLACE AND OTHER SHORT STORIES, Guy de Maupassant. 128pp. 27064-5 $1.00

BARTLEBY AND BENITO CERENO, Herman Melville. 112pp. 26473-4 $1.00

THE GOLD-BUG AND OTHER TALES, Edgar Allan Poe. 128pp. 26875-6 $1.00

TALES OF TERROR AND DETECTION, Edgar Allan Poe. 96pp. 28744-0 $1.00

DETECTION BY GASLIGHT, Douglas G. Greene (ed.). 272pp. 29928-7 $2.00

THE THIRTY-NINE STEPS, John Buchan. 96pp. 28201-5 $1.50

THE QUEEN OF SPADES AND OTHER STORIES, Alexander Pushkin. 128pp. 28054-3 $1.50

FIRST LOVE AND DIARY OF A SUPERFLUOUS MAN, Ivan Turgenev. 96pp. 28775-0 $1.50

FATHERS AND SONS, Ivan Turgenev. 176pp. 40073-5 $2.00

FRANKENSTEIN, Mary Shelley. 176pp. 28211-2 $1.00

THREE LIVES, Gertrude Stein. 176pp. (Available in U.S. only) 28059-4 $2.00

FICTION

FLATLAND: A ROMANCE OF MANY DIMENSIONS, Edwin A. Abbott. 96pp. 27263-X $1.00

PERSUASION, Jane Austen. 224pp. 29555-9 $2.00

PRIDE AND PREJUDICE, Jane Austen. 272pp. 28473-5 $2.00

SENSE AND SENSIBILITY, Jane Austen. 272pp. 29049-2 $2.00

WUTHERING HEIGHTS, Emily Brontë. 256pp. 29256-8 $2.00

BEOWULF, Beowulf (trans. by R. K. Gordon). 64pp. 27264-8 $1.00

CIVIL WAR STORIES, Ambrose Bierce. 128pp. 28038-1 $1.00

THE AUTOBIOGRAPHY OF AN EX-COLORED MAN, James Weldon Johnson. 112pp. 28512-X $1.00

TARZAN OF THE APES, Edgar Rice Burroughs. 224pp. (Available in U.S. only) 29570-2 $2.00

ALICE'S ADVENTURES IN WONDERLAND, Lewis Carroll. 96pp. 27543-4 $1.00

O PIONEERS!, Willa Cather. 128pp. 27785-2 $1.00

MY ÁNTONIA, Willa Cather. 176pp. 28240-6 $2.00

PAUL'S CASE AND OTHER STORIES, Willa Cather. 64pp. 29057-3 $1.00

IN A GERMAN PENSION: 13 Stories, Katherine Mansfield. 112pp. 28719-X $1.50

THE STORY OF AN AFRICAN FARM, Olive Schreiner. 256pp. 40165-0 $2.00

"THE YELLOW WALLPAPER" AND OTHER STORIES, Charlotte Perkins Gilman. 80pp. 29857-4 $1.00

HERLAND, Charlotte Perkins Gilman. 128pp. 40429-3 $1.50

FIVE GREAT SHORT STORIES, Anton Chekhov. 96pp. 26463-7 $1.00

"THE FIDDLER OF THE REELS" AND OTHER SHORT STORIES, Thomas Hardy. 80pp. 29960-0 $1.50

FAVORITE FATHER BROWN STORIES, G. K. Chesterton. 96pp. 27545-0 $1.00

THE WARDEN, Anthony Trollope. 176pp. 40076-X $2.00

THE COUNTRY OF THE POINTED FIRS, Sarah Orne Jewett. 96pp. 28196-5 $1.00

GREAT SHORT STORIES BY AMERICAN WOMEN, Candace Ward (ed.). 192pp. 28776-9 $2.00

SHORT STORIES, Louisa May Alcott. 64pp. 29063-8 $1.00

THE AWAKENING, Kate Chopin. 128pp. 27786-0 $1.00

A PAIR OF SILK STOCKINGS AND OTHER STORIES, Kate Chopin. 64pp. 29264-9 $1.00

THE REVOLT OF "MOTHER" AND OTHER STORIES, Mary E. Wilkins Freeman. 128pp. 40428-5 $1.50

HEART OF DARKNESS, Joseph Conrad. 80pp. 26464-5 $1.00

THE SECRET SHARER AND OTHER STORIES, Joseph Conrad. 128pp. 27546-9 $1.00

THE "LITTLE REGIMENT" AND OTHER CIVIL WAR STORIES, Stephen Crane. 80pp. 29557-5 $1.00

THE OPEN BOAT AND OTHER STORIES, Stephen Crane. 128pp. 27547-7 $1.50

THE RED BADGE OF COURAGE, Stephen Crane. 112pp. 26465-3 $1.00

A CHRISTMAS CAROL, Charles Dickens. 80pp. 26865-9 $1.00

THE CRICKET ON THE HEARTH AND OTHER CHRISTMAS STORIES, Charles Dickens. 128pp. 28039-X $1.00

THE DOUBLE, Fyodor Dostoyevsky. 128pp. 29572-9 $1.50

NOTES FROM THE UNDERGROUND, Fyodor Dostoyevsky. 96pp. 27053-X $1.00

THE GAMBLER, Fyodor Dostoyevsky. 112pp. 29081-6 $1.50

THE ADVENTURE OF THE DANCING MEN AND OTHER STORIES, Sir Arthur Conan Doyle. 80pp. 29558-3 $1.00

THE HOUND OF THE BASKERVILLES, Arthur Conan Doyle. 128pp. 28214-7 $1.00

SIX GREAT SHERLOCK HOLMES STORIES, Sir Arthur Conan Doyle. 112pp. 27055-6 $1.00

SILAS MARNER, George Eliot. 160pp. 29246-0 $1.50

DOVER · THRIFT · EDITIONS

NONFICTION

A MODEST PROPOSAL AND OTHER SATIRICAL WORKS, Jonathan Swift. 64pp. 28759-9 $1.00

UTOPIA, Sir Thomas More. 96pp. 29583-4 $1.50

THE AUTOBIOGRAPHY OF BENJAMIN FRANKLIN, Benjamin Franklin. 144pp. 29073-5 $1.50

COMMON SENSE, Thomas Paine. 64pp. 29602-4 $1.00

THE STORY OF MY LIFE, Helen Keller. 80pp. 29249-5 $1.00

GREAT SPEECHES, Abraham Lincoln. 112pp. 26872-1 $1.00

THE PRINCE, Niccolò Machiavelli. 80pp. 27274-5 $1.00

PRAGMATISM, William James. 128pp. 28270-8 $1.50

TOTEM AND TABOO, Sigmund Freud. 176pp. (Available in U.S. only) 40434-X $2.00

POETICS, Aristotle. 64pp. 29577-X $1.00

NICOMACHEAN ETHICS, Aristotle. 256pp. 40096-4 $2.00

MEDITATIONS, Marcus Aurelius. 128pp. 29823-X $1.50

SYMPOSIUM AND PHAEDRUS, Plato. 96pp. 27798-4 $1.50

THE TRIAL AND DEATH OF SOCRATES: Four Dialogues, Plato. 128pp. 27066-1 $1.00

THE BIRTH OF TRAGEDY, Friedrich Nietzsche. 96pp. 28515-4 $1.50

BEYOND GOOD AND EVIL: Prelude to a Philosophy of the Future, Friedrich Nietzsche. 176pp. 29868-X $1.50

CONFESSIONS OF AN ENGLISH OPIUM EATER, Thomas De Quincey. 80pp. 28742-4 $1.00

CIVIL DISOBEDIENCE AND OTHER ESSAYS, Henry David Thoreau. 96pp. 27563-9 $1.00

SELECTIONS FROM THE JOURNALS (Edited by Walter Harding), Herny David Thoreau. 96pp. 28760-2 $1.00

WALDEN; OR, LIFE IN THE WOODS, Henry David Thoreau. 224pp. 28495-6 $2.00

THE LAND OF LITTLE RAIN, Mary Austin. 96pp. 29037-9 $1.50

THE THEORY OF THE LEISURE CLASS, Thorstein Veblen. 256pp. 28062-4 $2.00

PLAYS

PROMETHEUS BOUND, Aeschylus. 64pp. 28762-9 $1.00

THE ORESTEIA TRILOGY: Agamemnon, The Libation-Bearers and The Furies, Aeschylus. 160pp. 29242-8 $1.50

LYSISTRATA, Aristophanes. 64pp. 28225-2 $1.00

WHAT EVERY WOMAN KNOWS, James Barrie. 80pp. (Available in U.S. only) 29578-8 $1.50

THE CHERRY ORCHARD, Anton Chekhov. 64pp. 26682-6 $1.00

THE THREE SISTERS, Anton Chekhov. 64pp. 27544-2 $1.00

UNCLE VANYA, Anton Chekhov. 64pp. 40159-6 $1.50

THE INSPECTOR GENERAL, Nikolai Gogol. 80pp. 28500-6 $1.50

THE WAY OF THE WORLD, William Congreve. 80pp. 27787-9 $1.50

BACCHAE, Euripides. 64pp. 29580-X $1.00

MEDEA, Euripides. 64pp. 27548-5 $1.00

THE MIKADO, William Schwenck Gilbert. 64pp. 27268-0 $1.50

FAUST, PART ONE, Johann Wolfgang von Goethe. 192pp. 28046-2 $2.00

SHE STOOPS TO CONQUER, Oliver Goldsmith. 80pp. 26867-5 $1.50

A DOLL'S HOUSE, Henrik Ibsen. 80pp. 27062-9 $1.00

HEDDA GABLER, Henrik Ibsen. 80pp. 26469-6 $1.50

GHOSTS, Henrik Ibsen. 64pp. 29852-3 $1.50

VOLPONE, Ben Jonson. 112pp. 28049-7 $1.50

DR. FAUSTUS, Christopher Marlowe. 64pp. 28208-2 $1.00

THE MISANTHROPE, Molière. 64pp. 27065-3 $1.00

DOVER·THRIFT·EDITIONS

PLAYS

THE EMPEROR JONES, Eugene O'Neill. 64pp. 29268-1 $1.50

BEYOND THE HORIZON, Eugene O'Neill. 96pp. 29085-9 $1.50

ANNA CHRISTIE, Eugene O'Neill. 80pp. 29985-6 $1.50

THE LONG VOYAGE HOME AND OTHER PLAYS, Eugene O'Neill. 80pp. 28755-6 $1.00

RIGHT YOU ARE, IF YOU THINK YOU ARE, Luigi Pirandello. 64pp. (Available in U.S. only) 29576-1 $1.50

SIX CHARACTERS IN SEARCH OF AN AUTHOR, Luigi Pirandello. 64pp. (Available in U.S. only) 29992-9 $1.50

HANDS AROUND, Arthur Schnitzler. 64pp. 28724-6 $1.00

ANTONY AND CLEOPATRA, William Shakespeare. 128pp. 40062-X $1.50

HAMLET, William Shakespeare. 128pp. 27278-8 $1.00

HENRY IV, William Shakespeare. 96pp. 29584-2 $1.00

RICHARD III, William Shakespeare. 112pp. 28747-5 $1.00

OTHELLO, William Shakespeare. 112pp. 29097-2 $1.00

JULIUS CAESAR, William Shakespeare. 80pp. 26876-4 $1.00

KING LEAR, William Shakespeare. 112pp. 28058-6 $1.00

MACBETH, William Shakespeare. 96pp. 27802-6 $1.00

THE MERCHANT OF VENICE, William Shakespeare. 96pp. 28492-1 $1.00

A MIDSUMMER NIGHT'S DREAM, William Shakespeare. 80pp. 27067-X $1.00

MUCH ADO ABOUT NOTHING, William Shakespeare. 80pp. 28272-4 $1.00

AS YOU LIKE IT, William Shakespeare. 80pp. 40432-3 $1.50

THE TAMING OF THE SHREW, William Shakespeare. 96pp. 29765-9 $1.00

TWELFTH NIGHT; OR, WHAT YOU WILL, William Shakespeare. 80pp. 29290-8 $1.00

ROMEO AND JULIET, William Shakespeare. 96pp. 27557-4 $1.00

ARMS AND THE MAN, George Bernard Shaw. 80pp. (Available in U.S. only) 26476-9 $1.50

PYGMALION, George Bernard Shaw. 96pp. (Available in U.S. only) 28222-8 $1.00

HEARTBREAK HOUSE, George Bernard Shaw. 128pp. (Available in U.S. only) 29291-6 $1.50

THE SCHOOL FOR SCANDAL, Richard Brinsley Sheridan. 96pp. 26687-7 $1.50

ANTIGONE, Sophocles. 64pp. 27804-2 $1.00

OEDIPUS REX, Sophocles. 64pp. 26877-2 $1.00

ELECTRA, Sophocles. 64pp. 28482-4 $1.00

MISS JULIE, August Strindberg. 64pp. 27281-8 $1.50

THE PLAYBOY OF THE WESTERN WORLD AND RIDERS TO THE SEA, J. M. Synge. 80pp. 27562-0 $1.50

THE IMPORTANCE OF BEING EARNEST, Oscar Wilde. 64pp. 26478-5 $1.00

LADY WINDERMERE'S FAN, Oscar Wilde. 64pp. 40078-6 $1.00

BOXED SETS

FIVE GREAT POETS: Poems by Shakespeare, Keats, Poe, Dickinson and Whitman, Dover. 416pp. 26942-6 $5.00

NINE GREAT ENGLISH POETS: Poems by Shakespeare, Keats, Blake, Coleridge, Wordsworth, Mrs. Browning, FitzGerald, Tennyson and Kipling, Dover. 704pp. 27633-3 $9.00

FIVE GREAT ENGLISH ROMANTIC POETS, Dover. 496pp. 27893-X $5.00

SEVEN GREAT ENGLISH VICTORIAN POETS: Seven Volumes, Dover. 592pp. 40204-5 $7.50

SIX GREAT AMERICAN POETS: Poems by Poe, Dickinson, Whitman, Longfellow, Frost and Millay, Dover. 512pp. (Available in U.S. only) 27425-X $6.00